Introduction

An Open Door by Gail Gaymer Mar[...]
Employed by a fashion magazine, S[...]
cover the spring fashion collection in [...]
complicated by a strange letter from [...] grandmother she has
never met. When she shares a cab into the foreign city, she
makes friends with a fellow American. But will Steffi be patient
enough to wait for God to reveal the import of these new people in her life?

The Lure of Capri by DiAnn Mills
Terri Donatelli has wanted to travel to Capri since she first
learned Italian and read her great-grandmother's letter tucked
inside an old Bible. She is looking forward to the month-long
trip for relaxation and adventure. She is not happy to find her
boyfriend has booked a room at the same hotel, though Ryan
gives her space. What does Terri think she'll find in Capri?
Can she trust God to direct her life?

To Florence with Love by Melanie Panagiotopoulos
Samantha Day is one of the highest paid movie stars in the
world, but she lives with a disquieting dissatisfaction that life
should be better. When she receives a letter addressed to
Florence Celini, she wonders who could know her real name.
The letter is from a lawyer in Florence, Italy, and it sends her on
a pilgrimage to discover exactly who the woman—Florence—is.

Roman Holiday by Lois M. Richer
Emily Cain had depended on her grandmother for guidance
ever since her parents died. Now her wedding has been can-
celled and her grandmother has passed away. When a letter
invites her to Rome, Emily hopes to learn more about her
grandmother's past, while putting her future on hold. Can God
enlighten her and use her to open up one man's soul?

from Italy with Love

MOTIVATED BY LETTERS, FOUR WOMEN TRAVEL
TO ITALIAN CITIES AND FIND LOVE

GAIL GAYMER MARTIN
DIANN MILLS
MELANIE PANAGIOTOPOULOS
LOIS RICHER

BARBOUR
PUBLISHING

An Open Door © 2003 by Gail Gaymer Martin
The Lure of Capri © 2003 by DiAnn Mills
To Florence with Love © 2003 by Melanie Panagiotopoulos
Roman Holiday © 2003 by Lois M. Richer

ISBN 1-59310-081-7

Cover image © Corbis

Illustrations by Mari Goering

Published by Barbour Publishing, Inc., P.O. Box 719, Uhrichsville, Ohio 44683, www.barbourbooks.com

Our mission is to publish and distribute inspirational products offering exceptional value and biblical encouragement to the masses.

ecpa Member of the
Evangelical Christian
Publishers Association

Printed in the United States of America.
5 4 3 2 1

from Italy with Love

An Open Door

by Gail Gaymer Martin

Therefore, as God's chosen people, holy and dearly loved,
clothe yourselves with compassion,
kindness, humility, gentleness and patience.
Bear with each other and forgive whatever grievances
you may have against one another.
Forgive as the Lord forgave you.
And over all these virtues put on love,
which binds them all together in perfect unity.
COLOSSIANS 3:12–14

Prologue

Steffi Rosetti clenched the black-banded letter in her trembling hands. Tears pooled in her eyes until they escaped and rolled down her cheeks. Anger? Sorrow? Confusion?

Her senses had numbed since she opened the letter, postmarked Venice, Italy, and the message tumbled through her mind like a grocer's can goods display falling to the floor. The clatter of words and emotions rattled all the way to her heart.

Steffi dragged her gaze, again, to the signature. Donata Rosetti. A grandmother she'd never met. The mother of her father she'd never known. Deep grief rolled over her. Grief. . . and what? Apprehension? Hope?

Steffi lowered her gaze to the graceful flourish of her penmanship, the uncertain wording, the unbelievable love that soared from the paper and wondered if she'd misunderstood, perhaps misread. Again she followed the sentences word by word.

My Dearest Steffi,
> *I pray you do not destroy this letter before reading it.*

I have asked a dear friend to search for you on, what he calls, the Internet. I have long lost your mother's address, having no need for it. . .under the circumstances.

I am sending you love and sad news from Italy. Though I promised your dear father to keep from his business, he has gone to God, and now I do what my heart has longed to do for years. I find you. Words cannot say what is in my heart. I ask God to bring you to visit me so I may tell you about your father and about your relatives in this beautiful country. If you find it in your heart to answer my simple letter, I will be most grateful and give to God many praise for His goodness. A visit by you to your father's homeland is my largest dream.

I am sorry to tell you of your father's early death, but it gives me opportunity to share with you my love and prayers for these many years. Please say you will come to Venice so I can meet you in person and hold your hand in mine.

With love from Italy,
Donata Rosetti

Tears dripped to the cream-colored stationery, smudging the ink into dark puddles, and Steffi wiped her eyes with the back of her hand. She'd known so little of her father, only that he'd left her and her mother to return to Italy when Steffi was two. Sometimes when she delved deep into her memory, she thought she remembered a handsome, dark-haired man who held her in his arms so many years ago.

But reality struck her with the truth. She'd once found a photograph—one her mother hadn't destroyed—and hid it in her treasure box. Though she loved her mother deeply, Steffi longed to know what had really happened. Why had her father abandoned her?

Please say you will come to Venice so I can meet you in person and hold your hand in mine. The words sent an unearthly prickle up Steffi's arms. The coincidence tangled in her thoughts. Her magazine editor had assigned her to cover the Italian designers' autumn and winter collections, and she would leave in another week for Italy. Not Venice, but Milan. . .and if she knew geography, Venice was not too far away.

And was the invitation a coincidence? Steffi knew God worked miracles. If the Lord could move mountains and turn sinners into pillars of salt, surely He could bring two people together—seeming strangers from two distant lands. But would the Lord heal Steffi's heart?

The thought sent fear skittering through her chest. Another disappointment. Another dashed hope. The trip to Milan flashed through her mind. Certainly she could add a couple of days to her venture. She could take a train to Venice.

The question was, would she?

Chapter 1

S teffi Rosetti gripped the handle of her carry-on case and headed for baggage claim. At least that's what she hoped when she saw the word *bagagli*. Other passengers were heading in that direction, so she plastered on a confident expression and trudged through the busy Milan airport.

With a relieved sigh, she found baggage claim, gathered her pieces of luggage, and made her way through security and customs. Outside, she maneuvered her bags toward the long line at the taxi stand.

The smell of fuel and warm concrete filled the air as she jostled her way to the end of the line. Steffi disliked this part of travel most. Long lines at the airport, passing through customs, and waiting for cabs were the worst part of travel. She'd done it before on a smaller scale, traveling for her work as feature writer for the fashion magazine, *Mode*.

Inching along, she bided her time, listening to the people around her talking with the speed of a race car driver, their voices riding on the air in a jumble of unique rhythms, syllables, rolled Rs, and punctuated with animated motions.

The line moved forward again. Now only one couple waited

in front of her. Steffi drew in a long breath, knowing she'd be next.

"*Scusi!*"

She heard a male voice and turned, thinking the man was speaking to her. Instead, the impeccably dressed young man was flagging the taxi-attendant. Steffi watched the man move to the young man's side, and they stood talking. The young man was obviously a seasoned traveler. He looked sophisticated, in brown slacks and beige wool sport coat, a brown hanky in the breast pocket. His sport shirt in earth tones lay open at the neck, giving him a jaunty look, like a man who knew fashion.

Steffi looked down at her faded jeans topped by an oversized sweatshirt and cringed. She had flown from the United States to cover a designer fashion show, and she looked like she'd won a competition at the state fair log rolling contest. She shrugged to herself. Who cared how she looked? All she needed to do was write a compelling article about the latest fashions.

Steffi noted the young man's impatience as he huffed and paced beside the taxi attendant. His voice punctuated the air. "*Vorrei un tassi. Presto!*" With a subtle motion, the young man slipped paper money into the attendant's hand. She felt a frown settle on her face, wondering why he'd paid the man.

Before she had a chance to contemplate, the attendant hurried to her side. "*Scusi,* Signorina. The signor is in great need of the next taxi."

"He what?" She turned her head to flash a scowl at the young man who averted his gaze, obviously noticing her annoyed expression.

Crimping the fingertips of his right hand, he flexed his wrist. "*Grazie*. It is urgent, he says. You will have the next taxi. *Capisce?*"

Steffi stood her ground. She wasn't born yesterday. The money had been a bribe to help the man move ahead in line, she figured. She riveted her gaze to his. "No. The next taxi is *mine*." She arched an eyebrow and stared at the man.

The attendant shrugged and stepped over to the young man who was now watching her with curiosity.

Steffi's shoulders tensed, and her pulse quickened, curious to see what would happen next. As she waited, shame settled over her. Perhaps the young man had a real emergency. The attendant had said it was urgent. Where was her compassion? Where was her Christian upbringing?

When the attendant glanced her way, Steffi beckoned him over. "If the man has an emergency, I'll be happy to share a taxi."

"Sì," he said, taking a step away.

Steffi grabbed his sleeve. "If he's going in my direction."

As she finished her statement, a cab rolled to a stop. The attendant opened the door and she slipped in. He spoke to the driver and hurried away. In a moment, the impatient young man slid in beside her.

"*Grazie*," he said, giving her a nod. He leaned over the seat toward the driver. "Jolly Hotel Touring."

The driver shifted into gear, and the taxi pulled away.

Steffi gave the gentleman a puzzled look. "That's where I'm going," she mumbled, not knowing if the man understood English.

He laughed. "You're American."

She heard his Midwest dialect and irritation rose up her

back. "Yes." She folded her hands in her lap and squirmed in the corner. She'd been duped by an American to share a cab, and she didn't like it one bit.

They rode in silence while she gazed through the windows at the wonderful sights that flashed past—buildings embedded in history and adorned with ornate facades, fresco moldings, and piazzas with magnificent statuary and fountains.

At a red light, her pulse skittered, seeing a unique art form that spanned both sides of the median. On one side a towering threaded needle rose from the ground while a strand of yellow, green, and red intercepted the needle's eye in a loop, then dangled to the ground. On the opposite side of the street, two strands of thread rose from a small fountain pool and knotted at the end. The whimsy was an amazing tribute to Milan, the center of the fashion industry. She nearly commented to her fellow passenger, but caught herself. The young man shuffled through papers in his lap, and she decided to curtail a taxi-ride friendship.

The hotel came into view off the via Turati, a pink and gray concrete structure with a black overhang sporting the hotel's name. When they came to a stop, the driver unloaded the baggage, and Steffi paid the driver and toted hers inside.

At the registration desk her irritation with the young man faded as her mind filled with her purpose in Milan. Covering the new couture fashions for *Mode* was a coup for her career, but more than that, her thoughts settled on the letter she carried in her shoulder bag. The letter from her grandmother had weighed on her heart—a grandmother she'd never met, yet a woman whose sadness and grief rose from the words on the stationery.

Steffi had fought the idea of visiting the woman. . .her father's mother, but curiosity and compassion nudged her to reconsider. Steffi's mother had filled her head with negative comments about her father, a man who'd forsaken them when Steffi was young. What could her grandmother tell her to make things better? How could the older woman excuse her son's abandonment of his family in the United States? The questions weighted Steffi's mind as she clasped her key and rolled her luggage to the elevator.

The young man from the taxi had vanished, and Steffi was relieved. Yet curiosity infiltrated her thoughts. He was an American, staying at the same hotel. A strange coincidence, she thought. No matter, she hoped she never saw him again.

She erased the last thought as her inquiring mind poked her with questions.

Paul DiAngelo dropped his bag on the bed and set his tote on the luggage rack. He gazed around the room—nothing luxurious, but pleasant. After tugging off his sport jacket and hanging it on the chair back, Paul slipped off his shoes and sank into a chair, thinking about his trip from the airport. He'd acted like a pompous jerk, slipping the taxi attendant money to move ahead in line. Why? He was no better than anyone else, but he'd watched others do it and he thought he would give it a try.

He'd certainly made a bad impression on the woman he'd met on the ride to the hotel, and he was disconcerted when he learned she was staying at the same hotel. For some reason, he figured she was a farmer's daughter returning home from somewhere or perhaps her family owned a small vineyard. Her casual attire—the baggy sweatshirt and jeans and her hair tied back in a ponytail—had thrown him off course. What he had noticed was her pretty face. . .until she glowered at him.

The vision made him laugh. Who was she? And why was she in Milan? His stomach rumbled, and he put his clothes away for the week's stay. From another bag, he pulled out his camera equipment. He'd carried it on the airplane rather than take a chance on having it misplaced in baggage or damaged. Cameras were his livelihood. Paul approached his new position with *Mode* filled with excitement and a sense of challenge. Shooting the new fashions in Milan would be his first assignment for the magazine, and he wanted to do well. His photographs would be published as a pictorial article on the latest Italian couture.

As he hung his clothes, he heeded his stomach's call for food, and when finished, he made his way to the second floor dining room and scanned the filled tables. His shoulders sagged, and he realized he shouldn't have wasted time unpacking. The airplane meal had been tedious at best—the typical thimbles of tasteless food. With an appointment in little more than an hour, he felt anxiety rise.

When the maître d' approached and explained he'd have to wait, Paul thought of tipping the man for a reserved seat he guessed was somewhere, but he stopped himself. He needed to ask God's forgiveness for his impatience as much as for his manipulation.

Paul scanned the crowd again, hoping to find someone ready to leave. Instead, his pulse quickened when he spotted his taxi partner. "I know that woman," he said. Before the maître d' could stop him, Paul hurried into the dining room.

As he approached her table, he saw surprise, then irritation, settle on her face. "Do you mind?" he asked, pulling out the chair. "I have an appointment in an hour, and I'm starving."

"You seem to have a lot of emergencies," she said, giving him a restrained nod.

He sank into the chair, wishing he'd made a better first impression. He found her interesting for some unknown reason. Before Paul could apologize, the waiter hurried over and stood while he scanned the menu, made a selection, and placed his order. When the waiter left, Paul folded his hands and gathered his thoughts. "I'm sorry. I've been rather impudent."

"Yes. You have, but thanks for the apology."

"I'm Paul DiAngelo from New York."

Her forehead wrinkled as a flush mottled her cheeks. "From New York?"

He nodded.

"Me, too. I have an apartment in Manhattan."

"I have a place in Jersey City," he said. "I drive through the Holland Tunnel, and I'm in Manhattan."

"Quite a coincidence," she said, extending her hand. "I'm Steffi Rosetti."

"You're Italian, then? Do you have family here?" He saw her wince, leaving him puzzled.

"I'm here for my magazine," she said. "I'm doing a feature article on the Milan Week fashion openings for *Mode*."

For *Mode?* Her statement took the wind out of him. He eyed her sweatshirt, trying to find his breath. "You're kidding," he said finally, motivated by both her attire and the coincidence. "I just hired on with *Mode*. I'm doing a pictorial feature on Milan's fashion week."

Steffi's mouth gaped a moment before she clamped her jaw. She studied his face and, finally, shook her head. "I took you for some kind of seasoned traveler in your sport coat and slacks. You don't dress like any photographer I know."

He shrugged, embarrassed that she caught him in his charade. "I like to dress well."

Her gaze fell to her own garb, then took a slow trip upward to his face. "You can see, I don't worry much about clothes."

Paul wanted to say she should, but he bit back his words. He'd already made a bad impression, and being a fellow coworker, he needed to mend his ways.

"So where are you off to in such a hurry?" she asked.

Paul was pleased she'd changed the subject. "I have a press conference in"—he eyed his wristwatch—"forty minutes."

"No one let me know about a press conference," she said, obviously annoyed.

The waiter appeared with their meals, and he halted his response. The man refilled their water goblets, then hurried away.

"Come along with me," he said. He managed to keep his gaze from shifting to her unkempt appearance.

"Looking like this? Do you think?" She tugged at her sweatshirt.

Honesty or politeness? He decided to go for honesty. "If you hurry, you can toss on something else."

She jammed her fork into the salad. "I suppose. . .if you think it's necessary."

He swallowed his answer and gazed at his food while his appetite drifted away.

With little conversation, they hurried their meal, signed the bill, and rushed off in the directions of their rooms with the agreement to meet in ten minutes.

When Paul returned to the lobby, he paced near the doorway, eyeing his watch and expecting her to be late. On the dot, Steffi stepped from the elevator, surprising him. Though she didn't look the picture of fashion, she had made an amazing improvement in her appearance. She wore a long purple sweater over black knit pants. She'd let down her hair—waves of long dark brown tresses—that took his breath away. Over her shoulder, she carried a large tote, her handbag, and a camera. A camera? He swallowed the question, not wanting to ask.

She hurried toward him, and for the first time, she smiled. Her face lit the room.

"Ready?" he asked.

She didn't answer but jiggled the tote and moved toward the door.

He followed, and they stepped outside into the warm spring air. Paul waved his hand at a passing taxi. "We could walk there, but we don't have time, I'm afraid."

A cab pulled up to the curb, and Paul motioned Steffi inside. "Piazza Meda. Starhotel Rosa," Paul said, climbing in beside her. He slammed the door as the driver pulled away. "The press conference is close to the Duomo, the main cathedral in Milan. It's magnificent."

"I'd love to see it. . .to sightsee for that matter," she said, her attention focused on the passing scenery.

Paul watched her out of the corner of his eye. In the hotel lobby, her smile had been fleeting, and now it had vanished. Her full lips pressed together as if in serious thought. He wondered why someone so young—he guessed in her mid-twenties—gave an air of someone weighted with concerns.

"Have you been on foreign assignments before?" he asked.

She kept her head turned, as if not hearing him. Finally, she glanced his way before turning away again. "Mexico City once. I've worked designer openings stateside most of the time."

"I came to Milan once, but as an assistant. I even speak a little Italian."

She gave him another glance. "I heard."

Her voice held a sarcastic note, and he cringed, remembering his obnoxious conversation with the taxi attendant at the airport.

"I hope you can forgive me for that," he said. "Could we start over again?"

He heard her chuckle.

"Why not?" she asked. "I have to thank you for dragging me along on this press conference."

Paul appreciated her willingness to overlook his past behavior. "You're welcome." But as he looked at her, his mind tangled in her long wavy hair and her moody ways. "I like having the company."

He watched the sunlight flicker across her features—her sculptured nose with a hint of freckles and her wide-set eyes as deep blue as the Mediterranean—and could envision her in his camera lens. . .if she would allow it. Still, it wasn't her beauty that caught his attention. Something about her grabbed his heart. Something deep weighed on her soul, and he prayed he could make a difference in her life and be a friend.

Chapter 2

S teffi slid her notebook into her tote bag along with her camera and waited for Paul to pack up his gear. She watched him, remembering their awful meeting, but pleased that she'd had a chance to learn a little more about the man. She had to admit he was generous. He'd invited her to join him at the press conference, and the experience of hearing the couturiers talk about the new fashion trends would give her a head start when she covered the upcoming openings.

In the hotel's large reception room, Steffi stood near the door, hoping Paul would be ready soon. She liked Paul's good looks, the way a sport coat looked just right over his knit shirt. His dark brown hair with a soft wave was parted on the right and had been cut short with a neat sideburn. Not too short. Just right, Steffi thought. She guessed him to be near thirty. His deep laugh lines were punctuated by deep dimples. She'd noticed his dark brown eyes always seemed to hold a smile—except when he was pacing. Then his brow furrowed and he hunched over like an old man. If she got to know him well enough, she would mention that patience is a virtue.

Who was she to tell him anything? She'd been muddling

along with problems of her own, not impatience but other flaws that a Christian shouldn't have. She let her mind slip into a prayer that God would uplift her and give her courage to face the challenge of her trip to Italy. Before she'd finished her talk with God, Paul's voice pierced her solitude.

"How'd it go?" he asked.

She drew her mind from her prayer with a quick amen and focused.

"I'm sorry," he said. "I interrupted your thoughts."

She shook her head and hoisted the tote back on her shoulder, avoiding the issue of her musing. "Can we walk back to the hotel?"

"Great idea. Can I carry that for you?" He gestured toward her tote bag.

"I'm fine," she said, struck by the realization that she wasn't fine at all. She needed to think. . .to plan whether or not she would visit her grandmother.

They followed the Via Pattari, and ahead, Steffi could see the magnificent gothic cathedral, its ornate spires, one after another, circling the building. When they reached the Piazza Duomo, she stood back, amazed at the size and beauty of the white marble structure. As she neared, she noticed, amid the spires, statues embedded in the ornate marble design along with gargoyles that hid the rain gutters.

Paul didn't seem to mind the delay as she gazed at the sight. He had delved into his camera bag and had begun to snap pictures from various angles, his lens expanding and retracting, as he changed settings. At times, Steffi sensed he had included her in the photo. She felt like a child, enthralled by the mass of people, the abundance of pigeons, and the many balloon men who hawked their wares to the tourists. She joined Paul, focusing and clicking the lens.

"Can we go inside?" she asked, when Paul drew closer.

He swung his arm, motioning her forward, and she hurried ahead, passing through the wide arched door. Inside, she stood in the darkness until her eyes adjusted from the bright sunlight outside. Awed by the murals and religious statues, Steffi moved into a pew and sat. Paul made his way ahead, stopping to lift his camera to his eye.

In the hush of the cathedral, Steffi let her mind return to her problem. She deliberated the letter from her grandmother— the woman's quest to meet her and comments about her father, a man she didn't remember and who only lived in her memory from her mother's bitter words. *Lord, guide me. Help me find compassion for the grandmother I don't know. Help me make a decision that's pleasing to You. Let it be Your will not mine.*

She lifted her eyes in time to see Paul flagging her toward the door. She eyed her wristwatch in the gloomy light and realized she'd been without sleep for more than twenty-four hours. Rest is what she needed. . .and God's guidance.

❧

Paul sat at the breakfast table alone. He'd invited Steffi to join him, but she wasn't ready, and he disliked waiting for people. He tapped his fingers against the tablecloth, stretching his neck to catch the waiter for a refill on coffee. As he looked, Steffi came into the hotel dining room, and he beckoned to her.

She lifted her hand, letting him know she'd seen him, and headed his way. Today her hair was bound back from her face, her ponytail swinging in rhythm to her steps. She wore cords and a red sweater that could have held two people, with a hem that hung to her knees. He wondered why she hid beneath such baggy clothes.

He rose, but she yanked out the chair and plopped down, dropping her tote bag beside her on the floor. "What's good?" she asked, picking up the menu and reviewing the options.

"I had the buffet," he said, studying her sullen face and brooding eyes.

She pivoted her head and peered at the selection of food spread over the long table—baskets of rolls and pastries, yogurt, cereals, fresh fruit. She closed the menu and slapped it on the table. "Me, too." She rose, and he watched her move to the buffet to make her selections.

The waiter finally arrived and refilled the coffee. Paul took a sip and pondered Steffi. She filled him with curiosity. He had so many questions that wanted answering. For one, why did she carry her camera? For sightseeing, yes. That made sense. But she took photographs at the press conference. Seeing her juggle her notebook and camera to take pictures irked him. Photography was his job.

Steffi returned, her plate filled with fruit and a container of yogurt. She positioned her breakfast on the table, settled into the chair and, for the first time, focused on him. "What are your plans for today?" She forked a piece of melon and lifted it to her mouth.

His mind thought *to get to know you better*, but he knew not to say it. "Walk around. Take a look at the quadrangle."

She lowered the fork and her brow furrowed. "What's the quadrangle?"

"The fashion quadrangle. The four streets that create a square of Italian designer shops that took the wind out of

Paris fashion. Want to come along?"

"Sure. I'd like that."

He liked it, too. Walking and talking was a good way to get to know her better. . .and perhaps understand the reason for the darkness in Steffi's eyes.

꧁

The March breeze brushed against Steffi's cheeks as she walked beside Paul. She'd been irritated earlier when he invited her to breakfast and then couldn't wait for her to get ready. But he'd asked her to join him on the walk, and she guessed that made up for it. Her sense of direction was not always perfect. . .though she hated to admit it, and taxis left something to be desired when trying to get the feel for a city.

"Tomorrow's the Armani showing. I'm excited," Steffi said. "I've done so many stateside shows in New York and other locales, but this is different. I'm honored they trusted me enough to do full coverage of Milan's fashion week."

"You must be good," Paul said, giving her a wink.

She shrugged, wondering herself why they'd chosen her to come. She'd worked hard and devoted herself to a project, but she didn't really think she was a great writer.

"What's that?" she asked, approaching a large arch over the street in front of her. Its multi-toned blocks of gray stone looked like a bulwark.

"I think it's the Porta Nuova. It closes the street. Some historical event, I've heard, but when we pass beyond it, the street name changes to Manzoni. That's where the fashion district begins."

They passed beneath the arch and, after a couple of blocks, turned onto Via della Spiga. Wending their way through the streets, they paused to look inside the boutiques, the shelves nearly bare, the counters polished wood and glass as sparkling as diamonds. Top designer names flashed past their eyes, and in the unique window lighting, Paul caught reflections of Steffi—her pouting mouth, her dark lashes that canopied amazing eyes that reflected a troubled soul.

He couldn't resist and lifted his camera lens to focus on her pensive face.

When she noticed him, she held up her hands. "Don't photograph me. Here," she said, dropping her tote to the ground and tugging out her camera, "let me take you."

He laughed and posed like a male model beside a shop window, blackened glass leaving only an oval of clear, like a cameo that framed one pair of leather shoes and matching handbag. Such opulence, he'd never seen in the States.

His curiosity got the best of him as they turned the corner and moved along Via Sant Andrea. "Why do take your own photographs at events? That's my job."

She shrugged.

"Do you think I should take notes in case you don't do your job?"

"That's different," she said, turning away and gazing into the windows.

He didn't think it was, but why argue? The situation was a trust factor. Trust. Was that an issue for Steffi? His spirit sagged. Perhaps trust was a clue to her problems. He thanked God for the small hint. One day maybe Steffi would trust him enough to open the door of her heart and let him in.

❧

On Sunday afternoon, Steffi experienced her first opening. The

Armani unveiling dazzled the crowd with slim jackets, column dresses, and soft leather pencil skirts. The color palette was a blend of gray and beige with splashes of richer hues used as accents. Steffi gawked at the famous personalities and wealthy citizens who sat in narrow rows along the catwalk, but she kept control of her excitement, knowing her role as a journalist and hoping to appear professional and unaffected by the glamour that surrounded her. Funny. She wouldn't be caught dead in one of the garments she saw. Steffi liked her loose slacks and over-sized tops. In a way, they kept her safe from many of life's ills.

Steffi wrestled with balancing her notebook while adjusting her camera. Paul's question came to mind—why did she take her own photos? To make sure, would have been her answer. She hurt his feelings, she suspected, remembering his comment about writing her story. She lifted the camera and followed the supermodel who strutted along the walkway, looking as if she hadn't eaten since the previous year.

Across the floor, Paul had settled into the perfect vantage point. She watched him when she had time to shift her attention from the notepad, admiring his concentration in the midst of madness. She'd admired him a day earlier at the press conference when she'd been jostled by a taller journalist. Paul had stepped in with tact and spoken to the gentleman. In a flash, the man apologized and made room for Steffi in her rightful place in a press area. She'd seen Paul's generous side so often, but yesterday he'd shown integrity. What he still hadn't revealed was patience.

The show ended in a burst of applause, followed by the hum of conversation. Steffi dropped her notes into her shoulder tote, then headed toward the door. Paul caught up with her, his camera still hanging around his neck. His shirttail had pulled out, and she grinned, happy to see him, for once, not his usual vision of neatness.

"What's the smile for?" he asked.

"You. . .and your shirttail."

He glanced down and gave it a quick tuck before eyeing her. "I've been meaning to talk to you about that."

"About what? Shirttails?"

Paul chuckled and took her arm as they stepped into the night air. "No, about your choice of attire."

She stiffened with his comment. "What's wrong with my attire?"

"Nothing, if you. . ." He shrugged. "Nothing." His voice lost its good humor.

"If I didn't look like I'd just climbed off a tractor?" She arched a purposeful eyebrow.

At that, he laughed. "Something like that."

"I like how I dress."

He didn't respond, and she ambled alongside him, wondering what he was thinking. She'd expected a comeback. She heard none.

"Ready to head back?" Paul asked.

"I'd like to walk for awhile. You can go on ahead." She sidled a glance, hoping he would walk with her.

"I won't leave you alone," he said. "It's a nice day. Let's walk back."

Steffi's mind filled with questions. She wanted to know why Paul cared how she looked. Didn't he know the most important part of a human was what was inside? Her mother had said that her father had been a handsome man. Dashing, she called him—well-dressed and well-groomed, but that didn't make him beautiful inside, where it counted.

❧

Paul wanted to kick himself for his comment about her clothes. The whole thing was self-serving. She didn't want to look like a supermodel. He wanted her to, but why? The question rattled in his head as they walked along the ancient streets toward the hotel. In the silence, an answer struck him. Because beneath her self-control, he sensed a woman tormented. . .a woman who did not like herself very much.

Another question fell into his mind. Why? How could an apparently talented woman with charm and beauty not have self-worth?

"You're the quiet one this time," she said, her soft voice puncturing his thoughts.

"Just thinking. . .about you." He swallowed the anxiety that rose from his comment. Would she now back away from him?

"About me? Why would you be thinking about me?"

"Loads of things, but right now I was wondering—"

"Why I dress the way I do?"

She'd finished his sentence incorrectly, and he breathed a relieved sigh. Why get into all the other puzzling things about her? "No. I wasn't thinking of that at all."

She didn't ask, and he didn't offer. He wondered how she would react if she knew about the photographs he'd taken of her—shots so lovely they took his breath away. He'd caught her in a blend of light and shadow. Her pensive downturned face tugged at his heart. Paul had been delighted when he realized he'd snapped a shot of a rare smile at the Piazza Duomo. Steffi's face had been upturned to the sun, and behind her a mélange of bright balloons filled the sky.

"I have something to show you when we get back to the hotel," he said, after sending a prayer to God to cover him with blessing.

"What?"

"Just wait. . .but it'll explain why you were on my mind."

She frowned, as if she didn't understand.

"I mean, you'll know why I was thinking of you," he said, answering her unasked question.

Their footsteps tapped along the concrete sidewalk, bouncing off the rococo facade of the building they passed, and at the Piazza Cavour, instead of turning, they headed up Via Manin, an indirect route to the hotel. They passed the elegant Belgioioso, at one time Napoleon's residence, and headed for the public gardens.

In the park, they ambled past ponds and shrubs, enjoying the spring flowers that blossomed from neat beds.

"It's beautiful," Steffi said, settling on a bench. She opened her tote bag and pulled out her camera, then stood back and focused on Paul.

"No fair," he said, giving her his brightest smile.

She laughed, and the lilt of her voice touched his heart. She should smile more often. He kept the thought to himself.

When she'd finished and turned toward the scenery, he pulled the lens cap off his camera. "My turn."

She swung around, and he brought the lens in close, catching her surprised look as the late afternoon sunlight played upon wisps of hair that had broken loose from their bonds and played against her cheek. When she realized what he'd done, she turned her back.

"I don't like pictures of myself," she said.

His heart sank, knowing he planned to show her the other photos he'd taken once they returned to the hotel.

Again, he was puzzled. Why did she dislike her picture being taken? She troubled him. . .concerned him. He wanted to know so many things about her.

God willing, he would.

Chapter 3

Steffi sat in the hotel lounge, sipping a soft drink and waiting for Paul, who'd run to his room to bring back the surprise he'd mentioned. She'd tried to guess what it might be, but she had no idea. Paul seemed full of surprises. They'd spent time together, enjoying the city and its history, and even with his limited Italian, he read signs and guided her to the most intriguing places, like today when he took her to the park.

When she looked toward the elevator, the door slid open, and Paul stepped into the lobby. He'd removed his jacket and now looked more casual in a knit shirt the color of milk chocolate, the same color as his eyes. Under his arm, he carried a folder. Awareness hit her. A portfolio. He'd wanted to show her his photographs.

His eyes smiled at her as he sank into the cushion at her side. "I hope you're ready for this."

The comment made her curious, and right away, she assumed he wanted to show her how terrific his pictures were, guessing that hers would not be nearly as good. "Mine aren't developed, yet."

Paul pressed his hand against her arm, keeping the portfolio closed. "I'm not trying to compete, Steffi. I want you to see something special."

His voice sounded tender, and the tone wove through her, wrapping around her heart. She placed the album on her lap and opened the page. She was struck by the exquisite detail, the play of light, the unique tilt of the lens. More than a fashion shoot, these photos were creative.

"Extraordinary," she said, turning the pages. "You have a great eye for exceptional photographs."

"Those aren't the pictures I was referring to," he said.

Paul's tone held a mysterious sound that caused her to turn and look into his eyes. With her gaze riveted to his, she felt him turn numerous pages. Then with the tilt of his head, he spoke. "These are the ones."

Her breath caught as she gaped down at the photographs. She flipped the pages, realizing each shot was her in the Piazza Duomo, in the fashion quadrangle, places she'd never known he'd snapped her pictures. The images amazed her. For the first time, she saw herself as he saw her—her pensive face, her sullen mouth, her rare smile looking into the heavens. She'd never liked her photograph taken, but the pictures intrigued her with the play of sun and shadow.

"You're a beautiful woman," he said, brushing his finger across her arm.

Steffi's chest tightened, hearing his words, and her immediate reaction was to run away from his flattery. He was mocking her, baiting her for something.

"Don't frown, Steffi. I'm only telling you the truth. I have no other agenda. . .than to get to know you better. You drive me crazy. You puzzle me."

"But I. . .I don't understand why you took these."

"I just told you. You're fascinating inside and out."

She felt the gentle caress on her arm, and the warmth traveled upward and nestled near her heart. He'd said he told the truth. Could she believe him? Could she trust him?

"I hope you're not angry. A photographer can't pass up an exceptional subject." He studied her face a moment before continuing. "You don't trust me for some reason. I wish I knew why."

Disappointment washed across his face like the sun fading behind a cloud. She'd doused his pleasure with her inability to say thank you, her fear to show approval. "They're very nice photographs. You've just surprised me. Thanks for letting me see them."

She placed the portfolio on the table in front of her, then took a sip of the soft drink.

"You're welcome," he said, disappointment reflecting in his voice.

They sat in silence before Paul flagged the waiter and placed his order. When the man had gone, he shifted his hip on the cushion to face her more directly. "Tell me about yourself."

His request sent tendrils of surprise and sadness weaving through her veins. "Why? What do you want to know?"

"Why you're so sad."

The blunt comment punctured her security. "I'm not sad. I'm thoughtful."

"Then why are you so thoughtful?"

⁂

Paul watched Steffi's expression shuffle through a myriad of emotion. Part of him grieved that he'd asked the question. Part of him rejoiced that he'd had the courage to speak the words that had lain in his heart since he'd met her.

"I have a lot on my mind, Paul."

"I realize we've just met, but I'm a good listener. What kind of things?"

"I don't want to talk about them." She pulled her gaze away.

Her blunt response whacked his curiosity, but he wanted to keep the door open, and he scuffled for a response. "Okay. Let's talk about me, then. Any questions?"

Her gaze shifted across his face as if trying to figure out if he was serious.

"Anything?" she asked.

"Sure, why not? Try me."

Steffi puffed out her cheeks, releasing a breath before she spoke. "Why are you so impatient? I've never met anyone who paces more or looks at his watch more than you."

She'd struck home with her question. He decided to go for a lighthearted response. "Me? Impatient?"

Her serious expression melted to a grin. "Then what do you call it?"

"Eager. Sensitive."

Her laugh surprised him.

"Really?" Her smile retraced itself to a serious look. "Are you a Christian? I have the feeling you are."

Paul wondered where that question came from. "All my life. I'm not always the best church attender, but God guides my steps." She'd piqued his own interest. "How about you?"

"Same as you," she said. "I believe in the Lord, but I probably don't demonstrate it as I should, and then there're things in my life that. . ."

Paul waited for her to complete the statement, eager to learn a little bit more about her. But she stopped. His mouth felt dry, and his attention shifted to the bar, wondering what had happened to his drink. He checked his wristwatch, and felt distracted for a moment, trying to remember how long it had been since he'd placed his order.

Steffi's silence broke with a chuckle. "I see you're being sensitive."

"Sensitive?"

"Oh, then it must be eager." She tapped her fingernails on the table, rolling them in a grumbling rhythm, as if taunting him.

He got the point. "Yes. I'm. . .*eager* for my drink."

A told-you-so grin curved her mouth, but he didn't give her the pleasure of response. Instead, he caught the waiter's attention and pointed to his empty hand.

The man nodded, and in a moment, he returned with a tumbler of soda. "*Scusi. Per fa ritardore.*"

"*Grazie,*" Paul said, taking his drink.

The man left, and Steffi looked at Paul with a frown. "What did he say?"

"He was sorry for the delay."

Steffi nodded. "So let's get back to this impatience thing. You can call it anything you want."

She looked uncomfortable, and Paul wondered what was on her mind.

She tilted her head and gave him a shy look. "If you're a Christian, then you know that God tells us to be patient. 'Clothe yourself with compassion, kindness, humility, gentleness and patience.' It's in Colossians."

"I know that scripture. 'And over all these virtues put on love.' That's my favorite part of the verse." Though he was teasing her on one hand, he truly believed love was what bound people together.

"Get serious. Admit you're probably one of the most impatient people on earth."

"I am being serious. I think without love we're nothing." He watched the same brooding look glaze her eyes. He'd hit home again, and he longed to reach out and touch her. . .to help her through whatever painful experience she had endured.

Yet, knowing better, he decided to talk about himself. Perhaps his example would open the door. "Okay. I admit it. I'm impatient. I don't know why, Steffi. Maybe because I was an only child and so I often got my way. My parents doted on me. I could do no wrong."

Her face paled as he spoke, and he could only assume that her childhood must have been part of the explanation for her sad eyes.

"When I got older, I realized that I could do wrong and I wasn't perfect, but I still liked having things come to me as quickly as they did when I was a kid. Not realistic, but truthful."

She nodded. "Many life expectations aren't realistic."

No expectations. No trust. No hope. Was this her life's motto? If so, he ached for her.

❧

Steffi jumped at the telephone's ring. She wrapped the towel tighter around her wet body and hurried to the telephone. "Hello," she said, eyeing the clock. Another opening would begin in less than an hour, and she was running late.

"Good morning." Paul's pleasant voice sailed across the

wire. "Ready? We need to get going."

"I'm not quite ready." She looked down at the white hotel towel and felt her wet hair cling against her back.

"How long?"

She listened for impatience in his voice, but she sensed he was making a valiant effort to control it. "Another fifteen." She knew she was pushing it, but she'd do her best.

"We'll be late. Even if we can catch a cab, the traffic will be horrible there today, and walking will take a good twenty-five minutes. I don't want to be late."

"Don't be so impatient." She grimaced at her ploy.

"I'm not being impatient. I'm being realistic. I can't miss the show and neither can you."

"So go without me." She tried to catch the drips from her hair with the corner of the towel. Her reflection in the mirror made her cringe. She would be late if she didn't fly. "I don't want you to be late."

She lowered the phone, feeling sorry as soon as she heard the click of the receiver on the cradle. He was right. She had to be on time. Flying back into the bathroom, she dried, pulled on her clothes, slid into her shoes, then faced the mirror. The comb slid through her hair with a few tugs to get out the snarls. She'd let it air dry on the way. She sent a praise to God for natural waves. After a daub of lipstick and mascara, Steffi took a final look, grabbed her tote, and ran out the door.

Paul wasn't waiting in the lobby as she'd hoped. Outside, she stood on the corner, trying to flag a cab, but each time they flew past as if she wasn't there. She glanced at her watch, then tugged her street map from her shoulder bag and studied it a moment. The Galleria was near the Duomo. She certainly could find her way. It was straight down Turati, which changed to Manzoni, and she would be almost there.

She struck out at a brisk pace, keeping an eye on her wristwatch. She waited at streetlights, her patience about as short as Paul's. As she passed La Scala, the famous opera house with its arched overhang to protect the carriages which brought the patrons centuries earlier, she saw the spires of the Duomo and the glass dome of the Galleria. Having nearly run the stretch from the hotel, she had arrived with five minutes to spare. The crowd jostled outside the building, but she paused a moment to watch the sunlight glint from the glass rooftop. It was one of those photo opportunities that Paul had mentioned.

She shuffled through her tote and pulled out her camera, focusing on the diamond glints that shimmered from the roof. She pushed the shutter release, hoping the photograph would capture the loveliness she'd witnessed. Hearing the rewinding buzz, Steffi realized she'd used her last picture. Frustrated at her lack of planning, she shoved her arm into her bag and pulled out a fresh roll of film.

"Signorina needs help?"

She looked up to see a nicely dressed gentleman standing beside her. "Thanks. I have to load my camera." She finagled trying to hold the camera while removing the film from the box.

"Let me help," he said, taking the camera from her hands.

She gave him a nod and, with two hands, removed the film from its housing. When she looked up, she saw the man's back running away. . .with her camera. Frustration at her own stupidity filled her mind. "Stop him," she yelled, remembering how many times she'd been told to watch out for pickpockets, and she'd fallen prey.

The man vanished in the bustling crowd, people heading for the opening and others toward the Piazza Duomo. Her shoulders sagged as she dropped the useless film into her tote. She didn't even have time to find a policeman.

She moved through the wide arched entrance into the street arcade. A glass ceiling with a central dome covered the way between Piazza La Scala and the cathedral. She made her way to the center where the temporary stage and catwalk had been constructed. The chairs lining the walkway were already filled with people, and the press area was crowded with journalists.

Steffi elbowed her way through the crowd, tears in her eyes from the loss of her camera and her own stupidity for not listening to the warnings she'd heard over and over. When she spotted Paul, her control left her, and tears rolled down her cheeks as quickly as she could brush them away with the back of her hand.

"What happened?" he said, his gaze shifting from her to the catwalk. She realized he didn't want to miss the show's beginning.

His voice could barely be heard above the music that reverberated from the ornate walls of the buildings that lined each side of the street and from the colorful mosaic tiled floor. "A pickpocket stole my camera."

Paul's eyes widened, and he leaned closer. "Stole your camera?"

With her throat knotted with emotion, she could only nod.

"I'm sorry, Steffi," he said, wrapping his arm around her shoulders and drawing her to him. He leaned closer to her ear. "Did you report it to the police?"

With her head buried in his chest, she only shook her head.

"We will later. . .after the show."

She knew she would never see her camera again, but she appreciated his effort to soothe her.

He lifted a hand and tilted her chin upward. She met his gaze, and a flutter in her chest made her breathless.

"I won't let you travel around here alone anymore," he said. "I'm sorry I left ahead of you."

"It was my fault," she whispered, as the music's pounding rhythm warned them the show was to begin.

"Let's not talk about fault," he said in her ear. "Let's talk about sticking together."

Chapter 4

Paul pulled out a chair and Steffi sank into it. He helped her scoot forward, then rounded the table and joined her. Frustration at himself and her permeated his thoughts. Why had he let her find her own way to the Galleria? Why had she been so unthinking to let a stranger hold her camera?

"Thanks for talking with the police," Steffi said, opening the menu and staring at the selections. "I know it's useless, but I appreciate the valiant effort."

"You never know." He agreed that it was hopeless, but at least he'd tried. "Why did you have your camera out anyway?"

Steffi told him the story of the Galleria roof and running out of film. She also relayed her inability to flag a cab. "I have to be honest with you. I wasn't at all ready when you called, and if you'd hung around I probably would have dawdled. I hurried, hoping to catch up with you in the lobby."

"Thanks for trusting me enough to tell me the truth." Her openness seemed one step closer to her confiding in him. If she didn't, how could he help her?

"I'd just gotten out of the shower. I was wet and my hair was sopped."

He grinned. "Next time, we'll both do better."

Her eyes searched his, then she smiled.

She refocused on the menu, and he did the same. They each selected a pasta, and once the waiter left, Paul took a drink of water and spoke the words he hated to say. "The fashion week ends in a couple days. Then, it's back to New York for you."

Steffi shrugged. "I'm not sure. I have another week. I might stay on."

"Really? I've taken vacation time, too. I figured, how often will I get a free trip to Italy? I might take a couple of side trips before going home."

Though she'd focused on him, he observed the faraway look in her eyes.

"Will you stay in Milan?" Paul asked. She needed to talk. It was obvious. *Lord, if You would only open the door to her heart, and let me in.*

"I'm thinking of. . .Venice."

Her voice had lost its momentum. "Venice. I've never been there, but I'd love to go. The Grand Canal, St. Mark's Square, Doges Palace. I've only seen photographs."

"Me, too." She kept her eyes focused on her water glass, her finger running along the edge.

He watched the unending trips her finger made around the rim, going nowhere. . .like Steffi's troubles. "There's more to it than that. I know you too well now."

Her hand continued to trace the circle, but it finally slowed, and she looked up. "Yes. There's more."

This time he knew better than to say *tell me.* She needed to make the decision for herself. Fighting the desire to ask questions and probe, he captured her gaze and waited. If Steffi ever recognized patience, it was now.

Silence hovered over the table until she released a ragged sigh. "It's a long story," she said.

He looked at his watch, then gave her a heartfelt grin. "We have all the time in the world."

Paul's patience paid off, and his hopes rose as Steffi began the story of her father's abandonment, her mother's bitterness, and the sorrow she'd felt throughout her life.

"I missed having a father," she said. "Now that I'm an adult it's not as important, but years ago, I felt to blame. He left after I was born. I was two years old. I figured he didn't want a child, or maybe, I was too whiny for his liking."

"Steffi." Paul shook his head, amazed she would think that way. "Hadn't you realized a two year old couldn't break up a marriage? Only teenagers can do that." He gave her a playful smile, trying to lighten the heavy conversation.

She grinned back, but her eyes didn't smile. "Kids don't think logically. Once rejected, it's hard to open up again."

Enlightened, Paul grasped the thought. "It's difficult to trust and to have expectations."

She nodded. "That's right. And my mother didn't help the situation, but I don't want to blame her. She was as hurt as I was. Worse, I'm sure."

Paul could only imagine. He'd come from a stable home with two loving parents. How might his life have changed if a divorce had occurred? He couldn't imagine it. "So your parents divorced?"

"No."

He gaped at her, his mind swirling with bewilderment. "You mean they remained married all those years?"

She seemed as puzzled as he was. "Yes. My father returned to Italy, my mother told me, and we never heard from him again. Mom never divorced him. I don't know why. Maybe religious reasons. Maybe not. She won't talk about it."

The information confounded him, and he could only imagine how it would be to spend your life without answers to probing questions. "So that's it, then." He reached across the table and touched her hand. The feeling seemed so right. Baggy shirts and jeans? Paul didn't care. Steffi was beautiful in his eyes from inside out. "You'll never know what really happened."

She closed her eyes, and he could see tears rim her lashes. "What is it?" he asked. "What's wrong?"

She turned away and delved into her shoulder bag, sitting between her feet. When she lifted her hand above the table, she brought up a crumpled envelope. "Here. Read this."

Confused and concerned, he pressed the creases from the jacket and pulled out cream-colored stationery, trimmed with a black border. The black tugged at his remembrance. In European countries, the black borders stood for death. Paul unfolded the letter, then thought better of it. "Are you sure you want me to read this?"

"I'm positive. I need advice. . .and a friend."

Her words lifted his spirit and tangled around his heart. He'd longed since he met her to hear Steffi say those words. He scanned the letter, emotion skittering through him as he read the plaintive words of the grandmother. When he finished, he lifted his eyes to hers. "What kind of advice do you need?" He prayed it wasn't what he feared.

"Should I go?"

Paul had been right. How could she not go to visit this

woman who'd opened her heart? "Do you have a choice?" He searched her face, hoping to see a flicker of an answer. "She's your grandmother."

She lowered her head, and before she lifted it, the waiter arrived with their meals. Paul thanked him and when he'd gone, he asked again, "Do you have a choice?"

Her eyes downcast, she released a deep sigh. "I could ignore the letter like my father did us twenty-three years ago."

Paul reached forward and clasped her hands in his. "Could you really do that?"

When Steffi lifted her gaze, tears filled her eyes. "I don't think so, but. . ."

"But it's difficult. I agree with you." Paul didn't release her hand, but held it captive. "I think what you have to keep in the forefront is that this woman"—he touched the letter—"isn't the one who left you years ago. She wanted to get in touch, but your father told her to stay out of his business. He had his reasons, Steffi. You'll only learn why when you go to see her."

She didn't respond, but he saw in her face the struggle that tormented her thoughts.

He gave her hand a squeeze. "Let's talk about this tomorrow. Work through your thoughts and tell me tomorrow what you're thinking. I want to help you."

Steffi agreed, and they both faced their plates, their appetites diminished by the tension that had wrought them for the past minutes.

"Dig in," he said, sending her a silly smile.

She laughed, and the lilt warmed him. He saw hope in her eyes. He would pray tonight that the good Lord would help her find the answer.

❧

"Two more openings," she released a puff of air from her lungs. "This is hard work. I've spent all my free time writing up my notes and trying to get them into the laptop. I've been sending reviews of the openings each night, but now they tell me they want a feature article on the full event."

Paul rested his back against the lounge chair and sipped his soft drink. "I wonder if they've changed their minds. Maybe they're using my photography to illustrate your article."

"They didn't say. Could be."

He frowned and rubbed his chin. "I'm not sure I like that. They sent me here for a pictorial feature. I'd hate—"

Steffi pressed her hand on his arm. "I'm sure it will be what they assigned. They may include a full fashion week review in the same issue." She felt her eyebrows lift, asking without saying the words. She'd never seen Paul appear so sensitive and unsure about his work. He'd always had an air of confidence.

"I suppose you're right. I sound like a spoiled kid."

Not spoiled in her eyes, perhaps more humble than she realized. He seemed to doubt his ability, and that surprised her. No matter what his flaws, she liked him anyway. She liked him a lot. Steffi sipped her coffee, getting her thoughts around the words she planned to say. The dark brew rolled on her tongue and warmed her throat. "I've made a decision."

His head lifted with the speed of a lightning bolt. He didn't ask. He reached over and took her hand. She loved the feel of closeness—a feeling she had avoided most of her life for fear of being hurt, of being forsaken by someone who meant too much to her.

"I'm going to Venice, but. . .I'll have to find the courage to visit her. I might just call."

"Oh. . .Steffi, I—" He shook his head. "It's not my business. You do what you must, but here's a thought. Let me go with you. I have the time, and I've never seen Venice. That's not a place to go alone."

"It's not?" She thought of the pickpocket who stole her camera. "You mean it's—"

"Venice is the city of love. Amore." He flashed her a heart-warming smile. "You can't be alone in a town like that."

His look sent a ripple through her chest. Paul had shown compassion for her, and it soothed her. He'd reached out to her and touched her life with his funny world of impatience—although she had to admit he was making an effort to improve—and optimism. She needed someone who could help her see the bright side of life. She'd asked the Lord for direction, but Steffi realized she didn't listen well to God's guidance. Steffi struggled along on her own until all else failed, then she turned to the Lord's bidding. When would she learn?

"I can't ask you to come with me. I'm too depressing."

He laughed. "And I'm the guy who can make you smile. You need me."

She did smile at his silliness. "I suppose it wouldn't hurt. You could help me find my way and then—"

"Then I'll leave you be. You need to visit your grandmother on your own, but I'll support you. Yes." His countenance brightened like the glinting roof she'd admired on the Galleria.

"Let's celebrate," he said. "We have another show today, and the final opening. Tomorrow night we could find a wonderful restaurant. . .a really special place to have dinner to enjoy our last night in Milan."

Steffi's stomach twisted with the truth. "I can't."

"You can't? But why?" His face faded from bright to dim.

She tugged at her sweater. "I have no clothes for a nice restaurant."

"Hmm?" he rubbed his chin as if in thought.

Steffi realized he was teasing her, but she waited.

"Let's see. We're in Milan, fashion capital of Italy. Perhaps we could find a shop where you could buy some new clothes."

"I couldn't touch the price with my whole savings." She shook her head, knowing that was the truth.

"Have you heard of designer outlets? Just like our shops at home. Exclusive stores that sell at a discount. What do you say?"

His eyes glowed with excitement, and she hated to disappoint him. Clothes were not her friends. She liked comfort, not style. He should know that by now. "We could eat at the fast food restaurant at the Galleria. The building's lovely." She gave him a feeble smile.

He grinned back but lifted his shoulders in defeat, then rallied. "Do you remember those photos I took, Steffi. Did you see your face? Your hair? You're so pretty, but you hide it all beneath those baggy things you wear."

She shrugged, hoping to dissuade him from talking about her looks. She'd worn dowdy clothes all her life to avoid relationships. He was trying to undermine her tactic.

"I understand now," he said. "You want to avoid getting attached to people so you make yourself as unattractive as possible, but you see it didn't work. You know why?"

She didn't, and she feared he would tell her something

about herself that she didn't even know. She shook her head.

"Because anyone of worth looks inside first. When they find the beauty inside, the outside doesn't matter. In your case, Steffi, you're lovely inside and out."

Tears pressed behind her eyes, and she lowered her head so other diners wouldn't see her emotion. He'd called her beautiful. . .inside. She never thought of herself as beautiful in any way, even though people often told her she was attractive—although they usually added, "If you'd fix yourself up."

He covered her hand with his. "I'm not trying to upset you. You want me to be truthful, and I am."

"Thank you," she whispered.

When she raised her head, she saw his eyes filled with concern.

"I'm fine," she said. "You just surprised me with your comments."

"You shouldn't be surprised, Steffi. People should have told you how good you are all along. Good to the depth of your being, not just surface. . .although that's nice to hear, too."

He lifted her hand and pressed it between his. "It's time you let your beauty shine. You want your grandmother to see the best side of you, don't you? Whether it gives credit to your mother or your father, she needs to see the real you."

His words settled into her thoughts. *The real you.* Did she really know who she was? Sometimes she wondered. Her life had been a blend of disappointment and bewilderment, of grief and bitterness. She wondered how Paul could see that she had beauty from within. He had made a good point, though. If. . .and that was *if* she went to see her grandmother, she might as well present herself in the best light possible.

No matter what had happened in the past, she wanted her grandmother to know that her mother had raised her well. Her mother had raised her to be a Christian despite her bitterness, and that was a gift in itself.

Chapter 5

Paul grabbed Steffi's hand and urged her into the intriguing shopping mall. Like a little Italian city, the shops stood behind arcades with covered walkways spanning the shops a story above the street. A large cupola rose above the roof, and as Paul tilted his head to see the dome, he noticed the wrought iron balconies that extended from the second-story shops.

"It's charming," Steffi said, craning her neck to catch all the sights. Designer names adorned the windows of the shops selling famous couture discounted up to seventy percent.

With Steffi's hand still in his, Paul drew her into a nearby shop. Though she resisted, she moved ahead, gazing at the price tags and lifting her eyebrows to announce the prices were still too exorbitant. As Paul wandered among the displays, he handed Steffi one garment after another, prodding her to give it a try.

Finally, she grudgingly headed into a dressing room. He sank into a chair and waited, confident he would be there awhile, but to his surprise, Steffi came through the doorway in a heartbeat. She wore a skirt and top that seemed meant for her. The black leather skirt nestled against her shapely frame, and the ruby-red knit top curved beneath her neck and swept down her arms, a perfect fit.

"Looks good," he said, giving her a thumbs up. But she looked more than good. She looked better than any supermodel he'd seen on the catwalk.

"If I buy this, I'll need boots." She lifted her foot and pointed to her made-for-comfort walking shoes.

"So?"

She shrugged and hurried back inside. In a moment, Steffi returned with the same skirt, but a different top, a silky blouse in black and teal shades, perfect for her dark coloring.

He sent her a wink. "I like it."

When they made the purchases, they moved on and visited store after store, wandering through the displays and weighing the value of one item over another. Steffi's taste in attire astounded him. She put together skirts with sweaters and vests that looked made for each other. He wondered how she could know so much about fashion and still wear those baggy clothes. Then he recalled their conversation and remembered her unorthodox appearance was part of her defense.

Today he rejoiced that she'd let down her guard, trusting him enough to add some new items to her wardrobe. . .for her grandmother and, just perhaps, for his admiring look.

Before they left, Steffi had added black stylish boots, a dress that sent his heart on a whirl, and more garments than he could recall. Paul had made two purchases—a new designer shirt for himself and a cashmere sport coat, but the best was a surprise for Steffi. He'd had one opportunity to steal away while she was preoccupied, and after purchasing the gift, he dropped the package into the other shopping bag so she wouldn't see the store logo.

Exhausted, they returned to the hotel, and in his room, Paul realized he needed to make reservations at Il Teatro. The restaurant was well known and in the fashion quadrangle. The setting seemed an appropriate place to celebrate their last night in Milan.

When Paul hung up the telephone, he leaned back in the lone chair in his room. He eyed the gift he would give Steffi before dinner when he went to her room to escort her to the restaurant. To him, the evening seemed their first official date, and he knew a gentleman always picked up the woman at her home.

He smiled to himself, thinking of the happiness he'd felt the past week with Steffi in his company. Their unpleasant meeting had faded in his memory, and he was grateful. She'd been kind to forgive him, and he prayed the Lord had done the same. He'd acted pompous and rude. With the Lord in his thoughts, Paul slid his Bible from the table beside him. He opened the pages and let his eyes rest on God's Word.

With all that had passed, Paul sensed in his heart that the Lord was at work in his life. In New York, he'd allowed his social life to become mundane. Nothing excited him except his work. No woman had caught his eye, and as far as he had been concerned, he didn't need anyone. But since he'd arrived, he'd learned something new. He didn't need anyone. Instead, he yearned for someone with whom to enjoy life. He remembered a Bible verse from Ecclesiastes that said something about two people are better than one. He'd begun to feel the same.

Two are better. Like Noah and the ark, two were company,

two were support, two were partners in life's joys and trials. He wanted to wipe away Steffi's tears and give her the love she'd avoided for so long. Paul sensed the Lord had brought their paths together for that purpose. *And over all these virtues put on love, which binds them all together in perfect unity.* The scripture summarized the deep feeling that had been growing in his heart.

Cautioning himself, Paul closed his eyes, realizing he'd only known Steffi a week, but in that week, he'd given more and accepted more than he had in years. Since he and Steffi worked together at *Mode*, he knew that God was offering them time for their relationship to grow. With confidence, Paul accepted the thought.

He could only hope that Steffi would someday feel the same.

෧

Steffi slid her hands beneath her hair and clasped the delicate choker she'd found in the hotel's boutique. A chain of black beads between rows of gold links looked perfect with the new dress she'd purchased. Paul had admired the gown, and though she'd never dreamed she would wear something so lovely, she'd tried it on and agreed. The black lace bodice and sheath skirt veiled a shimmering deep rose lining. The material slid over her like gossamer threads, making her feel special.

Paul had been good for her. He'd brought out her best qualities that had lain deep inside her, afraid to come to the surface for fear of rejection. When she thought of going back to New York, sadness filled her—not that she wouldn't see Paul again, but that life would get in the way and they would drift apart.

Steffi slipped on the black-strapped pumps she'd brought from home, a last-minute decision, and took a final look. She likcd what she saw. When she turned away from the mirror, she heard a rap on the door. Her heart jigged through her chest, and she grinned at the silliness of her emotions. The caller was only Paul. But as she thought the words, she knew she was fooling herself. He'd come to mean so much to her.

She peeked through the hole and seeing his face, Steffi pulled open the door.

Paul's eyes widened and he gave her a slow whistle. "Where have you been all my life?"

He stepped inside and took a quick look at the room before returning to her. "You look lovely."

"Thank you," she said, wanting to press her hand against her chest to hold back the intense beat of her heart.

"Your room looks exactly like mine. Big surprise." He flashed her a grin and held up a package. "I didn't bring a corsage, but I have a present for you."

She looked at the package, wondering if she'd heard him correctly. "A present?"

"You know. . .a gift." He extended the tissue-covered item.

She shook her head. "When did you buy me a gift. . .and why?"

"Because I like you, and I bought it when you weren't looking."

She chuckled. "Obviously." She sat on the corner of the bed and pulled off the wrapping. When she saw the gift, tears welled in her eyes. "Paul, you shouldn't have." She studied the new camera, so much better than the one she'd owned. "You didn't have to do this."

"How can you take photos of your grandmother without a camera?"

His tender look took her breath away. "What can I say?" She placed the camera on the spread and rose, placing her arms around his neck. She drew him into an embrace, loving the feel of him in her arms and lost in the spicy scent of his aftershave.

He held her tight, and when she eased back to look in his eyes, she couldn't move. His gentle face said so much more than words. His gaze lowered to her mouth, and he moved forward, his lips brushing hers so sweetly, her knees weakened.

"You're welcome," he said, holding her in his embrace. "I thought you'd like it."

His kiss had flustered her and thrilled her at the same time. She opened her mouth to speak and found her wits had taken a vacation. Finally, her senses returned. "I more than like it. I love it."

"I'm glad. I wish I could give you everything your heart desires."

His words touched her deeply.

"Are you ready?" he asked.

She grabbed her black wrap and followed him through the door.

❧

As Paul organized his gear for a final shoot, he could not forget the previous evening. Steffi dressed in a shimmer of black and a rich flowery pink hidden beneath the lace. Her hair had fallen around her shoulders in a billow of waves, her dark blue eyes looking at him with trust in one of those wonderful moments. He'd taken a chance and kissed her. The gamble had been worthwhile. She'd accepted his lips and his embrace beyond his expectation.

The restaurant had been as perfect as he'd imagined. Lodged inside the Four Seasons Hotel, the area was surrounded by columns and frescos from a fifteenth century cloister. Inside, Steffi's eyes widened as she gazed at the murals, lavish bouquets of fresh flowers, and the porcelain and brass decor. The tables were covered with white linen and set with elegant china and crystal stemware. Paul had paid a handsome sum, but seeing the wonder in Steffi's eyes made the cost worthwhile.

Today, Paul faced his final couture opening. Taking one final review of his equipment, he picked up the receiver and punched in Steffi's number. No answer. Concern settled over him, but he pushed it away. He hoped she wasn't still in the shower. She'd been late so often. Instead of calling again, he headed for the elevator. If necessary, he would call her from the lobby, but when he stepped into the registration area, Steffi was waiting for him by the door.

He grinned, realizing she had met his need for being on time. Compromise, he thought. Part of a relationship. The thought struck him. Was this a relationship? He felt it growing in his heart. Could it be blossoming in hers?

"Hi," she said. "I'm ready, for a change."

"I noticed."

They went through the doors into the morning sun, and Paul stopped at the curb. "We'll need a taxi for this one."

"It's too far to walk?" Steffi asked.

He nodded and flagged a taxi. Inside the cab, Paul spoke across the seat. "Palazzo Acerbi."

The driver nodded, and Paul settled back, enjoying Steffi's company and watching the landscape pass. He felt relieved that the bustle of the fashion week had reached its end and more so that tomorrow was a new beginning with Steffi.

"I ordered our train tickets for Venice," Paul said. "We pick them up at Central Station tomorrow."

Mentioning the tickets, he noticed her hands tighten in her lap. "Don't worry. Once you're there, things will fall into place. I'm positive."

She sent him a faint grin. "I'm glad you're so confident. I'm still working on courage."

His heart went out to her, but he'd prayed so often that meeting her grandmother would open doors and windows, letting her heart fly free.

"Thanks," she said, shifting her tote bag. "*Palazzo* means palace?"

"Yes, and this one's a beauty. When I realized we were going there, I read about it. It was the home of a marquis in the seventeenth century. Now it's used for exclusive fashion shows like this one."

The cab made a turn and came to a squealing stop. Traffic blocked the thoroughfare and moving ahead looked hopeless. Paul rolled down the window, and exhaust fumes invaded the inside of the taxi. He cranked it closed and breathed a sigh, wondering if they were near the location.

Paul looked at Steffi, and without asking, she gave him a nod, as if she understood. He leaned over the driver's seat. "*Parla inglese?*"

"Sì," the driver said.

"How much further?" Paul asked.

"Two, three blocks," he said, holding up two fingers.

"We'll walk the rest of the way," Paul said, pulling out his wallet and handing the appropriate bills to the driver.

Paul slid out on the curbside and helped Steffi. The driver sat while they moved forward along the rough concrete. Ahead they saw the monumental gate, wide enough for coaches to pass through. When they showed their press cards and entered into the colonnade courtyard, Steffi came to a stop and grabbed his hand with a squeeze.

"It's beautiful." She gestured toward the main rococo staircase decorated with stucco and bronze work.

He agreed, and they followed the crowd upward to the second floor. Paul gaped at the extravagant room. He leaned closer to Steffi. "Do you have your camera?"

She lowered her eyes, then raised them. "I don't need a camera."

"You don't? I thought you always took your own photographs." He remembered the hurt he'd felt when he thought she didn't trust his ability with a camera.

"Not anymore." She gave him a tender smile.

"And why not?"

"Because I have you," she said. She slid her arm around his waist and gave him a squeeze.

Her admission was all he needed to hear. He called that real progress.

Chapter 6

The train swayed as it sped through the Italian country-side, nearly rocking Steffi to sleep. Her mind filled with the wonderful time she'd had in Milan. She'd been pleased with the feature articles she'd sent to the magazine via the Internet, and she'd received accolades that lifted her spirit.

Meeting Paul had been a gift from God. Not only had he been kind and helpful, but also he'd become her friend, one of the best friends she'd had in a long time. She'd always been afraid to form attachments, fearing she would be hurt again. Today Steffi chided herself for her fear. Why hadn't she given the problem to the Lord? Since she'd come to Italy, she'd drawn closer to her faith. . .perhaps an influence of Paul's.

When the train had made a short stop at Verona, Steffi had longed to get off and make her way through the ancient city streets and visit the setting of Shakespeare's play, *Romeo and Juliet*, but time didn't permit. Instead, she'd admired the church steeples and tall fountains visible from the train station.

"How much longer?" she asked Paul. The closer they came to Venice, the more her heart palpitated and her hands trembled.

He grinned. "You sound like a little kid. I don't know, but we're close." He lifted her hand from the armrest and held it in his. "Are you getting nervous?"

"Yes. I suppose it's silly. My grandmother's not waiting for me at the station."

"That's right. We'll get there, and you can take time to collect yourself. I know in my heart, Steffi, that you'll be happy you did this."

"Thanks for your confidence."

She returned her attention to the passing scenery while her mind sorted through a myriad of questions and imaginings, trying to guess what her grandmother would look like and be like. Would she be as loving as her letter indicated? Would she have the answers to the questions that burned in Steffi's heart?

The conductor passed by, calling out, "Venezia." Venice. Steffi's heart stopped, and she caught her breath. She was being foolish, she realized, but anxiety wrapped around her chest like barbed wire.

The train pulsed to a stop, and passengers rose, pulling baggage from overhead bins. Steffi sat still, unable to make her legs move.

Paul rose and stepped into the aisle, then pulled down their carry-ons. "You're staying onboard? Where are you headed? Florence?" His voice was teasing.

She lifted her gaze and tried to smile, but her face had frozen in place. "I'm petrified, Paul."

"We're in Venice," he said, taking her hand and urging her up. "Think of the city, not the mission. You can take a day to catch your breath."

His suggestion made standing easier. Steffi roused herself

and slid into the aisle, then grasped her bag and followed him from the train. Outside the air felt damp, and puddles attested to a recent rain. She breathed in the fresh air and watched the sun peek from behind a cloud, sending rays of golden light shimmering into beads of moisture clinging to everything.

She followed Paul as they collected their bags and headed toward the taxi sign. Forgetting where they were, Steffi gawked at the line of people standing along the water's edge. "This is it?"

"Taxi or bus. That's your choice."

"In the water?"

He gave her a poke. "Venice has no streets. I thought you realized that. It has canals. It's water taxis and buses. . .or walk. Those are your choices."

"I never gave that much thought," she said. "I figured we had options. . .like Amsterdam. I'm just surprised."

The line moved closer, and they settled into a water taxi.

"Venezia Splendid Hotel," Paul told the driver.

The man acknowledged him, and Paul moved toward the back. Steffi chuckled when he had to stoop to ease his way beneath the low opening into the interior. They settled on a hard bench inside, and when the taxi filled with eight passengers, they headed along the canal.

The sight was more than Steffi had imagined. Ancient buildings of stone and brick lined the waterway with small piers—some covered with canopies—for passengers to disembark or to wait for a water taxi. Poles lined the dock where boats or gondolas could moor to the building. Shuttered windows, some with small wrought iron balconies, looked out over the winding canal.

They wended their way through narrow channels with walls

so close Steffi could almost touch them. They turned right and left, like city streets flooded with water. Unique bridges, each different in appearance, spanned from one side to the other. Pedestrians passed overhead while some hung over the railing waving to them as they motored beneath. Homes, hotels, apartments, and businesses lined the way, and at an occasional stop, a passenger or two left the taxi.

When the canal widened, Paul squeezed her hand. "This is the Grand Canal."

Steffi eyed the expanse of water, and her pulse raced when the taxi sped past a gondola, with its unique shape like ancient Persian shoes with toes and heels curving upward. The lone oarsman stood at the back, his long pole cutting through the water. He dressed in a black-and-white striped shirt, wearing an Italian sombrero with long black ribbons wrapping the crown and hanging down in back. Steffi had seen them in photographs but never imagined she'd see the real thing.

"This is amazing," she said, her heart in her throat. Yet at the same time, she was filled with sadness. Why couldn't she be this excited to meet her grandmother? She felt her body shrink into the bench, weighted with guilt and sorrow.

"Something wrong?" Paul asked, eyeing her with concern.

She shook her head. "I'm just overwhelmed." Steffi had told the truth, being engulfed in a mix of emotions on both ends of the spectrum.

"You would have missed this if you'd decided not to come. See what God can do." He slid his arm around her shoulders and gave her a squeeze. "He directed you to Venice."

Paul looked sincere, and his words hung in her mind. "Do you really think it was God's work?"

He raised her clasped hand and brought it to his lips. "Steffi, I believe this whole adventure was God's bidding." He lowered his lips and kissed her fingers.

She warmed inside at this gentleness. . .and his faith.

Again they left the Grand Canal and wove their way down another narrow channel. Steffi looked ahead and saw a bright red awning and thin red-and-white poles, like a barbershop.

"Venezia Splendid Hotel," the driver called. The motor rumbled as they stepped from the taxi and loaded their luggage onto the pier. In a moment, the boat sped away, leaving a soft ripple of waves in the brackish water.

Paul gathered his luggage, and she followed, stepping into the hotel—her first step in Venice and her first step toward facing the woman who called herself grandmother. That step was far wider and more frightening than any other Steffi had ever taken.

❧

Paul held the city map he'd been given at the reception desk and gave it a quick look. The streets appeared like a maze, divided only by the snaking width of the Grand Canal.

Steffi eyed the plan and shrugged. "You know me," she said. "I'd get us lost in a minute."

He chuckled as they stepped through the doorway to the outside, his camera hung from his neck on a wide strap. To the left, he spotted a footbridge to allow people across the canal where narrow streets rambled into wider walkways and piazzas. Not one bicycle or motor vehicle interrupted the pedestrian streets. Only the waterways buzzed with the sound of the water vehicles.

He looked to the right, where the sidewalk wended off into

a maze, and grasped Steffi's arm, steering her in that direction. They ambled past glass and silk shops, boutiques, and cafés, stopping on occasion to glance into the colorful windows displaying lace, embroidery, and silk garments. Finally they reached an ornate fountain marking the entrance of Piazza San Marco, the largest square in Venice.

Steffi hurried ahead, like a child chasing the ice cream man, her hair blowing on the breeze and her trim body twirling like a sandstorm. She faced him and ran backward, beckoning him to join her.

Paul hurried to catch up, laughing at her exuberance. When he came to the center of the amazing square, he stopped, letting the magnificence settle over him. Steffi came to his side and slid her hand in his. His heart lifted at her open acceptance. He squeezed her palm, praising God for allowing them this time together in such a perfect place.

After removing his lens cap, Paul framed in the surrounding buildings and artists on the square selling their paintings of well-known Venice scenes. He set up his shot, adjusted the exposure, and captured the moment. When Steffi wasn't looking, he photographed her awed face, taking in the beauty.

Paul replaced his lens cap, and they ambled, hand in hand, to the outside tables that spread along the square. Violinists filled the air with music, and people walked past, taking in the beauty of the day and of the ornate buildings that surrounded the piazza.

"It's breathtaking," Steffi said, gesturing toward the magnificent structures. In front of them stood the Basilica of San Marco—Saint Mark in English. The ornate facade covered with Romanesque carvings had five archways leading into the church. On the right stood the Doges Palace, a gothic structure built of white and pink marble. Paul felt as awed as Steffi, but his masculine pride kept his excitement under control.

"I'd like to go inside the cathedral," Steffi said, asking with her eyes.

He took her hand, and they joined the crowd making their way into the massive edifice. Inside, Paul marveled at the beautiful mosaic columns that lined the walls and the mosaic-tiled floor that echoed the sound of their footsteps. A reverent hush hung over the sanctuary as tourists admired the Byzantine enamel paintings and the goldsmith art that adorned the altar screen. As they crept along, Steffi sank to a pew, her head tilted upward and her facing glowing with amazement.

Paul opened his mouth to speak, then closed it, seeing she had bowed her head in prayer. He could only speculate that the prayer related to their quest. He longed to support her and show her how much he cared, but she had to make the decision alone. The delicate balance between finding love and clinging to bitterness was a journey Paul could not walk. Steffi, alone, with the Lord's blessing, had to be moved by the Holy Spirit to gift the older woman with a visit.

Lowering his head, Paul joined in Steffi's prayer. Where two or three are gathered, the Lord had said, and Paul clung to those words of hope.

When Steffi lifted her head, Paul rose, and they wove their way through the transepts and passed in front of exquisite altars, retracing their steps into the pleasant sunshine.

"Well?" Paul asked, having no real question in mind.

"I feel better," she said. "It's not my kind of church, but the magnificence drew me closer to the Lord and helped me imagine how much more glorious heaven will be. It was awesome."

They wandered away from the crowd past the government buildings and headed through the narrow streets to where the Grand Canal twisted through the city. When they reached another stretch of the wide canal, they stopped to watch the gondoliers propel their oars through the water in perfect rhythm.

"I know they're expensive, but I'd love to take a gondola ride," Steffi said, holding her hand above her eyes to block the sun, now low on the horizon.

"One day, maybe you will," he said, knowing he'd planned to do just that.

Paul raised his camera and focused on the gondoliers. When he lowered the lens, a thought struck him. "Let's find a photo shop where I can get these rolls developed. I'm anxious to see them."

Steffi gave him a playful pout. "You hurried me out so fast I didn't bring my camera along."

"Tomorrow's another day, and it'll give us a reason to come back."

She grinned, and he led the way, searching for a professional photo shop. Not too far along the canal, he spotted one. Inside, Paul was pleased to learn they had one-day service. He left the film and walked outside. Drawn by the tempting aroma of pizza drifting from a nearby stand, Paul realized they hadn't eaten for hours. He gestured toward the small café.

"Pizza?" he asked.

"Love it," she said, joining him at the window to order a large slice. They found a table and sat beside the canal. To the east, the Rialto Bridge spanned the wide channel with small shops lining its arch, and to the west, the sinking sun reflected in the calm water.

❧

Steffi took a bite of the cheesy topping, then ran her tongue along her lips to capture the wayward sauce. "Delicious and beautiful, too." Her free hand motioned toward the velvet sunset that spread over the buildings and rippled on the water.

They sat quietly, eating pizza and sipping soft drinks. From across the water, a concertina sent a soft wave of music, and from an occasional gondola, a tenor's voice drifted to their ears, singing an Italian love song. She watched the gondoliers dipping their long oars into the water in an easy rhythm. They stroked and glided with precision—the right depth, the proper speed, confident in knowing the pathways through the maze of canals and sensing the beat and cadence of each stroke.

Sometimes she felt as if she were heading downstream with one oar, unable to keep her boat on course and not always knowing the way. She needed direction and confidence. If only she sat in the passenger seat and let the Lord be her gondolier, she, too, would glide along life's canal knowing she was in good hands. She would have no assurance that her course wouldn't be rough, but with a pilot who knew the way, she would come through it safely. In the hush of conversation, she sent up a prayer, asking God to give her courage to let go and let God be her navigator.

"It's been a perfect day, Paul. I can't imagine what I'd be doing if I was here alone."

"You'd be lost in this maze," he said.

She laughed, and the sound warmed his heart.

"I can't imagine being here without you." He looked into her eyes and, for the first time, saw promise, a hint of hope and happiness he'd never seen before.

Paul slipped her hand in his and felt the quiet ticking of her pulse. They gazed at each other as the sun touched the rooftops, then sank below them, leaving only a shimmer of gold on the red tiles.

When the cooler air drifted off the water, Paul stood and Steffi joined him. No longer shy, he held her hand as they wove their way back to the hotel.

"What did you plan for tomorrow?" Paul asked, hoping the Lord had guided her answer.

"I—I'm not sure," she murmured. "I'm thinking about it."

"And praying?"

She gave him a crooked grin. "And praying about it."

"It's the only way, *cara mia*."

The tender words sprang from his heart, and Steffi's loving look lighted the evening darkness.

Chapter 7

Steffi stood in the window of her hotel room, looking at the canal that passed beneath her window. The moon lay like soft satin on the water, beautiful but leaving her with a sense of melancholy. Now she wished she had opened her heart to Paul and told him the fears that punctured her resolve. In her heart, she had come to meet her grandmother, and now she felt herself backing away from her purpose.

Closing the curtain, Steffi forced herself away from the window and sank onto the bed. She wanted to talk. Would Paul be asleep? She peered at her watch and gave a ragged sigh. *Have faith*, an inner voice whispered. The words startled her.

She walked to the telephone and punched in Paul's room number.

He answered in a heartbeat.

"It's me," she said.

"Hi. Can't sleep?"

"I'm doing the thinking I mentioned."

"How about the praying?" he asked.

His question knocked the air out of her. She'd already forgotten her promise to pray. "Guess I let that one slip."

"Time you changed."

His voice sounded gentle without reprimand, and she sensed he understood. "Pray for me, Paul. I need to let God take charge."

"You got it, my sweet."

"And speaking of help." She hesitated, knowing what she was going to ask, and drew in a calming breath. "Are you still dressed? Do you have time to talk?"

"Always. How about the café downstairs?"

"Thanks. I'll be there in a minute." She hung up the phone and grabbed her handbag.

Paul was waiting when she arrived. "I shouldn't have dragged you down here."

His tender look surprised her. "Losing your courage?"

He knew her too well. "Let's walk. Anywhere."

Paul nodded, and she suspected he knew she wanted the cover of darkness to ease the conversation.

They left the hotel and followed the walkway to San Marco Piazza. As they walked, Paul held her hand, and his touch brought her comfort. Entering the piazza, they found a bench near the fountain away from the bustle of the square. In the shadows, Steffi felt protected.

Paul slid his arm around her shoulders and drew her closer. "You need to talk, *cara mia*."

The loving phrase wrapped around her heart, and the fears that had weighted her spirit lifted, allowing her tongue to release it. "You're getting to know me too well."

"Never," he said, nuzzling her closer to his shoulder.

She found courage to gaze into his eyes. Though dimmed by the darkness, his concern—his gentle look—gave her confidence.

"I've lived in fear of rejection, Paul. I've pushed people away all my life before they abandoned me. I realize why, and I know it's not logical, but I was ingrained to feel bitterness and to dwell on rejection. My mother didn't mean to do that, I know, but it happened."

He didn't speak, but his silent touch let her know he was listening and feeling her emotion.

"When I get close to people, I hold my breath waiting for them to find out that horrible flaw I must have to chase them away." Her voice quivered, and she knew she was losing control.

Paul grasped her hands in his. "You know better. I learned to enjoy your flaws."

The lighthearted tone gave her a moment's reprieve from her sorrow. "Thanks, and I like yours."

His smile faded and a serious expression took its place. "Remember. You've been open enough to tell me this, and I thank the Lord that you have. It's what I've been praying for. You're changing, and you're growing."

He had been honest, and she wanted to give him a straight answer. "That's because I trust you. You're different and special."

"And so are you. God has made us all such wonderful promises. All we need to do is believe in them. In Romans, He tells us that all trials and tribulations are conquerable through Christ's love. You just need to have faith."

"My good sense does, but my irrational mind says no."

"Do you know what you've done all these years?"

Steffi shook her head.

"You've closed the door of your heart and bolted it, fearing who might come in. You've locked out not only the enemy but also friends. Jesus has knocked on your door, but fear has kept you from letting Him in. You've closed the door to love, Steffi."

He drew her around to face him, his eyes filled with sadness. "How can anyone let you know how much you mean to them when you hide behind a locked door? Open it, *cara mia*.

Tears welled in her eyes and rolled down her cheeks. Paul had been right. He'd seen through her scam of confidence; he'd understood her attempts to protect herself in shapeless clothes; he'd recognized her deep yearning to be loved. She'd spent her life feeling unhappy and insecure. Today was a first step. Paul had given her the key, and God would help her open the door.

"Everything you've said is true." She touched his face, feeling the prickle of a growing beard. "How can I thank you?"

He looked at her without response, and her heart froze for a moment, wondering. Then he captured her hand in his and kissed her fingers. "This is all the thanks I want. . .just looking into your eyes."

She sensed it coming. His lips neared hers, and she greeted them with pleasure, her spirit soaring at his touch. His mouth moved in a gentle caress, and she returned the kiss, enjoying the sense of joy and friendship that they shared.

Tomorrow. A new beginning. A new day. She'd made her decision.

⤮

Paul stood beside Steffi in her hotel room, his hand resting on her back to give her courage. He watched her fingers tremble as she punched in the numbers on the telephone. When she told him in the morning she would call her grandmother, he could not describe the joy. In his heart, he knew it was not only the right thing to do but that it was the key to opening the door for Steffi.

"Are you sure you don't want me to leave?" he asked, feeling uneasy about listening to her first conversation with her grandmother.

She shook her head, her ear pressed to the receiver.

Though he preferred to give her privacy, he stayed, as she wanted. He watched Steffi with her ear pressed to the receiver, and from the look on her face, Paul knew when someone had answered the telephone.

"Donata Rosetti, *grazie.*" Steffi hesitated. "Oh. . .*buona sera.*" She gave Paul a frantic look. "This is Steffi Rosetti. . . your granddaughter."

Her face paled while her eyes misted with tears. She stared at the receiver, then covered the mouthpiece, tears rolling down her face. "What should I do? She's crying."

Paul closed the distance between them and held her close. Her body trembled as she clung to him. "Talk to her, Steffi." He caressed her cheek and wiped away the moisture.

She pulled her hand away and spoke. "I'm in Venice with a friend. I've come to see you."

Her voice quavered, and watching the scene tore at Paul's heart. Though he couldn't hear the grandmother's words, he could sense her joy. Steffi's tension seemed to ebb as she spoke, and Paul shifted away again, praising God that she had chosen to take the path toward healing.

He sat on the only chair in the room, and when he refocused on Steffi, she was beckoning to him.

"Would you talk to her and get directions?" Though tears misted her eyes, she gave him a faint smile. "You know me."

He did know her and realized Steffi would never find the way to her grandmother's house alone. Paul took the receiver and spoke to Donata Rosetti. Though the woman had a strong Italian accent, she spoke in almost perfect English, and while he waited, Steffi scrambled for a scrap of paper, and he scribbled the directions to her villa in the Santa Croce district.

When he'd finished, Paul returned the telephone to Steffi, and she set a time then said good-bye. She placed the receiver in the cradle and turned to face him.

He saw it coming. The flood of joy and sorrow she'd controlled broke from its well and spilled down her cheeks. She rushed to Paul's arms, and he nestled her close as she sobbed on his shoulder. When Steffi calmed, she lifted her head and used his handkerchief to wipe her eyes.

"I'm sorry. It's—"

"Don't feel embarrassed. It's natural to cry," he said. "Your grandmother sounded thrilled. You've brought her joy. . .just by your telephone call."

"I know, but—"

He pressed a finger to her lips to halt her apology. He meant what he'd said. "What time is she expecting you?"

"For lunch. . .at one."

"I'll walk you there. Hopefully you can find your way back." He asked God's assistance on that one. The thought caused a grin.

"Why are you smiling?" she asked.

He caressed her cheek. "I'm happy for you, *cara mia.*"

❧

Steffi lingered on the sidewalk outside her grandmother's home. She'd never been to a villa and had no idea what to expect. She gazed outside the gray stone building, adorned with only slate-colored window shutters and door. Steffi read the address on the building again to make certain she hadn't made a mistake. Anxiety tugged at her nerves and tightened her chest. Her grandmother had sounded warm and loving on the telephone, and Steffi's heart had opened to the woman, but she'd learned that life held surprises—some bad and some good, and Steffi wasn't confident that the welcome wouldn't change to feelings she didn't want to face.

"Go ahead," Paul said, standing near the bell. "Ring it. You'll never meet her this way."

"Maybe that's for the best." She rubbed her hand along the tight cords of her neck. "I really want to leave."

"No, you don't." He stepped closer and, in the empty street, brushed a kiss across her lips. "You're here now. Have faith." His gentle touch sent a comforting warmth coursing through her chest, unleashing some of her fear.

She studied Paul's sincere face and gentle gaze. Harnessing courage, she stepped forward and pushed the bell.

"I'm proud of you." He squeezed her arm. "I'm leaving now, and I'll see you back at the hotel."

"No, don't go. I'll never make it back without you."

"Yes, you will. Straight down this sidewalk to the canal and a left will lead you to a water taxi or bus. They'll drop you off at the hotel dock."

"But—"

Her sentence was shortened by a noise at the door. Before she could move, an elderly woman swung open the gate and stood in the threshold, her eyes wide and pooled with tears. Steffi had no doubt. She recognized her father's features in the woman's face—her father's face she'd seen only in a single photograph now brought to life in the lean, attractive woman.

No words passed between them. Donata Rosetti opened her arms, and Steffi stepped into the embrace. The movement seemed so natural and felt so right.

"It has been too long. Too long," her grandmother said, her eyes searching Steffi's face, her voice trembling with emotion. "I've waited a lifetime for this moment."

Steffi nodded, unable to speak without sobs bursting from her bound chest. When she found her voice, she gestured toward Paul. "This is my friend, Paul DiAngelo." The words caught in her throat. "This is my grandmother," she said to Paul.

Donata greeted him, then took Steffi's hand and led her forward. "Come in. . .both of you."

Paul shifted back, then remembered his manners. "Thank you, Signora Rosetti. I wanted to make sure Steffi arrived here safely. I'm heading back to the hotel."

Steffi looked at him with longing, wanting him to stay, but she had no right to invite him in.

"No," Donata said, beckoning to him. "I have too much food for two ladies. Please, join us for lunch. It is nearly ready."

She stretched out her arm to him, and Steffi relaxed when she saw Paul step toward her and follow them through the doorway.

Inside the courtyard, Steffi faltered. From the outside, she hadn't expected such charm. In the center of the yard, beds of flowers surrounded an ornate fountain. Two shade trees stood near the U-shaped house, their branches giving shade to a wrought-iron table, bench, and chairs. A cobblestone path circled the yard and led to an arched doorway.

"This is lovely," Steffi said.

"This was your father's home." Her grandmother's voice

was weighted with sadness.

Hearing reference to her father, Steffi's heart knotted, and a thin edge of fear worked its way into her thoughts.

"Come," Donata said, opening the thick wooden door.

As soon as Steffi stepped inside, luscious scents of meat and sauce drifted from the kitchen. The foyer opened to a large living room with furnishings that had probably been in the home for many years—sturdy and well crafted. Donata motioned them inside, and they seated themselves on a tapestry sofa while she excused herself for the kitchen.

Steffi drew in a deep breath and looked at Paul. "I can't believe I'm here. Thank you for prodding me to come."

"God did all the work. I had little to do with it."

Steffi knew it was God's work, but Paul's faith and confidence had helped her more than she could say.

Within a few minutes, Donata returned and beckoned them into her dining room. An antique buffet and sturdy table shone with china and crystal. They gathered around the table, and Donata prayed, praising God for Steffi's visit. Anticipating their upcoming conversation, Steffi had a difficult time swallowing the wonderful food her grandmother had prepared. Yet Steffi grinned watching Paul enjoy the feast that arrived at the table in such abundance—salads, pasta, antipasto, chicken, roasted potatoes, fruit, and cheese. When the last course had ended, Donata rose and invited them into the living room.

"If you don't mind," Paul said, "I'd like to walk for awhile." He gave them a wry grin as if admitting his reason. "You both have years to cover, and I'd like to give you some time alone."

"Paul, you don't have to—" Steffi touched his arm.

"I don't have to. I want to," he said. "I'll enjoy the fresh air."

Steffi knew she was defeated, and with a wave, Paul stepped outside. Through the open window, she heard the street door swing closed.

"Why not enjoy the sunshine, too?" Donata said, rising. "Let's go into the garden."

Steffi rose and followed her grandmother into the courtyard. She led her to the chairs beneath the tree. Steffi selected a chair in the sunlight, while her grandmother settled onto a wrought-iron bench in the shade.

Donata turned her face toward the outside door and gestured. "He seems like a fine young man." Her tender gaze filled with understanding.

"He's wonderful. We don't know each other well, but we will." Feeling she needed to explain, Steffi told her grandmother about her work at *Mode* and how she'd met Paul.

"Surely the Lord's doing," Donata said, her slender hands clasped in her lap as if in prayer.

Steffi's pulse skipped, hearing her grandmother's reference to her faith. She knew so little. "Was my father a believer?"

Her grandmother's face grew melancholy. "Your father was a wonderful man who knew the Lord well. He was a good man, Steffi, and he loved you dearly."

The unexpected words rattled through her and shook her to the core. Steffi knew she should take her time and allow her grandmother to speak at leisure, but couldn't hold back her curiosity. "I don't understand how he could love me and. . ." She let the words trail off, seeing the look that filled her grandmother's eyes.

"So much sorrow has passed through this house," Donata

said. "Your father not only loved you, he loved your mother."

As if struck by a hammer, Steffi winced with confusion and disbelief. How could this be? She searched her grandmother's face, looking for an explanation. "But how can that be? Why was he here and not in New York City?"

"Sit here beside me," Donata said, patting the bench seat. "Let me tell you about your father and the love he had."

Her grandmother's look drew Steffi from the safety of the chair. She rose, her heels clicking on the cobblestone, and settled beside her grandmother. The older woman clasped Steffi's hand in hers. Donata's skin was creped with age but as soft as velvet.

"Your grandfather, Rocco, was a good man. Hardworking. Generous. He loved children, but the Lord only blessed us with one, your father, Antonio. We called him Tony. He gave us such joy, and when he was ready for college, your grandfather allowed him to go to America for his education. That's where he met your mother."

Steffi listened, her mind filled with questions.

"My Rocco had a good business head. He bought land outside of Venice and grew olive trees. Rosetti Olive Oil was the best, and the business grew to be successful. He bought this villa, and he could afford a college education for Antonio in the United States.

"We were disappointed when Tony called to say he had fallen in love with a beautiful American woman." She lifted her hand and guided Steffi's face toward her. "You must have your mother's eyes, but you are so like your father. He was a handsome man."

"I don't remember him," Steffi said, "but my mother always

said he was good-looking."

"When you were a baby, your grandfather died, and since your father was our only son, I asked him to bring his family here so he could take over the business." Donata tapped two fingers against her temple. "I have no business sense, and I didn't know what to do."

The news inched into Steffi's mind. She had never known the reason her father had abandoned her. "But why didn't he bring us here? Why didn't we hear from him?"

Her grandmother patted Steffi's hand. "Your father told your mother about his homeland. You see how beautiful it is in Italy. . .and Venice is most lovely."

"It's charming," Steffi said. "It's a city of romance."

"Ahh, yes. The city of romance. Tony tried to convince your mother to come to Italy. She told him to go and promised she would follow."

Promised she would follow. "Are you sure?" Steffi asked.

"As sure as my heart beats. I overheard his telephone calls. I saw the tears in his eyes through the tears in my own. I had never met your mother. . .only through photographs."

Sorrow knotted in Steffi's chest. "I only saw one photograph of my father."

"Only one? I have many, Steffi. I will show you." She rose. Her face looked tired. Steffi knew the stress of their meeting had taken its toll on both of them.

Donata went into the house and returned with a thick album. Steffi held the book in her lap, and as she turned the pages, her heart leaped with each photograph—snapshots of her father as a child and another as a teen working amidst the olive trees. She drew the album nearer, seeing one of her father and mother looking into each others eyes, their love so evident. The vision touched her but left her bewildered.

"Your father sent us these pictures from America. New York," Donata said, running her finger over the photo in a caress.

Steffi pressed her hand against her heart and turned the page. She faltered while tears rose in her eyes and blurred the photograph—her mother stood beside her father holding Steffi, a toddler, in his arms, his face beaming at her. She tried to speak but only tears flowed.

Donata drew her closer, and they let the years of hurt and sadness flow from their heart in the form of tears.

When Steffi gained control, she wiped her eyes and studied the snapshot. The look of tenderness dumbfounded her. Her father loved her. She saw it in his face.

"This picture was taken shortly before your father came back to Italy," Donata said. "He brought the photos with him."

Steffi studied the images, admiring his strong build and his classic features, but most of all, she cherished the look in his eyes as he gazed at her in the photograph.

"This was the last picture I saw of you," Donata said.

Overwhelmed, Steffi sat a moment trying to gather her thoughts and settle the questions that had lain on her heart all her life. Despite the unknown details that still remained, she knew that her father loved her. "If he loved me, I don't understand why he didn't keep in touch and why I never heard from him when I grew old enough."

"You were never abandoned by your father, dearest Steffi. . . not your earthly father or your Father in heaven who has watched over you these many years. When your father could not be with you, he kept you in his prayers and in God's loving hands."

Confusion rattled through Steffi, wanting to comprehend and wanting to believe.

Donata lifted her finger and rose. "Come with me. Bring the album with you." Steffi nestled the photographs in her arms and followed her grandmother into the house. While Donata made her way across the room, Steffi returned to the love seat, still clutching the album. She ran her hand across the smooth leather, then placed it on the table in front of her.

She watched her grandmother bend to open a door beneath a large cabinet against the wall. When she returned, Steffi saw she carried a box. Donata placed it in Steffi's lap, then sank beside her. "Open the box. It will answer your questions."

Her hands shaking, Steffi lifted the lid and looked inside. A bundle of letters filled the bottom, and her heart lurched when she focused on the handwriting. Her mother's address was written on the front with bold strokes. The return address was this one—the villa. Steffi stared at the letters, postmarked and stamped, but marked return to sender.

"He wrote to us, and my mother sent them back?" Unable to handle the new information, Steffi closed her eyes, trying to comprehend what it all meant.

"I took the liberty to open these after your father died," Donata said. "Your father was adamant that I not interfere in your mother's life. . .or yours. He was a beaten man." Donata drew closer to Steffi and rested a hand on her shoulder. "My front door and my heart have always been open to you." She clasped her free hand to her chest. "I so wanted to offer the invitation, but I honored your father's wishes, but now, it is different. You are here."

With tears pooling in her eyes, Steffi grasped her grandmother's hand and pressed it to her cheek, then shifted her gaze to the box. Steffi lifted one of the yellowed envelopes and studied the date. She selected another. Time after time her father had written, and the letters were returned unopened.

"He never divorced your mother," Donata said. "Your father remained faithful to her all of his life."

The tears that rimmed Steffi's eyes rolled down her cheeks and dripped on the yellowed paper. "May I read one?"

"Read them all, my dear. They will help you to know that your father loved you both. The answers—if there are any—rest with your mother, but let me say one thing." Her grandmother touched Steffi's hand again, then clasped it between hers. "I forgive your mother. I trust she had her reasons, whatever they may be. God tells us to forgive so that our sins may be forgiven. We have all sinned. We have all made mistakes. I may never understand what happened in the United States, but I no longer need to know. I'm so filled with joy to meet you at last."

Steffi held her grandmother's hand and leaned over to kiss her cheek. Like a healing balm, the moment spread over her and cleansed her heart.

When Paul returned, Steffi was still reading the letters. In them, she heard the love and devotion her father held for them. She had felt his plight and experienced how his yearning turned to despair, then to sorrow until finally he'd lost hope. The last letter had been dated the year Steffi had turned fourteen.

"I'll make tea," Donata said, leaving them alone.

"Are you okay?" Paul asked, his face filled with concern.

Her eyes blurred again, and she nodded until she contained her emotions. "I'm fine." But the word seemed so inadequate. "Not fine. I'm much more than fine. I'm whole."

Paul's worried face brightened as he moved to her side and kissed her cheek. "I've prayed for this. All the time I walked, I asked God to help you find the answers."

"I found more than answers. I found healing. . .and forgiveness."

Chapter 8

Steffi walked beside Paul, her hand in his. The afternoon with her grandmother had been more than she had dreamed, and she'd left with promises to return to spend the following day. She and her grandmother had so many years to share in such a short visit.

As they ambled along the sun-warmed streets, Steffi told Paul all that she'd learned. In her shoulder bag, she carried photographs of her father that her grandmother had insisted she take with her—photographs to help her get to know the father she never knew.

"I wish I'd known him," Steffi said, weighted by melancholy.

"You do," Paul said, squeezing her hand. "Through your grandmother's eyes and in your own. She opened the door to the past and let you in. When I look at the photos, I can see your father in you."

She was touched by his thoughts. "Time seems so short, though. Three days to share a lifetime is impossible."

"Now that you've met, you can come anytime. Your grandmother would love it. . .and maybe one day she could come to New York to visit you."

Steffi couldn't imagine her grandmother in the bustle of New York City, but perhaps it was possible. Her grandmother had spunk and perseverance. She could do just about anything if she set her mind to it. Her letter to Steffi attested to that. "Today has been. . ." She paused unable to express the joy she'd felt.

Paul slid his arm around her shoulder and didn't try to find the words. Steffi knew he understood, and no words could express her gratefulness to God and the healing that she'd felt after so many years of sorrow and bitterness.

"Thanks for being here and letting me share all this," she said, gazing at his face, haloed by the setting sun.

"Coming here was an honor, and I mean that." Paul watched Steffi's gaze shift behind him, and he turned to catch the golden colors melting on red-tile rooftops and reflecting in the gray water of the canal. He raised her hand to his mouth and kissed her fingers. "I have an idea. . .the perfect way to top off an exceptional afternoon."

Steffi gave him a questioning look, but he didn't respond. Instead he drew her forward, weaving their way through the narrow walkways with shops on each side selling Murano glass and Italian silk. The walks opened to a small piazza beside the Grand Canal. Paul moved her forward.

"Get in line," he said.

"In line?" She swung her arm forward. "For the gondolas?" He saw the excitement in her face. "Yes. It's my treat."

"It's too expensive. You've done too much for me already."

"You let me be the judge of that." Paul grinned and urged her forward.

When they reached the front of the line, the boatman helped Steffi into the gondola.

"Venice Hotel Splendid," Paul said.

Walking carefully, Steffi made her way across the flat bottom to the upholstered chair covered with teal fabric and fringe. Paul followed, helping her sit. When he settled into the seat beside her, he pointed to the bow of the barge, where a crystal vase had been attached and held a bouquet of yellow flowers.

"Pretty," Steffi said.

"And romantic," Paul added.

The gondolier pushed away from the pier. With his single oar, he steered the barge into the center of the Grand Canal. Paul slipped his arm around Steffi's shoulders, and she nestled closer as they glided along the canal with only distant music and the dip of an oar breaking the silence.

The colors of the sunset spread along the water like an artist's palette, daubed by the shimmer of red, white, and brown brick buildings standing on the water's edge, and in the distance, the white arches of the Rialto Bridge neared.

In time, the gondola followed the twisting path and glided past San Marco Piazza, and in the sinking sun, lights of buildings came on along the canal, adding a sprinkle of glitter to the darkening water.

"Paul, this is beautiful. It is a perfect ending to a perfect day."

"Not an ending. Remember? It's only the beginning."

Awareness shuffled across her face, and she nodded. "A special beginning."

The gondola veered left and floated from the Grand Canal to a narrow waterway, heading toward their hotel.

"What's that?" Steffi asked, pointing to an ornate enclosed bridge that spanned the canal and connected two gray brick buildings. Two wrought iron-covered windows looked out over the canal. "I've never seen a bridge like that one."

"It's the Bridge of Sighs. Many years ago, the bridge was used to transport prisoners to the place of execution."

Her smile faded. "I suppose it was the prisoners' sighs that gave it the name. That's sad."

"Now it's just a beautiful bridge not used for prisoners anymore," he said, hoping to cheer her. He felt her shoulders relax.

"You know, today was like getting out of prison for me," Steffi said. "Finally, I'm free. I've unlocked the door that I kept closed so long."

"You've unlocked another door, too."

She tilted her head and gazed at him. "My grandmother's?"

He grinned. "Her, too, but I meant me, Steffi. You've unlocked the door to my heart. I've prayed for days that you'd feel the same."

"I do, Paul. You're wonderful. You've helped me find my way around Milan and Venice. . .and now, you've helped me find my way home to my grandmother. I don't think I'd have done it without you."

"I think you would have. God wanted it to be. You came all this way. I don't think you'd have given up."

"Maybe you're right, but you've become so important to me. Sometimes I wonder if God had this all set up."

Paul chuckled. "I've said that to myself so many times. The Lord works miracles and opens windows and doors. I realize we've only known each other a couple of weeks, but look how it worked out."

"We both work at *Mode* and spend our time in Manhattan," she said.

"God's fixed it so we have time to get to know each other better, but. . .to be honest, I know I've fallen in love with you."

"And I love you, Paul. You're the key to my heart."

A tenor's voice drifted across the water, his love song intermingled with the music of a concertina, while Paul drew Steffi into his arms and kissed her. His heart surged with the feeling of her lips on his and the beating of her heart against his chest. God had guided them to find each other and opened the doors of their hearts.

Dear Reader,

Two years ago, my husband, Bob, and I left our home in Lathrup Village, Michigan, and stepped off an airplane in Milan, Italy. There, we began our journey, visiting so many well-known cities such as: Venice, Florence, Rome, Pisa, Naples, Sorrento, Pompeii, and the Isle of Capri. As we entered some of the glorious churches, we were awed by the magnificent Christian art work created by such men as Michelangelo and DaVinci. We were amazed at the power we saw in the statue of David and the beauty of the ceiling in the Sistine Chapel. We stood beside DaVinci's *The Last Supper* and viewed the bell tower the world knows as the Leaning Tower of Pisa.

I am always awed by God's good gifts to us, including our talents. When I began writing fiction in 1997, I had no idea what abundant blessings the Lord would give me. I was published with Heartsong Presents in 1998 and since have signed contracts for thirty-one novels or novellas. The Lord has allowed me to witness about Him through stories that make people laugh and cry, stories that touch hearts and lives with the glorious truth of our salvation through Christ Jesus. I praise God daily for His abundant blessings.

Visit my web site and view the photographs of our trip to

Italy under the section called About Me. I love to hear from you. So please drop me a line and say hello. I wish you God's richest blessings.

In Him,
Gail Gaymer Martin

The Lure
of Capri

by DiAnn Mills

Dedication

To Beau and Allison for all of their research and help.

Prologue

Terri Donatelli blew the dust from her great-grand-mother's worn leather Bible and reached inside for the familiar yellowed slip of paper. She'd read the Italian words hundreds of times until she had them memorized. Each twist of the pen had drawn Terri into the world of her great-grandmother in the early 1900s on the Isle of Capri and the anguish of lost love.

Taking a deep breath, Terri unfolded the fragile letter.

My darling Giovanni,

How foolish and wrong I've been. Please forgive me for the pain I've caused you. Believe me, I never meant to hurt you. You brought so much love and laughter into my life, a precious gift from heaven, and all I've offered in return is heartache. You gave me your heart and a promise of a lifetime of devotion. I gave you tears and pleadings for you to join me in Venice. Always I begged for my way until now I fear it is too late. My selfishness eats at my soul; my tears declare my guilt. My joy, my love, I pray you still have love for me.

I thought I couldn't leave my family, but God in His infinite wisdom has shown me I can do anything with Him. Giovanni, we can be together, forever as God intended. I love you more than life, and I want to live out my days with you. I pray this is not too late.

Visions of Capri are before me. I remember the sound of the waves breaking against the shore, the salty scent of the blue Mediterranean, the cry of the seagulls, and the lure of the mountain peaks. Most of all, I remember your arms around me asking me to be your wife.

Oh, how you have captivated me along with the beauty of the island. Please answer me, my Giovanni! I long to be with you. Tell me you still love me!

Teresa

Chapter 1

Terri Donatelli stared at the colorful travel brochure describing the Isle of Capri and realized she might never return to Kentucky. She'd dreamed of this trip since high school, and tomorrow she'd actually board a plane en route to this ancient island. There, she'd live for a month among her ancestry. A fluttering exploded in her stomach at the mere thought.

Terri lived with the knowledge—and sometimes the loud and crazy antics—of a large Italian family. She loved them fiercely, and she understood their protective nature. But only when her great-grandmother revealed the beauty of the isle of Capri and the story of her first love, did Terri appreciate her heritage. The island drew her to explore all of its charm, wonder, and the exquisite people.

Her great-grandmother's recollections came alive with sights, sounds, and the anticipation of smells and tastes that surpassed any book or picture. Unfortunately, Teresa Donatelli passed away the summer after Terri's freshman year in high school, but the faded and worn letter to her first love lived on in the old, Italian Bible passed on to Terri.

Placing the travel brochure on her bed alongside her passport, airline tickets, and travel itinerary, Terri glanced at her cell phone and knew she had to call Ryan. The dreaded call had loomed over her the past week. Ryan had discovered her plans for a summer vacation to Capri, but he didn't know her departure date. Once she told him, he'd be considerate and shy away from any confrontation, but deep inside he'd be devastated. If she took the initiative to probe deeper, he'd admit his worrisome nature and his reluctance to let her go. Separating herself from Ryan Stevens was the only part of the trip that her family supported.

"Maybe you can find an Italian husband," her father said the previous night. "You certainly can't find one here in Louisville." Naturally, he made the comment while her older brother visited with his four boisterous sons.

Maybe God did plan for her to fall in love with a handsome Italian. What a legacy her great-grandmother had left for her. Giovanni might live on after all!

"Dad, I want to see Capri as Grandmother Teresa did. I don't know if anything else will happen. I'm going for the experience, not to find a husband."

"Sounds like a bad idea to me," Dominic said, a replica of their father, with high cheekbones and large dark eyes. "Who is looking after you?"

"I'm with a Christian tour group, and in case you haven't noticed, I'm a college professor with plenty of intellect to take care of myself."

"You should be raising kids." Dad lifted baby Josh onto his lap.

"Hush," her mother said, scooping up the toys from the

floor. "Terri has prayed about this, and she believes God wants her to take the trip."

"At least Ryan is not in the picture," Dad said. "Nice man, but not Italian."

Later, Dad found her alone in the kitchen and gathered her into his arms. He smelled of spice and garlic, and she loved it. "My sweet Terri, I want you to be happy. Naturally, I think you would be happier with an Italian man, but I want the man God wants for you. Am I forgiven for what I said about Ryan?"

"Of course. I love you, too, Daddy. I'll have a wonderful time and take lots of pictures."

"You are too much like my grandmother—ready to take on the world." He planted a kiss on the tip of her nose. "How does Ryan feel about your leaving?"

Terri hesitated. "I haven't told him yet."

Dad's huge shoulders raised and lowered. "Terri, he has a right to know. I've seen the way he looks at you. Honey, I'm disappointed. That man is going to be hurt."

"I'll tell him tomorrow night. I promise."

This was tomorrow night. Terri snatched up the phone and stared at the numbers. A big part of her wished Ryan wouldn't answer, but prolonging the inevitable made matters worse. He deserved to hear her plans. She owed him that.

Ryan Stevens taught English at the same university where she taught Italian. She'd met him three years ago, and instantly his considerate, thoughtful mannerisms attracted her. At the time, two popular coeds had cornered a young man who lacked social skills. They were teasing him about dating a sorority sister, and all he could do was stammer. Just when Terri stood ready to give the girls a lesson in propriety, Ryan stepped forward.

"Ladies, I'm sure this guy is flattered with your attention, but since he outdid both of you last semester, give him a break. He has better things to do." Ryan proceeded to escort the coeds to the end of the hall.

Later, when the young man disappeared, she congratulated Ryan on his rescue mission.

"Those two have no idea the damage they're doing to a shy kid who is speechless around a pretty face. Besides, they were brought up in church and understand perfectly what our Lord expects from us." He chuckled, and his green eyes sparkled. "I have them in my college Sunday school class and know their parents." He stuck out his hand. "I'm Ryan Stevens."

Terri smiled and introduced herself. "I started teaching Italian this semester."

"I know. I've been looking for a way to meet you."

Flattered, Terri braved forward. "How about coffee?"

Terri and Ryan had been together ever since. Their friends called them comfortable opposites, extreme personalities that appeared to balance. She lived up to every story about volatile Italians, while he never allowed things to bother him.

Ryan hadn't mentioned love, no doubt waiting for her to make the first move. His reluctance to initiate anything frustrated her, but he could be sweet with unexpected flowers and special gifts. Sometimes Terri's demonstrative family threatened her sanity, but Ryan always calmed her with infinite patience. On the flip side, Ryan's unpredictable moodiness drove her to distraction. Clamming up and preferring solitude when she loved the mere sight of people sometimes caused arguments. Left to him, she felt sure they'd date forever, when in fact she wanted to be wooed and wowed to the altar.

Terri wanted more from a relationship than an introvert and an extrovert seeking stable ground. Terri craved excitement and adventure, and she'd find it for sure in Capri. Without another moment's delay, she speed dialed Ryan's phone.

"Hey, what's happening in your world?" she asked.

"I might ask the same," he said.

She heard the edge in his voice. "Sounds like you're in a great mood."

"I'm trying to be."

"Ryan, what's wrong? You know how I hate to play games."

He expelled a heavy sigh. "I'm not the game player here. I saw your sister today, and she asked me how I felt about your upcoming vacation."

Terri inwardly groaned. "My trip is why I'm calling."

"To say good-bye before you whisk away to Italy?"

"You're not being fair. You knew I was going to Capri this summer." She should be apologizing, but the words refused to form.

"I see a big difference between talking about a trip and making the travel arrangements without informing me. I thought we had better communication than this."

Guilt assaulted her, but not enough to take total blame. "Maybe if you had encouraged me to pursue my dreams, I wouldn't have kept it from you."

"And I thought we'd honeymoon in Capri—visit the spots your great-grandmother spoke about."

His words stunned her and irritated her at the same time. "How nice to inform me. And when did you plan the wedding? Was this before or after your declaration of love?" Instantly she regretted her outburst. "I'm sorry, Ryan." She plopped down on the bed. "I'm behaving like a spoiled kid. Please forgive me. I intended to tell you weeks ago about the trip, but I assumed you'd try to stop me."

She heard his radio playing contemporary Christian music in the background. The song spoke about finding time in a busy schedule for God.

"I'm sorry, too. Honestly, I'm disappointed, and I don't understand your obsession with the island."

"You never have."

She heard the music lower. "Do you think you'll find the man of your dreams there, like your great-grandmother left behind?" She envisioned his eyes narrowing and his fingers combing through amber-colored hair.

"Ryan." She stopped the flow of words before she did more damage. Actually, his question hit closer to the truth than she wanted to admit.

"For what it's worth, I love you."

Why didn't he tell her sooner? "I don't know what to say." Why couldn't he have planned a romantic dinner with music and candlelight, instead of blurting it out in the near heat of an argument? She couldn't appreciate the words without atmosphere.

"What time is your flight? I'd like to take you to the airport," Ryan said.

As usual, we don't talk about the real issue. "I need to be there around ten in the morning."

Right then Terri believed she'd made the right decision in not telling Ryan sooner. She didn't want to be around when he withdrew into his little moody world.

❧

Now Ryan understood Terri's moodiness over the past few

weeks. He thought she'd planned to break off their relationship. In reality she had. He tried to give her space, honor her independence, and not smother her, but most of the time she interpreted his responses as indifferent. On the other hand, when he began deep subjects about their relationship, she took two steps backward by claiming he didn't understand her.

He hoped this separation sealed their relationship and didn't destroy it. He'd prayed about his love for her and planned a proposal complete with a honeymoon package to Capri. Better Terri be sure about them than hold on to this fairy tale of everlasting love in the arms of an olive-skinned Italian.

On Saturday morning, as he drove to Terri's house with her favorite coffee drink safely in tow, he talked himself into optimism. He did love this woman, even if the right words never formed his heartfelt emotion. For certain, a month without her would be endless, but he could utilize the time to plan for a dynamic proposal—one he knew she dreamed of.

Terri possessed a vivacious love for life that he wished fell in his gene pool. He treasured the intensity of her olive-colored skin, smoldering, dark eyes veiled in a curtain of lashes, and lips perpetually curved in a smile. They quarreled occasionally, but their differences were what he valued about their relationship. Granted she loved people and thrived on them, while he preferred quiet times with dinner or a play, but he could fit into either situation. Terri called him the balanced one. Ryan smiled. Definitely he'd miss her, and he could only pray God brought them back together in a solid relationship.

Once he pulled into her driveway, he laughed aloud at the cars parked up and down the street. Every relative in Louisville must have shown up to wish her bon voyage. He shouldn't be so amused. His family lived in the hills of Kentucky, and he found new cousins at each family reunion. Both sets of families were ready to get together at a moment's notice.

"Hi, Ryan." Dominic Donatelli, Terri's dad, answered the door. "We're having a little going away party for Terri, but I believe she's ready to head toward the airport."

Ryan hugged Matelda Donatelli, Terri's mom, and shook her dad's hand. From amidst an enthusiastic crowd of well-wishers, Terri emerged with a single carry-on attached firmly to her shoulder and dragging a Pullman. A pint-sized nephew dragged another suitcase behind her.

"So glad you're here." She glanced about with a pasted grin and added, "I need quiet and space."

He laughed and brushed a kiss across her cheek. He would have kissed her on the lips, but the whole family was watching.

"Do you have everything?" her mother asked. She held a huge checklist in her hand.

Terri continued through the door. "Yes, Mom, you checked my suitcases twice. I'm prepared for any emergency known on the face of the earth."

"Mount Vesuvius might erupt," her mother said.

Ryan held his amusement. Once they drove away, Terri closed her eyes and leaned her head back against the headrest.

"Why didn't I choose a weekday to leave?"

"Because you didn't want any of them missing work."

They laughed as though the two were headed out for a sun-filled day rather than a month-long separation by the Atlantic Ocean. The sobering thought reminded him of his parting words to her.

"I have a few things I want to say." Ryan punched off the radio.

"Is this a lecture, Professor?" Her words hinted of sarcasm.

"Possibly. Would you like to hear my version of Hamlet?"

"No thanks, but let's get this over and done."

"Simply stated, I want you to have a good time. I want you to see and do all the things you've dreamed about. Leave no rock unturned. Make a million friends. Take a ton of pictures and download them to me at night—if you have the time. Soak up the Mediterranean sun and swim in the Grotto. Pick a few lemons and buy some souvenirs."

"Why thank you, Ryan." Her gaze registered surprise. "How sweet."

"I have a reason."

Her eyes widened.

"I love you, and I don't want you to have any regrets when you return."

Terri failed to reply but stared ahead at the road.

"Unless you don't plan to return."

Chapter 2

Terri stood on the long dock at Naples waiting for a boat to transport her to Capri. In the early morning, she munched on a cold, hard roll and sipped on the strongest coffee she'd ever tasted. She inhaled the smells of the sea and locked it into memory. Back in Louisville, she'd have tossed the roll and dumped the coffee, but here in the land of her dreams, she savored every bite and repeatedly told herself the coffee tasted of old world atmosphere. Her friends would have laughed at the unsavory meal arising out of years of saving for this trip.

Terri could barely contain her excitement. She'd arrived in Naples yesterday about noon, but the Capri tour group didn't leave until Monday morning for the island. This gave her time to convert money into euros and journal about her flight from Louisville. She'd managed a walk with a couple bound for the same tour and even shared dinner with them.

To think, in an hour she'd be in Capri. Excitement spiraled up and down her spine. If the water didn't look so choppy, she'd be tempted to swim. The tour guide, Lisa, suggested taking motion sickness medication, but Terri ignored her warning.

She'd never had a problem before, and her enthusiasm refused to allow anything to dampen her adventure.

She finished the roll and placed her hand over her shoulder bag while glancing into a sea of faces that represented many nationalities. Pickpockets roamed the area, and she anticipated keeping everything she'd brought.

The warm Mediterranean air bathed her face in a mixture of light sprays. Sea gulls dived and soared ahead, now and then grabbing up a piece of crusty bread. Great-grandmother had once been here. She might have stood on this very dock and waited anxiously for a boat en route to Capri. The turquoise-colored water welcomed Terri to a world unlike she'd ever seen, only imagined. Like her great-grandmother, she would live the island's magic.

People began to board the double-decked boat for the approximately forty-minute ride to Capri. Terri shuffled her baggage in line. All those ahead of her left their luggage below on seats then ventured to the open top with its fabulous view. She stood below for a few minutes, wondering if someone might steal her bags, but when everyone hurried upstairs, she followed them. A few of the passengers headed for something to drink, but she didn't want to waste a single moment.

Finding the perfect seat with a wondrous view of the island in the distance, she eased down, allowing the wind to tease her face in a refreshing expectancy of the days ahead. In a few moments, Lisa sat beside her.

"So, do I get a firsthand report of our arrival to Capri?" Terri asked. She had quickly warmed to the darkly tanned young woman from the Bronx.

"I'm up as high as I can be in hopes my motion sickness

tablets work." Lisa touched her stomach. "Every time I take this ride, I never know if I'll feel like quitting my job when we dock."

Terri frowned. "You must have a queasy stomach."

"Don't tell me you didn't medicate yourself."

"I didn't see any point in it."

"Take my word, this trip is unlike any you have ever experienced."

A strange fluttering flitted across Terri's stomach. The boat lunged ahead before she could conjure an intelligent reply as to why she'd ignored the warnings. "I may live to regret it."

Before long Terri vowed to adhere to every suggestion Lisa made for the remainder of the trip. The boat jumped over choppy water that left her hard roll and coffee somewhere in the Mediterranean depths. Still, she attempted to tune her senses in to the first glimpse of the island, a towering mountain rising in a blue-gray and silver haze.

By the time the boat reached Capri forty-five minutes later, Terri trembled with the assault on her body. Next time, she'd water-ski.

Nothing compared to seeing the island for the first time—even if she felt greener than the lush grasses and really wanted to crawl into bed. The island's dock was walled up against the mountain, which meant the boats coming and going used only one side.

"Are you going to be okay?" Lisa placed her arm around Terri's shoulder. "I'm a bit wobbly inside, but nothing like you look." The brunette had a unique accent, which amused Terri despite the current status of her body.

"Thanks. I had plans to enter the local beauty contest this

morning." Her attempt at humor sounded flat.

"I'm normally encouraging, but don't spend any of the winnings yet. We'll get to the hotel, and you can rest a little before we start our afternoon activities."

Terri closed her eyes. "Remind me of what we're supposed to do."

"A train ride straight up to a level where we catch a bus to Anacapri. The island is known for its steep hills and narrow winding roads."

Terri tossed her a wry smile. "I'm sure I'll enjoy it."

Lisa patted her shoulder then pointed around the upper deck. "You are not the only one who's had a rough time. We'll linger in the shops and restaurants for awhile until everyone feels better."

Terri nodded. If Ryan had been there beside her, he'd have done everything but thrown up for her. He'd also have insisted she take the motion sickness medicine back at the Bay of Naples. Right now he was sleeping peacefully in his condo in Louisville. Odd how her thoughts turned to him, when she wanted to concentrate only on her vacation.

With Lisa's help, Terri secured her luggage and hobbled off the boat. She wound her way through the various shops, sidestepping the restaurants, and making a mental note to sample the *gelato*—Italian ice cream—when her stomach settled.

When she took the time to study the other tourists, she saw all of them had at least one companion to share the adventures. For a brief moment, she felt a twinge of regret in not having Ryan beside her. But she had Great-grandmother's letter in her shoulder bag, and God promised to never leave her or forsake her. Terri and Lisa had established a friendship of sorts, and a small group of college girls had included her in their conversation. Terri didn't have the heart to tell them about her professorship at Louisville University.

"The train leaves for Anacapri in thirty minutes," Lisa said. She left Terri and the college girls, who introduced themselves as Tami, Heather, and Ashley, outside a bakery while making a round to notify the rest of the group. The scent of fresh bread didn't hold its normal appeal.

Terri scrutinized the train and the track ambling up the side of the mountain. Again her stomach protested. Forty-five degrees up looked precarious. Terri knew about the mode of transportation, but at this particular moment all she wanted was level ground. The seats inside the train were positioned in such a way that the angle of the train did not affect the passengers—a pleasant surprise. The higher the train climbed the more she could see the water and the many lemon trees. Ten minutes into the incline, the passengers moved from the train to a bus. Lisa had been correct in her description of the narrow, winding roads. At each curve, the bus honked to alert any vehicles traveling in the opposite direction.

Repeatedly, Terri told herself she would grow accustomed to the island's transportation, especially if she chose to stay permanently.

"The bus will drop us off at our hotel. It's the second stop on the left past the statue of Augustus Prima Porta," Lisa announced to the tour group. "This statue portrays Augustus as a victorious general posed in the ancient Roman fashion of delivering a speech. Note his stance and body proportions are to reflect an ideal man, athletic and commanding."

Terri remembered from the brochures that this statue was

a common sight in Italy. When it came into view, she felt the old excitement tug at her senses. Would the hotel be even more beautiful than the travel brochure depicted? Suddenly a list of all she wanted to see and do toppled across her mind: the villas, the Faraglioni, a yacht tour of the island, Mount Solaris, the Blue Grotto, the churches, and so much more. She yearned to speak Italian to the handsome people living in Anacapri and to delight in the easy lifestyle—so many memories to make in one month's time, and perhaps for a lifetime.

The breathtaking view from the hotel confirmed her trip— twisted rock and cliffs, patches of green, picture-perfect water. She snapped picture after picture, especially the view of Mount Vesuvius from her balcony. Later she'd download the pics and E-mail them to her family and Ryan. He had a special interest in volcanoes, and the story of Pompeii had always fascinated him. The eruption occurred in 79 A.D., and now two million people lived there—not her idea of the perfect home site.

Terri caught her thoughts in a gasp. Why did Ryan have to enter into her magical world? She'd left him in Louisville where he belonged. For that matter, she had no idea what her feelings were for him and didn't care to analyze her heart while on vacation. A moment later, his picture flashed across her mind. She did care for him and at times believed she loved him, but he was a boring English professor. Terri couldn't help but believe her great-grandmother would have insisted upon more.

She stepped into the open hotel onto a turquoise-tiled floor. It reminded her of the sea waters against walls and tall ceilings of white. Her room was typically European: a little small, a tiny bathroom, and no air conditioning. She opened double doors and inhaled the salty air from the balcony. Oh, the glorious atmosphere. Terri didn't need to dream any longer. She could touch, taste, and smell her dream!

Terri felt a need for adventure. Just like her namesake, she desired to experience Capri and whatever it held for her.

Without warning, heaviness pressed against her heart. What did God have in mind for her during the next month? A twinge of fear picked at her, reminding her of a little girl on the brink of opening birthday gifts. What if she didn't receive the treasures she wanted?

❧

The next morning after a breakfast of fruit, hard rolls, and strong coffee, Terri and the tour group headed for a lift that would take them to Mount Solaris. From the moment she began the trek up, the lush green of the hillsides and the lemon trees held her spellbound. At the top, she looked down on Anacapri, more beautiful than her imagination could fathom. Houses dotted the hillside, along with elegant villas, exquisite flowers, and the architecture of centuries old churches—their grandeur invited all to worship. A panoramic view of the water encompassing the bay and Mount Vesuvius rising like a huge cone moved her to click picture after picture. In another view, she captured the Faraglioni rocks, rising out of the water as though they were centurions guarding that portion of the island's jagged edge.

At lunch, the group wandered through Anacapri to sample the local food. Lisa strolled with Terri.

"Where are Tami, Heather, and Ashley?" Lisa asked, gazing at the throng of tourists like a mother hen keeping a watchful eye on her chicks.

Terri laughed. "They found out I'm a college prof. They

thought I was closer to their age."

Lisa's mouth curved into a grin. "What a compliment."

"Oh, they're sweet girls, but I made them feel uncomfortable."

"Can I ask you something?" Lisa asked.

"Fire away."

"Why did you take this trip by yourself? And I understand you plan to stay past the week tour." Lisa shrugged. "It's really none of my business."

Terri stood outside a restaurant and inhaled a sundry of enticing foods. The bakeries drew her inside as though the Pied Piper played a tune just for her. "It's a little complicated, but in short, my great-grandmother found the love of her life here, and I wanted to see Capri for myself."

Lisa's eyes widened. "So she met your great-grandfather on Capri, married, and eventually ended up in the States?"

"Not exactly. She was supposed to meet him here but couldn't bring herself to leave her family. They never met again."

"How sad. Did she tell you all this?"

"Yes, and I found a letter in her Bible. It was returned when the man couldn't be located."

"So you came alone."

Terri thought of Ryan and his plan for them to honeymoon on Capri. Irritated at her remembrance, she pushed his face to the farthest corner of her heart. "I'm the daring type."

Lisa studied her curiously. "How about lunch? Are you up for a ham and mozzarella panino?"

"Is that the sandwich with little mozzarella cheese balls?" Terri asked.

"The same, and you'll love the thick wonderful bread."

Late in the afternoon, the group returned to the hotel. Terri had hiked everywhere, and her leg muscles screamed with what the next day would bring. She looked forward to a leisurely bath before dinner. The romance of the atmosphere and anticipation for the evening left her tingling with excitement. Standing in the hotel lobby, chatting with a few of the tour group, she spotted a familiar face.

Ryan.

❧

Ryan knew once Terri discovered he'd made the trip to Capri, she'd be angrier than when she learned her favorite brother had eloped with an Anglo high school dropout. Ryan did not misjudge her reaction.

Fire blazed from her dark eyes. He saw the betrayal, the accusations, the invasion of her Capri escapade. Instead of approaching her, he merely smiled and headed for the elevator. What had once seemed like a wonderful idea now looked like a stunt from a love-struck kid. Humiliation crept up his neck and face.

He stepped into the elevator, but not before Terri scooted in beside him. A middle-aged couple chatted with her, and for the moment, relief washed over his battered nerves. At his floor he exited, and she trailed after him.

"Ryan, what is the meaning of this?"

He whirled around. "I'm on vacation. I figured since I had an empty summer planned, that I might as well check out Capri."

"You followed me here?" Her words fairly exploded.

He pressed his lips together. "Actually, no. Despite what it looks like, I had all the trip information about the island, and

I decided to check it all out for myself. I had no idea we'd be staying at the same hotel. For that, I do apologize."

"I don't appreciate this at all." Her face reddened, but when she opened her mouth to say more, a trio of young women interrupted them.

"Hi, Terri. Want to have dinner later?"

Ryan saw her professional façade take over. "Sure. I want to take a long bath, first."

"Great, how about sevenish?"

Terri nodded and watched them disappear. She whipped her attention back to him. "Are you trying to spoil my day? Are you going to destroy my vacation, too?"

Ryan crossed his arms over his chest. He had never understood Terri's unpredictable, extreme emotions, and this was another one of those times. "Terri, I'm here and I intend to stay." He raised his hand in defense. "I have no inclination of disrupting your vacation. I have my own agenda, which means we will be seeing each other only in passing."

"I don't believe you for an instant."

"That's your choice. I really don't care. You made your feelings quite evident at the airport. I realized in Louisville that you had lost your commitment to our relationship. I'm a single man who has set his sights on a great vacation." He turned to head down the hall toward his room.

"If you plan to act unattached, then I will, too."

Ryan pulled the room key from his khaki pocket. "I never doubted you would do otherwise."

Chapter 3

Terri thought the hot bath would soothe all those things ailing her mind and body, but the fragrant lemon bath salts, native to the island, only relieved the muscular stress, not the choking lump in her throat. Ryan's deliberate plan to ruin her vacation infuriated her. In the next instant, a dull throb developed across her forehead. Did he think she was fool enough to believe he didn't purposely make reservations at this hotel? How could he mask it all by stating he wanted to see Capri and wouldn't get in her way?

I'm a single man who has set his sights on a memorable vacation. She didn't believe those words for one minute. Like a love-struck puppy, Ryan had followed her half way around the world to keep tabs on her behavior. Even her family hadn't gone to that extreme. She held high expectations for this trip, and she'd enjoy every minute of it no matter his devious interventions. After this, the two of them might not have a salvageable friendship. In fact, she might need to transfer to another university.

How could Ryan betray their relationship like this? For the past three years, they'd been inseparable. They'd laughed together, cried together, celebrated their victories, and prayed through the many trials threatening to separate them.

Terri drew in a breath and held it. They hadn't prayed about this trip. She'd chosen to alienate him from the entire matter. She'd even thought of leaving without telling him good-bye. She'd dreamed of a permanent location in Capri where she might meet the man God intended for her to spend a lifetime.

Terri knew she must pray. Her anger had caused her thoughts to veer in a sinful direction, and her past actions proved deceitful. She needed to ask God and Ryan's forgiveness and to forgive Ryan for attempting to ruin her vacation.

Lord, what is happening here? I don't dislike Ryan. In fact, I care about him very much, but why is he here? Does this look immature to You, or am I overreacting? She took a deep breath. *I'm sorry for the things I said, and I'll apologize.*

With a towel draped around her head and before she applied makeup, Terri phoned the front desk and asked to be connected to Ryan's room. He didn't answer.

Tami, Heather, and Ashley, who Terri had inwardly nicknamed the coed trio, joined her and Lisa for dinner. Like the previous night, the meal consisted of pasta in a tomato sauce, seafood, fresh vegetables, and more of Italy's wonderful bread. Unfortunately, the meal seemed tasteless in light of her tangled emotions.

"Who was that great-looking guy in the hallway?" Tami tossed a lock of platinum hair over her shoulder.

Lisa raised a brow and all attention turned to Terri. She wished she could crawl under the white linen-covered table. Nearby, a violin and soloist crooned a romantic melody, setting a mood for romance. She glanced about the room but didn't see Ryan. He must have elected to eat elsewhere.

"His name is Ryan Stevens, and he's an English professor at Louisville U."

"Where you teach?" Heather asked, a darkly tanned blonde. Terri nodded.

"Why do I think there's more to the story?" Lisa took a sip of water. "Your face is redder than my sauce."

"Seeing him surprised me." Terri straightened her shoulders. How could she change the topic of conversation?

"So are you two going to hang out together?" Tami asked. Only Ashley, the petite brunette, chose to keep silent.

"No. He has his agenda, and I have mine." Thankfully, the violin and the soloist strode their way, snatching up everyone's attention with a sweet song about a man in love.

At the end of dinner, Terri listened to the others chatter on about the next day's yacht tour of the island. The talk encouraged Terri to push aside her woeful misgivings about a spoiled vacation and look forward to another day.

The waiter, a handsome local wearing a name tag that read Dino, brought them all fresh fruit. He smiled, but he couldn't speak English. Lisa and Terri took turns ordering for them all, and Tami remarked about his perfectly white teeth and model-material smile. Heather stated she'd like to take him home in her suitcase. Ashley merely agreed, while Lisa pointed out the waiter most likely had a new girlfriend each week.

"Let God select the man for you," Terri said. "He already has one picked out for each of us."

"Can't I help Him along?" Tami's blue eyes sparkled.

Terri shook her head and laughed. "I think you're hopeless."

The waiter picked up Terri's uneaten dish of fruit and

walked toward the kitchen.

"Excuse me, I'm not finished," she said in Italian.

He didn't hear her and continued across the dining room. Terri rose from her chair and followed him. She tapped him on the shoulder and repeated her earlier statement. Dino flashed a smile that could have melted granite.

"I was teasing you," he said in perfect English. "You and your friends amused me, and I couldn't help myself." He handed her the fruit.

Humiliation crept over her. Terri saw a trickle of silver woven through his thick hair. Handsome did not even begin to describe him. "Thank you." She pointed to her table. "You understand those ladies are going to be mortified once they learn you heard everything they said."

He chuckled. "But I did like what you said about allowing God to pick our life partners. Do you really believe that?"

"Most certainly."

"I do, too."

"Mr. Vitulli?" a waiter asked.

Dino gave the young man his attention.

"Sir, you have a phone call in your office."

He turned to Terri. "Excuse me, Miss. I'm the manager of the hotel. Sometimes I like to work alongside my employees. That way I can appreciate their work. I'll appoint another waiter to your table."

Terri felt her smile coming from her heart to her lips. She nodded and turned to return to her table.

"Miss?" Dino's voice sounded more musical than the violin strings. He stepped to her side. "Since I see you are not in the company of a gentleman, may I ask to see you again?"

Her toes tingled. How long had it been since she'd been noticed by another man? "I think that would be fine."

"Would you care to join me here later on tonight, around eleven?"

Weariness tugged at her, but Terri refused to pass on Dino's invitation. "I'll be here."

Back at the table, she saw her friends once more had their attention fixed on her. This time, she didn't mind. Terri sat and purposely ignored them.

Tami, with her overwhelming sense of curiosity, broke the silence. "I can't stand this. What happened with that gorgeous waiter?"

"Oh, I learned he speaks perfect English."

The three coeds gasped. Words of humiliation spilled from their mouths while Lisa laughed and threatened to tell the entire tour group about the night's antic. Terri couldn't disguise her pleasure with the invitation, but she chose to keep the later meeting to herself. Great-grandmother's letter danced in her memory: Dino, a charming, handsome Italian and a Christian. God had blessed her indeed.

☙

Ryan ate dinner in his room rather than upset Terri with her friends. He'd gone for a long walk shortly after the argument and focused on his motives in coming to Capri. Had he traveled to this isle paradise to make Terri miserable or to win her affections? At this point, he didn't have a clear answer, and it frustrated him. Traipsing to another continent after her sounded like something a sixteen year old would do. At first when the idea struck him Saturday morning after dropping Terri off at the airport, he refused to consider it. By nightfall, he didn't care about the cost or what she might think. He'd planned for months to take her to Capri either as his wife or separately in a tour group. Instead she decided to vacation without him. He'd decided to travel alone and see the sights for himself, even take on a few days in Naples. If they met, he'd deal with the coincidence in a mature manner. Maturity would not get tossed into the sea.

Maybe his stubborn nature stopped him from admitting Terri had hurt him. He loved her with all his heart, and the proof lay in a black velvet box in his carry-on. Why he brought the diamond bewildered him, especially since she'd relayed her feelings for him on the road to the airport. Was this ridiculous venture his last effort to save their relationship?

Ryan couldn't save a one-sided love. With a sigh he stepped out onto his balcony and watched a half moon reflect on the water. In the background he heard the soft sounds of violin music and the hum of low conversations and laughter. He was in Italy, and he had no problem taking in the tourist attractions by himself. But the whole thing made him look foolish—like a stalker instead of a godly man.

All right, Lord, You have my attention. I'll talk to her tonight and apologize. I can easily reroute my trip to Naples and a few of the other cities and not make Terri feel uncomfortable. For certain, only You can orchestrate love between us. I give this relationship to You, where it should have been from the beginning.

Ryan allowed the beauty and the atmosphere of the Mediterranean night to thoroughly relax him. The time escaped him and before he realized it, the clock read a little past eleven thirty. He phoned Terri and hoped she hadn't gone to bed. Her normal metabolism had her falling asleep before nine thirty.

She didn't answer, and he didn't feel comfortable leaving a message of this importance. Restless, he grabbed his room key and headed for the restaurant. Maybe Terri and her friends had shared a long, leisurely, dinner. He'd politely interrupt her for only a moment.

❦

Terri gazed into Dino's dark eyes. In a way, he looked like all the men she'd grown up with, and in the next he resembled a storybook version of Prince Charming.

"Tell me about your life in America," Dino said. "I'm curious about your Italian family."

"We are demonstrative, loyal, and loud," she said. "We love each other to the point of a fault, and when we argue, we are just as passionate."

He folded his arms on the table. "Sounds like us here."

Terri wanted to know everything about this kind man. She'd gladly sit here all night and listen to the sound of his voice. "How many brothers and sisters do you have?"

"Ah, you didn't ask if I had any brothers and sisters, you asked how many—the mark of a true Italian. I have two brothers and four sisters."

"And you are the youngest?"

He leaned closer. "How did you guess?"

"I imagine your sisters spoiled you horribly, and you learned how to be charming and manage your own way."

"Absolutely. Now, let me guess. You were surrounded by brothers who protected you from any man who ever showed any interest."

"They still do." A giddy feeling enveloped her.

"I don't blame them." Dino picked up his water glass. "If

you were my sister, I'd have guarded you with my life."

"Dino, there's no need to pour on the flattery. I may be an American Italian, but still Italian."

He acted as though pained and patted her hand. She lifted her gaze and saw Ryan across the room. He stood at the entrance of the dining room, while she and Dino shared a table for two tucked away under an alcove. Luckily, the room appeared deserted. She expelled an inward sigh, but too late. He spotted her. In the dim lighting, she couldn't read his green eyes, but the emotions wafted through the air. She'd most certainly hurt him—again.

She turned her attention back to Dino with Ryan's drawn face playing before her. This was Ryan's fault; he should have stayed in Louisville. Between dinner and the meeting with Dino, Terri had convinced herself the relationship had long since died. She and Ryan could have avoided this if she'd insisted upon closure last Saturday. Reality checked in. This wasn't all Ryan's fault; she'd deceived him and needed to apologize.

"Does your tour guide have big plans for you tomorrow?" Dino scooted back his chair and gestured for a waiter to check on Ryan.

"The Blue Grotto and a yacht tour in the afternoon."

He nodded as though approving the plans. "The Grotto is quite beautiful. Sometimes, when I'm not too busy I swim there in the late afternoon, like a tourist. The water is incredibly clear, almost hypnotizing." Observing the waiter escort Ryan to a table, Dino moved around to face her again. "Would you like to have dinner tomorrow night? About nine? We could eat here or in my private quarters."

Having this wonderful man all to herself tempted her, but

Terri cautioned herself against a made-for-order entrapment. "Nine, and here would be fine."

"Good. By then, I will have extra help for the busy evening."

Relieved, she urged the trembling in her body to cease. She'd been with Ryan too long, and the business of getting to know someone else made her nervous. Terri yawned and felt herself redden.

"My lovely lady is tired and needs her rest. Let me bid you good night so you can be refreshed for tomorrow." Dino stood and reached for her hand.

It suddenly occurred to her that she and Dino would pass right by Ryan's table. A wave of guilt assaulted her. She'd betrayed him! Should she greet him like an old friend? Stop and chat for a brief moment? Introduce him to Dino? She cringed. She refused to be rude, but what should she do? Terri attempted to form a semblance of proper words, but just as she and Dino passed by his table, Ryan turned his attention in the other direction. Relieved, she moved toward the elevator where Dino charmed her with an endearing smile.

Terri adored the dimples on Dino's right cheek and his impeccable manners. Her stomach did a little flip. How long had it been since she felt this way about Ryan? Granted Ryan opened doors and displayed a special sentimentality that she appreciated, but he wasn't a handsome Italian and Dino wasn't a boring English professor. Ryan even owned a tweed jacket with leather elbows.

She fairly floated to her room. Words and laughter lingered in her ears. Once inside the confines of her Capri palace, she wondered how her heart would ever stop racing long enough to sleep. Readying herself for bed, she remembered the apology she owed Ryan. A glance at the clock revealed the lateness of the hour. Tomorrow, she'd talk to him. As her body relaxed and she bordered between reality and the dream world, the phone rang.

The shrill sound alerted her senses and woke her instantly. Reaching into the darkness, she answered on the second ring.

"Terri, I know it's late, but I need to apologize."

Ryan. "About what?"

"This trip."

"So you admit you followed me?"

"I'm not sure. It's not how I planned things. . .but I don't want to go into all that now. I want to reiterate my earlier statement. I will stay out of your way."

"Thank you." Terri started to say good night, but remembered her own admission of guilt. "I apologize for losing my temper."

"Which time?"

She heard the teasing in his voice and eased onto the pillow. Ryan could find something amusing no matter how dire the circumstances. "Tonight when I first saw you, and my behavior last Saturday when you took me to the airport. Deceiving you about the trip makes me feel. . ." She squirmed. "Feel disappointed in myself. I regret not having a long discussion with you about the whole thing."

"Do you want to break off our relationship?"

Terri hesitated. After deliberating about this for weeks, why did she feel reluctant to end it now?

"Terri?"

"I heard you. Ryan, I don't have an answer. I came here

looking for guidance in many areas of my life." She took a deep breath and exhaled slowly. "My inability to give you an answer is not right either. I certainly am not going to ask you to wait while I sort out my heritage and God's will for my life."

"I want His will, too, but you're right. I won't put my life on hold while you find yourself."

The bitterness in his words implied what he felt about seeing her with Dino. He was angrier than she ever remembered, and he had no right. "Don't put your guilt feelings on me. I'm perfectly content." A tear trickled over her cheek. Why didn't she believe her own words?

Chapter 4

The Blue Grotto had enticed Terri since she first saw the pictures from the travel agency, researched the marvel at the library, and searched for more information online. She'd read every word, savored the descriptions, and imagined herself indulging in every drop of blue water. This morning, she shivered in anticipation of the tour.

Terri glanced around the dining room looking for Ryan. She expected him there since he rarely skipped breakfast. A pang of something pricked at her heart, an indefinable feeling that she refused to dwell upon. Nevertheless, it took residence in her heart and instantly zapped her excitement for the day.

By the time the tour group boarded a bus outside their hotel and took the winding road down to the Grotto, she'd captured the enthusiasm from the others and felt better.

"Some refer to the Blue Grotto as a symbol of Capri. I'll let you be the judge." Lisa stood at the front of the bus. "First let me describe what you'll see. It may take a few moments for your eyes to adjust to the cave. The sun shines through the cavern and reflects off the blue water lighting the walls in a blue cast. It is probably the most spectacular experience of the entire island." She grabbed a pole behind the driver as the bus jerked with a curve. "Ancient Romans enjoyed the Blue Grotto, and their statues were found inside. As time went on, the inhabitants avoided the area in the belief witches and monsters lived there. Enjoy your boat ride—the cavern is filled with beauty and history. I assure you that Capri will always bring memories of the Blue Grotto."

"Can we take a swim?" a teenage boy asked.

"Not until after five when the boats are finished with their tours. You're on your own during that time, so feel free to venture back. Let me remind you the water is cold."

Terri planned to take her swim after the tourist group left for the week. Today, she and Heather chose to be the first to enter the water-filled tunnel. They stepped into the rowboat while those behind them waited to climb into the other waiting ones.

"You'll need to lie down to get through the narrow entrance," Lisa said.

"I'm too old to get into that kind of a position," a middle-aged woman said. "You didn't tell us about the inconvenience."

Lisa smiled. "It's only for a moment, and I believe once you're inside, the difficulty with the entrance will add to the beauty and charm."

"You can manage this," the woman's husband said. "I'll be right there beside you."

The man's encouraging words to his wife caused Terri to glance about. His comments sounded like something Ryan would say. Faced with meeting his family and nearly backing out when she learned they headed for a family reunion, Ryan made a point to tell her he'd not leave her side. He kept his word. Terri ended up having a grand time.

The scent of a popular and intensely strong perfume from Heather attacked her senses. Terri sneezed. A bit of regret nibbled at her. Ryan should have been there in the rowboat with her instead of Heather. The coed giggled as they passed through the entrance. Ryan would have stolen a kiss.

Instantly Terri shoved away her thoughts. Being comfortable with a man didn't mean she should spend the rest of her life with him. Ryan fit into her life like an old shoe, when in fact she needed a new one. Tonight she'd share dinner with a delightful, charming Italian man. For certain, she'd never consider Ryan's memory after this evening.

As soon as she rose to a sitting position, the grandeur proved more than blue light illuminating the walls of the cavern. It became an atmosphere of worship. All the other concerns around her faded in the beauty of God's handiwork, as though a writer of the Psalms had used the Blue Grotto to express His creativity.

For great is the Lord and most worthy of praise.

Never had a sight appeared so awesome. An ethereal light—holy and matchless to anything she'd seen before surrounded her. To even whisper might break the moment.

Lord, where are my thoughts? Why have I been consumed with things that do not glorify You? Here within this breathtaking light, I am humbled by Your greatness. Forgive my ugly thoughts about Ryan, and lead me in Your path.

༄

Ryan slept fitfully and rose long before dawn. He ordered the typical breakfast of rolls, fruit, and coffee to his room, and from his balcony he ate and basked in the beauty of Capri's sunrise. No painter could ever bring this mystical isle to canvas; one must live the encounter. Now he understood why the Russian writer, Maxim Gorky, spent a number of years here. Curzio Malaparte, the Italian writer, claimed Capri as a paradise. Ryan felt those words were quite an understatement. Given the money and time, he'd gladly play out his years writing from a villa balcony.

He planned to tour the Casa Malaparte villa later on today and remember every aspect of it for his students. The momentary diversion from Terri might be just what he needed to pull out of this horrible mood.

Normally, a good quiet time with the Lord helped him to see that focusing on himself was a horrible waste of God's time. However, the sinking feeling today had him more baffled. He feared he'd lost Terri, and he didn't know whether to attempt to win her back or assume she'd find happiness with someone else—like the suave fellow in the restaurant last night. She'd certainly not wasted any time in replacing Ryan.

Whatever had Ryan been thinking when he announced his intentions to conduct himself as a single man? Beginning a relationship with another woman sounded ludicrous, nearly repulsive, from his point of view. The best attitude for him to take came from his parents' era: if you love someone, set them free. If they're yours, they'll come back. Ryan didn't have the saying word for word, but he understood the meaning of it. With this realization, he knew the logical position meant staying away from Terri and not forcing her to make a decision about their fading love.

When Ryan checked into the hotel, he'd picked up the tour guide's schedule. This way he could plan all of his activities and be assured he wouldn't be in Terri's way. She'd have her own itinerary once he returned to Louisville anyway. He didn't want to think about how horrible the days would be while waiting for her to return.

Shaking the despairing thoughts, he studied the tour group's schedule. He could easily seek out the Piazza Umberto today and see for himself why the small, historical square was called the heart of Capri. Along with the stores and cafes, he could visit the San Stefano Church. Ryan had an interest in the churches there, so after grabbing lunch, he could tour them, too.

Enjoying this vacation came from a state of mind—away from Terri.

✺

Lisa encouraged the tour group to mingle along the Piazza Umberto and enjoy lunch on their own. A problem had arisen with the yacht tour, and plans for the rest of the day had been shifted. While in the ancient piazza, they could take in the sights for most of the afternoon. Terri had considered visiting some of the old churches and mentally listed the ones that piqued her interest.

"No matter how many times I take a group here, I always enjoy the Piazza Umberto," Lisa said. She'd worn her hair in a ponytail and with her tanned skin, she looked like one of the locals.

Terri glanced about. "I like the narrow, winding streets, although this all would be nicer if there weren't so many people."

"I agree. Aren't the flowers gorgeous? Makes me wish I could paint."

"I have little talent in that arena—or anything creative

with my hands," Terri said. "If I close my eyes, I can picture ancient people going about their daily business, the women with baskets and jars on their heads and children playing about their feet."

"Some scholars claim the walls of these structures date back to one thousand years before Christ and others much later. No one is really sure, but the architecture of the limestone blocks is about the fifth or sixth century."

"You are a walking storehouse of information." Terri laughed. "What do you do in your spare time?"

"Collect stamps." Lisa burst into laughter. "Not really, but I do enjoy fly fishing." She glanced to the right of them. "Isn't that guy staying at our hotel?"

Terri swung her gaze in the direction of the bell tower in the square. The three coeds stood with Ryan. Tami leaned into him and Heather touched his arm. Only Ashley kept her distance, but her tank top dipped short of decent.

Lisa peered at the foursome. "It's embarrassing how those girls throw themselves at guys."

"Right, and he doesn't seem to mind a bit."

"Why, you're angry," Lisa said. "Have you taken those girls under your wing?" She peered into Terri's face then back at the coed trio and Ryan. "Frankly, I see this all the time."

"It doesn't honor God." Terri stared into Ryan's smiling face. How could he do this to her? Was he flirting simply because he knew she'd watch his every move?

"You're right. I'll have a talk with them later."

"Good," Terri said. "I'm sure their parents would be appalled."

Lisa urged her to walk away from the sight. "Do you have plans for dinner tonight? I thought of eating at a cozy restaurant in Anacapri and wondered if you might want to join me."

Terri toyed with the truth, but what did she have to hide? "I have a date for dinner."

Lisa stopped in the middle of a crowded group of people. "Who? None of the men on the tour seem to be your type, especially since they're all married or too young."

"He's the manager of the hotel."

"Oh. The cute one with the dreamy eyes."

Terri nodded. "We met last night for coffee and he asked me then. You and I can have dinner tomorrow night, if that's okay."

"Sure, but you're avoiding the obvious. Did you speak to him in Italian and sweep him off his feet with your brilliant accent?"

"Are you kidding? I haven't spoken a word of it since I arrived."

"Then tell me how did you get such a handsome guy to ask you out?" Lisa waved her hand. "I didn't mean that. You're a great-looking woman, but what's your secret?"

"He knows a beautiful Italian woman when he sees one."

The two walked beyond the Piazza Umberto, laughing and talking about their lives. Terri fought the urge to turn around and see if Ryan and the coeds were still lingering. The thought of him dating one of those college girls infuriated her.

"Ready to head back to the others?" Lisa asked. "Some of them panic when they can't find me."

During her student teaching, Terri taught junior high. She knew exactly how Lisa felt. Truthfully, Terri wanted to see if Ryan had left the area. The short walk revealed him and the girls still chatting away.

"I've had enough of this," Terri said.

"What?"

Terri didn't reply. Instead she headed straight for Ryan. He was a disgrace to the teaching profession, and she intended to let him know about his inappropriate behavior. She gave her attention to the girls. After all, Lisa planned to handle them.

"Excuse me for disturbing you." Terri pasted on a smile. "May I have a word with Ryan?"

"Oh, hi, Terri," Tami said. "Ryan is so funny and cute, too."

"Actually, he's a great guy," Heather added.

Ashley said nothing. Her scooped neckline spoke for her.

"I'd like to discuss something with you girls," Lisa said, her voice laced with sweetness. "Let's grab something to drink first."

The coeds and Lisa moved toward a café, leaving Terri and Ryan alone. His face displayed no emotion, but she'd known him long enough to recognize the depth of his feelings.

"What can I do for you?" Ryan's green eyes cast yellow flecks in the sunlight. His hair looked lighter, too.

Terri patted her foot against the stone street. "Stop this foolish behavior. I'm embarrassed."

"Why? I'm staying out of your way, and I was here before your tour group arrived."

"I don't believe that for an instant."

Ryan pulled a folded piece of paper from his pocket and slapped it against his palm. "This is your tour group's itinerary. Look at today's schedule; it says Blue Grotto in the morning and yacht tour in the afternoon."

Terri swallowed. Regret began to weave an uncomfortable path through her body. "That doesn't excuse what you've done."

Rarely did Ryan exhibit anger, but lines buried across his

forehead and his jaw tightened. "Are you asking me to leave Capri? What's the deal here?"

She closed her eyes. Looking at him only fueled her anger. "The way you threw yourself at those college girls is disgusting."

"I'm not so sure it's any of your business, but they approached me."

"You certainly seemed to enjoy the dialogue."

Ryan nibbled at the inside of his mouth. "Really, Terri, green is not your best color."

Her pulse raced along with her temperature. "How dare you? I'm referring to your reputation. LU might not like the idea of their prized English professor linking up with coeds on an island paradise."

He moistened his lips and studied her face. "I have done nothing to warrant this outlandish accusation."

"Looks to me like you picked up a couple of younger women to make me jealous."

Ryan laughed, an artificial, irritating laugh. "I can't make anyone jealous who doesn't feel anything. And while we're on the subject of immature behavior, what about you throwing yourself at the waiter?"

"That's none of your concern. We are adults who are enjoying a friendship."

"Let me get this straight. You want to control any woman who talks to me, but you can go about your vacation however you wish. Something doesn't sound right."

Terri realized she couldn't talk sense to Ryan. "I was merely pointing out the dangers ahead by associating with naïve young women."

Ryan nodded in Lisa and the girls' direction. "At this point, they are more mature than you are."

Terri wanted to throw rocks at him. She'd merely tried to help him regain his senses. Glancing at Lisa, she hoped her friend had experienced better luck with the coed trio.

"I'm continuing my day," Ryan said. "I suggest if you want to ensure our paths not cross then leave a note for me at the front desk when your tour guide changes plans."

Chapter 5

Sweat streamed down Ryan's face. His shirt stuck to his back, and he clenched his fists. Never had he been this furious with Terri. First with her obvious jealousy—the only time she'd ever displayed such disappointing emotion—and secondly with what she thought he and those college girls were discussing. Granted young women tended to flirt as much in Capri as they did on American soil, but he knew his stance as a highly regarded professional and a godly man.

The three had questions about the history of Capri. They were part of a two-month tour of Italy as an extension of their college studies. Their knowledge of Mount Solaro and the Piazzetta equaled his. The girls were respectful, and their conversation continued on with the differences in Italian food, drink, and mannerisms. Laughter rose when a small boy and his sister struggled over the ownership of a shiny rock. Then one of the young women mispronounced the name of a villa, and the other two found the mistake amusing. Ryan felt discretion needed to be taken and excused himself from the conversation. But before he could walk away, Terri approached him with her accusations.

He didn't understand her one bit. They'd agreed the night before to enjoy their vacations separately and now this. Immaturity embedded in his mind. Terri's behavior involved a healthy dose of selfishness. She wanted a dream vacation complete with an Italian escort, while Ryan said and did nothing but act like an eighty-year-old professor. Besides, if she didn't care what he did, then why the show of jealousy?

Ryan stepped into one of the many tourist shops. He wanted to pick up something lemony to take back to his mother, probably bath salts like the ones in his room. He'd heard about the yellow lemon-flavored chocolate, a sure treat for his dad. After making his purchases, he made a decision. Once back at the hotel, he'd look into spending a couple of days in Naples. He wanted an opportunity to check out Mount Vesuvius and a host of other scenic and historical spots in and around the city.

Later on today, when he cooled down, he'd try to talk to Terri about this afternoon. He planned to apologize—again—for losing his temper. If he dwelled very long on his anger and not his direction from the Lord, she owed him one huge explanation.

Shaking his head, Ryan elected to tour the churches in the area. The one there in the Piazzetta, San Stefano, had its origin at the end of the seventeenth century. He'd already seen the marble inlay floor and the wooden picture of the Madonna and child, which, historically, had been thrown from a cliff by pirates and later found intact. With his interest piqued, Ryan moved on to tour the other churches. Some dated as far back as the Middle Ages. The Church of Saint Maria of Constantinople claimed to be the oldest parish on the island. It dated back to the eighteenth century, but the original church beneath it was built in the fourteenth. Odd how Americans grew excited about historic landmarks from the late seventeenth century, while the rest of the world hailed ancient structures, some built before Christ. Ryan often wondered how the ancient civilizations managed such feats.

Midafternoon found him at the Church of Saint Michele Arcangelo. He studied the magnificence of the tile floor depicting the banishment of Adam and Eve from the Garden of Eden, painted by Francisco Solimena. From the corner of his eye, he saw Terri and the tour guide slip into the back of the church.

He caught her eye and nodded. She moved his way, and he wondered if she intended to make another scene. Earlier this woman proved not to be the one he loved and cherished in Louisville. Was she about to confirm his earlier findings? What about this beautiful island had transformed her into. . . into someone he didn't know? His miffed feelings returned at the sight of her, but as she neared, all of his resolve to stand up for himself faded.

"Ryan." The sound of her voice sent his heart racing. His heart betrayed him.

Jamming his hands into his pockets, he forced a tight-lipped smile. "I'm just leaving."

"Could we talk?"

"I'm leaving, and right now is not a good time to discuss anything."

She shifted her camera bag and moistened her lips. "About today."

He strode past her. "Not now, Terri."

"I have some things I want to say."

"Not now!"

"You don't need to shout."

"I'm sorry." Ryan nearly bit his tongue, stopping a caustic remark.

"When?"

For a moment he thought he heard the old Terri—the gentle lift of her voice. He whirled around, anxious to see if the light of love still flickered in her eyes. Ryan braved forward. If they shared another argument, perhaps it would be closure for their dying relationship. If they got along fine then he could see hope for the future. "Tonight, around nine or so sounds good."

She sucked in a breath. "I have plans."

The words flew to his mouth before he had time to stop them. "A date?"

Terri's face hardened. "Let's not quarrel."

"You're right. I believe I was leaving."

Terri watched the man she thought she knew walk away. Ryan's back stiffened as he headed to the rear of the church. He greeted Lisa as he left. *Turn around, Ryan, please.* Terri no longer knew the English professor, the calm man who always put her cares and feelings first. Something about this island had changed him into a rude and obnoxious person.

She'd made a little mistake back there with the coeds, and he wouldn't even give her time to apologize. Maybe this was better. At least she found out here and not after a wedding. Perhaps her destiny was here on Capri and possibly with Dino.

Determined to hide the turmoil raging through her, Terri blinked and focused her attention to the front of the church. A moment later she felt a hand on her shoulder.

"Why don't you tell me what's going on? I've got a good ear." Lisa's Bronx accent that had sounded almost comical in the past now offered comfort.

"I can't. I don't even understand it all myself."

"Maybe by talking you can sort it out."

Terri released a pent-up sigh. "It might take awhile."

"Everyone is on their own, remember?" Lisa waved her hand around the church. "We're in the perfect atmosphere for a heart-to-heart talk, and when you're done, we can pray about the problem."

Terri crossed her arms and paced across the tiled floor. Tears threatened to flow, and she wasn't sure if they were for her or the lost relationship with Ryan. She thought she could trust Lisa, believing God must have put her in Terri's path for a reason.

"Let's sit down," Terri said. "This may take the rest of the day."

Without a word, Lisa acquiesced, and they slid into a pew.

"Before you begin, I'd like to ask the Lord to bless our time together," Lisa said. Without waiting for a response she began. "Heavenly Father, something has my friend upset. I want to help her work through this. Please use me to bring her to an understanding that You love her and want the best for her, amen."

"Thanks." Terri took a deep breath. "I've known you for only a few days and I'm about to reveal things I wouldn't want my own mother to know."

"Whatever you say goes no farther than me."

Terri considered the situation for another moment then plodded ahead. "Ryan and I have dated for the past three years.

We've talked of marriage, but nothing has ever been mentioned about love—sort of like the cart before the horse. I didn't tell him about this trip until right before I came. Needless to say, that was wrong."

"Then he shows up here."

"I hurt him badly, and I apologized, but he doesn't really understand why I came to Capri alone."

Lisa took her hand. "Was this your way of breaking off the relationship?"

"Maybe. . .I'm not sure. I thought my trip was to be a part of my great-grandmother's legacy, but now I'm rather disgusted with myself." She focused her attention on Lisa, hoping the truth might resurrect in her friend's eyes.

"Are you expecting to meet the man of your great-grandmother's dreams?"

The perpetual lump in her throat grew bigger. "I wish I knew. This sounds horrible, but I just wanted to do what she couldn't. Now hearing myself say the words makes me sound childish and foolish."

"Pardon me, but Ryan sounds a bit childish, too."

Terri hesitated. "He said he'd already looked into the trip for this summer either as a honeymoon surprise or the both of us booked separately in a tour. I blew his plans."

Lisa nodded. "So he came anyway."

"Yes, but he says he came because he'd already planned it. In fact, he's carrying around our tour group itinerary so we don't cross paths." A tear slipped down her cheek. "I'm not sure what to believe."

"Do you love him?"

How often had she asked herself the same question? "I'm

not sure about that, either. When I left him at the airport back home, I couldn't get away fast enough, but—"

"But today you overreacted when you saw him with Tami, Heather, and Ashley."

"I was really out of line. I must have made him furious, because he wouldn't even let me attempt an apology." Terri's stomach churned. "Looks like I want to have this fabulous vacation, and when it's over I can decide if I want to spend the rest of my life with Ryan."

Lisa said nothing.

Terri leaned back on the pew and massaged aching neck muscles. "I'm pretty despicable. My actions don't say much for my value of him or God."

"So what do you want to do about it?"

"I want to tell Ryan I'm sorry, but from there I don't know."

"Do you really want to find out what God wants?"

Terri stiffened. "Of course! I haven't slid that far back."

"Are you still having dinner with Dino?"

"Absolutely."

"I don't advise going, unless you're sure you don't have feelings for Ryan. It's not fair to either of them if you're undecided."

Terri felt the liquid emotion flow freely. She buried her face in her hands. "How can a Christian, educated woman like me be so torn with her life? I really want to have the dinner."

Lisa hugged her shoulders. "I think it's called distraction."

Lifting a tear-glazed face, Terri sensed the conviction in her spirit. "Instead of dinner with Dino, I need to spend time with the Lord."

"I think that's a splendid idea."

Terri peered at the altar. How many other people had

graced this church, looking for answers? Love seemed so complicated, especially when it meant a commitment for life. "Oh, Lisa, how could I ever think a fairy tale romance with someone I didn't know could compare with what God has planned for me? I don't know if the man for my life is Ryan, but I'm not doing one more thing until God gives me direction."

"Good. I need to get back to the bus soon and check on the rest of our group. Do you want to come along or stay here awhile longer?"

Terri expelled a heavy sigh. "I believe I'd like to sit here. I can always take a taxi if I miss the bus."

Lisa rose from the bench. "I'll see you soon."

"Thanks. Do you always counsel your tour group?"

Lisa smiled. "You'd be surprised."

"If you see Ryan, would you tell him I really want to talk—anytime he chooses?"

Lisa agreed and departed from the church. The quaintness of the centuries-old building left Terri feeling peaceful. *God, You are here with me, aren't You?*

She didn't expect an answer, but she did feel the incredible love surrounding her.

Forgive my childish ways. I'm ashamed of my actions and how I've hurt Ryan. Lord, if he is the one for me, please tell me. Right now, I don't even know if he'd forgive me for the hurt I've caused. I pray for the right words to convince him of my sincerity. Thank You, Lord, for always loving me—even when I'm not loveable.

Terri studied the tile floor. How fitting for her sin—Adam and Eve cast from the garden of paradise into a world that would battle against them to the day they died. In retrospect, Capri held the title of paradise, but the likeness didn't mean sin had escaped the island. Real paradise came only from God, whether the believer emerged from the slums of a large city or a tropical isle.

When Terri left the church an hour later, she flagged down a taxi to the hotel. Once inside, she promptly gave her regrets to Dino.

"Can we reschedule? Perhaps tomorrow night is more to your liking." He tilted his head, as though crushed beyond imagination.

"Dino, I wouldn't be good company."

"Ah, the problem must be another man."

Terri hesitated. "Yes, it is. I hope you understand."

He took her hand into his. "Affairs of the heart, we Italians always understand, but if you change your mind, you know where to find me."

Terri's next order of business came in contacting Ryan. He neither answered his phone nor his door. She double-checked every possible area of the hotel property, but nothing. Ryan often spent time on long walks at home, which gave Terri some consolation. Yet apprehension gripped her heart.

She left another message on his room phone about ten o'clock. When only silence greeted her, she decided to write him a note and slip it under the door. After midnight, Terri went to bed, tossing and turning until the brilliant Mediterranean dawn moved her to the balcony.

Oh, Lord, have I ruined things? Have I hurt him so badly that he can't bear to hear my voice? I can't blame him, but I'm begging for a chance to tell him I'm sorry.

Chapter 6

Terri pulled out her great-grandmother's Bible. In her haste to pack, she'd neglected to bring her own English translation. How sad, for Terri's Bible had notes written in the margins and several passages underlined.

Picking up the worn book, she searched through the Psalms. After reading several and praying the verses aloud, she turned to the front and stopped at I Kings, chapter nine. She had no idea why the accounting of Solomon's reign captured her attention, but suddenly she became immersed in the story. In the beginning of his rule, Solomon honored God with obedience to His commands. As the news of his wisdom spread, he accumulated more wealth than any man before or after him. Terri read on through chapter ten, silently cheering King Solomon and his fame—all because of his love and respect for God. Chapter eleven started out with the beginning of his downfall. The king had seven hundred wives and three hundred concubines. By the end of the chapter, King Solomon had sunk to great deprivation. He allowed his wives to manipulate him into serving other gods.

Terri closed the Bible and wondered why the story had held her interest, unless it served as a distraction from the turmoil going on around her. She pondered the similarities of Solomon's downfall and her desire to forget her problems. It all summed up in one word, the same word spoken today in her conversation with Lisa. Distraction.

A fluttering in her stomach caused Terri to once more focus on Solomon. He'd become distracted with the desires of his pagan wives. As a result of not following God's commands, his family eventually lost the kingdom.

Did Solomon's sin have anything to do with her? Had she been so preoccupied with great-grandmother's letter that she neglected to see God's blessings? She massaged the shivers on her arms. The thought of losing Ryan permanently frightened her. She'd literally run him off with her self-centered ways. When she compared his good qualities to his bad, an unbalanced scale set in her mind. So what if he taught English? Ryan's excellent mind and superb teaching skills earned him national acclaim. He might not have said he loved her in the conventional way, but he proved it with his endless devotion. Not that Ryan suffocated her. He'd always stood in the background and silently tended to her needs.

I've been such a fool. Lord, forgive me.

An hour later, she gave up on Ryan returning her call.

❧

"Ryan Stevens checked out yesterday afternoon," the clerk said.

Terri felt the bottom roll out of her stomach. "Did he say where he was going?"

The clerk looked at her like she'd asked when Mount Vesuvius would erupt. "Not to my knowledge."

"Thank you." Terri trembled and turned away. "Did he leave any messages?"

The clerk studied her closely. No emotion creased his face. "No. Nothing."

"May I talk to the desk clerk who checked him out?"

"I personally took care of Mr. Stevens."

Disheartened, she thanked him again and headed to the elevator. In exactly twenty minutes, the bus pulled out of the hotel with the tour group en route for the yacht tour. She couldn't go, not with this news.

Lisa met her at the elevator. "What's wrong? You were in much better spirits at breakfast."

Terri lifted her chin, determined not to cry. "Ryan checked out of the hotel yesterday afternoon."

Lisa sucked in a gasp. "Oh, Terri, I'm so sorry."

"I had this big speech prepared. I was ready to beg and crawl for his forgiveness."

"I'm sure he's somewhere on Capri. You could try calling all the hotels after we get back."

Terri's mind raced with the possibilities. Ryan had always been predictable, until he came to Capri. "You don't think he decided to head home?"

Lisa glanced around the hotel lobby before answering. "You know him better than I do. I'd rather think he's staying at another property."

"What do I do now?" Terri asked. "I'm confused and miserable."

Lisa linked her arm into hers. "Join us on the yacht tour. You can try to locate him later."

"I think I should stay here and make calls."

"And I think you should be with people and not alone."

The elevator door opened and the two women stepped

inside. "Get your things and meet me at the bus," Lisa said. "This is a beautiful day and no one should be shut up inside—"

"Feeling sorry for themselves?"

"Exactly."

❧

Ryan grabbed his luggage and lined up behind the passengers at Capri's dock. After yesterday, he wanted to get away from the island and never set foot on it again. All this trip had done was prove him short of insane for following a woman halfway around the world who didn't want him. He'd spent money that could have been used for something else instead of a useless trip to an island paradise. This was once designated as a honeymoon. Who ever thought a honeymoon came in singles? Stupid, purely stupid. All this time, he'd kept kidding himself about the real reasons for hopping on a plane and flying to Italy. His dad was right; men did crazy things because of women. At least being a boorish professor had kept him sane.

He could have taken the money spent on this trip and the two-carat diamond and purchased a new car—without all the heartache. Ryan stiffened. He could have pursued another Ph.D., added hardwood floors to his house, donated the money to a third world country with people starving to death, given it to church, anything, absolutely anything, besides blowing it on a woman who didn't care a whit about him.

An attractive redhead flashed him an ineffable smile. *Don't even bother, Lady. I'm finished with women unless God plants one in my front yard wearing a sign that says, "I'm Eve and you're Adam."*

"Are you traveling alone?" the redhead asked.

"Yes." Ryan tugged on his luggage. He refused to look at her.

"Spending time in Naples?"

"Yes." He scratched his whiskered chin.

"Alone?"

"Yes." With his final reply, he dumped his luggage on a lower seat and made his way to the upper deck. The last trip on these rough waters hadn't bothered him, but he'd again taken the recommended motion-sickness medicine. Right now he didn't care if the whole crew witnessed his dissatisfaction with the Mediterranean Sea.

Bitterness isn't a sign of a godly man.

Ryan found an empty seat and plopped down. He hated being reminded of his sin.

Love is patient.

He knew all that. The passage came from I Corinthians thirteen. He felt a nudge against his spirit to read the verses, a shove to read it right then. Ryan reached inside his carry-on and fished his way through his camera, passport, lip balm, sunscreen, and travel brochures to his New Testament. While the boat jolted and jumped, he read and reread the definition of love.

Love is patient, love is kind. It does not envy, it does not boast, it is not proud. It is not rude, it is not self-seeking, it is not easily angered, it keeps no record of wrongs. Love does not delight in evil but rejoices with the truth. It always protects, always trusts, always hopes, always perseveres.

In short, love was unconditional. Taking a deep breath, Ryan decided to do some heavy-duty praying while this boat bounced across the waves to Naples. The ride couldn't twist and turn his insides worse than his spirit felt.

Once he docked at Naples, he realized the futility of harboring bitterness against Terri. That type of sin promised to fester in him, with a guarantee of making him an angry, resentful man.

Forgiveness was in order. . .soon. Although he hadn't gotten to that point yet—he wanted to be there. Until then, he intended to focus his thoughts and spirit on cleaning up his heart.

Stubbornness was not a godly characteristic either.

Ryan tugged on his luggage and waved down a taxi driver. He loved Terri and didn't expect those feelings to vanish. Tonight he intended to rest and take care of a little matter between himself and God.

The following morning, Ryan phoned Terri's hotel, but she'd already left with the tour group.

"Has she left a message for Ryan Stevens?" he asked.

"No, Sir, but she does know you checked out."

Ryan's heart plummeted. "Would you connect me to her room?"

A moment later, the beep sounded for him to leave a message. His initial goal to sound strong and in control squeaked out like a weak monotone. "Hi, Terri. I'd like to talk to you at your convenience. You can reach me in Naples at. . ." Ryan searched the phone and the pamphlets around the room, but couldn't find the number. Before he could finish, his time expired. Frustration picked at him. He called the front desk of his hotel, but the clerk couldn't speak English. With a deep breath, he phoned Capri to leave another message. "Hi, Terri. Would you believe I can't find the number here at the hotel? And the front desk attendant doesn't speak English. I need you here to translate." *That wasn't a smart thing to say.* "Anyway, I'll try your room later." He disconnected then palmed his hand against his forehead. He still hadn't said what he intended. One more time, he dialed Capri.

"May I have Terri Donatelli's room please?"

"Most certainly."

Ryan waited until he realized his phone charges would equal the national debt.

"I'm sorry, Sir, but I'm unable to connect you to her room. Our phone system is experiencing problems. Can you please try back later?"

Ryan replaced the phone as gently as his rising temper would allow. He remembered Terri stating how he never grew intensely angry or charged up with enthusiasm. Something about Italy had pushed that characteristic over the top.

He snatched up his camera and headed downstairs. This would be a perfect time to visit the site surrounding Mount Vesuvius. He and the volcano, which had erupted more than fifty times since it first destroyed Pompeii and Herculaneum in 79 A.D., were sleeping time bombs. Luckily Ryan found strength in the Lord to control his new-found anger. Although the thought of God racing after him with hot volcanic ash at the speed of a hundred miles an hour did make him feel a bit warm.

Thank You for hearing my confession last night, Lord. I know the situation between Terri and me will work out according to Your perfect will.

Ryan boarded a bus and headed toward Mount Vesuvius. He'd been interested in the volcano since childhood, mostly because of the excavation of Pompeii. It puzzled him as to why two million people now lived in the area, as though challenging the mountain to shower them with ash, stones, and pumice while ushering in a river of molten rock. He remembered excavators finding bread in stone ovens preserved for over two thousand years. Right now he felt like his unconfessed sin had hardened for that length of time.

He shivered. Looked like God had a good reason for paving the way to Italy. Back home, he wouldn't have noted the analogies.

He toured the Museo Archeologico Nazionale, one of the greatest museums in the world, housing many of the relics of Pompeii and Herculaneum. The collections captured his attention, but he couldn't rid his mind of Terri.

As soon as he returned to the hotel, he called Capri. Their phone system was still unable to transfer calls. Ryan swallowed the words forming in his mind and thanked the desk clerk.

"Would you like to leave Miss Donatelli a message?"

"No, thank you." He wanted to talk to her personally. Surely by tomorrow he'd reach her. The longer the hours away from her, the more he felt his love grow. Strange, but true.

The following morning, he received the same information. Determined to find patience, he elected to seek out historic churches and take a tour of the catacombs—the underground burial grounds used by Christians in ancient times to escape persecution. Those dank and dark tunnels made him appreciate living in a country that allowed freedom of religion.

In the late afternoon, Ryan tried Capri again. By this time he felt sure the phones had been sabotaged.

"When do you expect the phone system to be in working order?" Ryan asked the clerk in Capri.

"Soon, Sir. Very soon."

Ryan replaced the phone and glanced about his hotel room. Sitting there waiting for modern technology to take control of his forgiveness issue with Terri seemed like having scientists figure out the origin of man. First thing in the morning, he'd take the boat back to Capri.

Chapter 7

Terri listened to Ryan's message repeatedly until she memorized every word, including how he said them. A lot of good it did her since his voice contained no emotion. If only he'd indicated why he needed to talk to her. When he didn't call back, the grueling situation grew worse. She contacted the various hotels, villas, and rental properties to see if Ryan Stevens was registered as a guest, but nothing. Of late, she wondered if he'd gone home. Even with allowing travel time, Ryan should be in Louisville by now. There his phone rang endlessly until the answering machine kicked in, and then she heard this long hum indicating a trail of messages. She'd left two and saw no reason to leave any more. Where could he be?

She considered everything from Ryan using an alias to the possibility he didn't want to hear from her or anyone else. Not that she could blame him.

"You're driving yourself nuts," Lisa said. "If you don't talk to him before you leave Capri, then you'll see him when you get home."

Terri groaned. "That's what I'm afraid of. This trip means

nothing until I can talk to him."

"Girlfriend, you might have to cut your stay short."

"I know, and I'm considering heading back to the States. I'll give him a few more days before I make a decision."

The two women walked into the hotel after a day of touring villas. The styles and gardens were breathtaking, but Terri ached to have Ryan there beside her.

"Miss Donatelli," the desk clerk said. "May I have a word with you?"

Instantly she wondered if Ryan had called.

"A Ryan Stevens has called here several times, but our phone system hasn't been able to transfer calls."

"Did he say anything else, leave a number?"

"No, only that he'd call back later."

Terri's heart sped ahead. "When was the last time you talked to him?"

"On my shift. . .last evening."

"Are the phones working now?"

"Yes," the clerk replied, "as of a little while ago."

Terri seemed to float to the elevator. Ryan repeatedly tried to contact her! The knowledge sent her spiraling upward instead of into the crevice she'd crawled under.

"Okay, so it's good news," Lisa laughed. "Doesn't look like he'll quit trying until he talks to you."

"I'm not leaving my room tonight. Do you want to have dinner with me?"

"Sure. Are you going to be too excited to eat?"

Terri hesitated. "I'm the type who eats when they are up, and this is definitely an up."

Hours later, after Terri and Lisa shared dinner, dessert, and coffee, the phone still sat silent.

"Lisa, there's no point in you baby-sitting me all night."

"I'm here because I want to be."

Terri stood and paced the room. "You're here because you're loyal and caring. I'm an adult and can handle what does or doesn't happen."

Lisa took a deep breath. "I have a big question, one you don't have to answer only think about."

"Okay. How badly is this going to hurt?"

"Depends." Lisa stared at her until Terri offered a brief nod. "You told me Ryan always catered to you—the places you wanted to go, restaurants and things."

"He treated me like a princess, a spoiled one I might add." Lisa glanced around the room.

"Go ahead. I'm asking for your thoughts. If Ryan and I ever mend our relationship, I don't want to run him off again."

"Do you think you controlled the relationship to the point he basically had enough?"

"Oh, yes." Confused by the obvious statement, she plunged ahead. "I've already admitted to driving him away."

"But why? That's what I think is the core of you and Ryan's problems."

Terri poured herself a glass of water and took a sip before anchoring it on the table. Her mind raced with Lisa's evaluation of the whole situation. "I don't understand. I did everything for him, even told him when to buy me flowers and suggested how his career should proceed."

"My point."

Terri rubbed her temples. She failed to see how Lisa viewed the situation, and it irritated her. Lisa spoke as if she knew Ryan personally, and she didn't. Terri peered into her friend's face. She didn't see any malice, only an earnestness to help. The truth, even more painful than what she'd done, embedded in her mind and latched itself onto her heart. "I. . .I'm a control freak."

"Possibly so."

"You believe control is the issue, not one single incident?"

"Only you and God have the answers."

The ugliness in Terri physically hurt. She wrapped her fingers around the glass of water and brought it to her lips. "I thought I'd worked through all of this, but I haven't." Terri saw where her glass had left a watermark. If she set the glass precisely over it, no one would ever see until the glass moved. The thought was repulsive.

Lisa interrupted her realization. "Are you okay?"

"I don't particularly care for this picture of me."

"Do you want me to leave?"

Terri picked up the glass and viewed the water spot. "Not for the reasons you might think. I need to talk to God about turning everything over to Him. If I don't and Ryan and I come to an understanding, I'll push him away again." She shrugged. "He may have already decided my overbearing personality is too much for him."

"Girlfriend, you can turn the issue over to God tonight, but it could take awhile to change your life patterns."

"I understand. Looks to me like I need to start somewhere and then commit to not falling captive to it again. It makes me sick that I've been trying to play God."

"The reason why He sent Jesus."

A light rap at the door startled Terri. "Yes?"

"It's Tami and Heather and Ashley."

Not exactly who Terri wanted to see, but the girls had been especially sweet the last few days. She opened the door and welcomed them inside.

"We don't want to stay." Tami's gaze darted between her friends and back to Terri. "We just wanted to tell you that we know you're upset, and we hope it's not something we've done."

A lump rose in Terri's throat. "Not at all. Please come in. Lisa and I are talking and we'd love for you to join us."

The girls slipped inside. Heather touched Terri's arm and Ashley offered a smile.

"Really, we don't want to bother you," Heather said, "but we've been praying for you."

All the critical remarks she'd made about the three inched across her mind. "Thank you so much." Terri gestured to the bed. "Have a seat." She noted how Ashley's sundress looked adorable, and told her so.

"Thanks. When Lisa suggested I might not be representing my parents or my college in an appropriate manner, I decided to be more conservative." She reddened. "More importantly, I know God was disappointed."

The girls exchanged looks. "One more thing. You were right about Dino."

She'd been so absorbed in her misery over Ryan that she couldn't remember what she'd said about Dino.

"We're going to wait until God puts the right man in our lives and concentrate on school," Tami said.

It's what I should have done. "What happened?" Terri asked.

"Dino asked each one of us to dinner. We realized he wasn't for any of us."

Suddenly Terri found the admission hilarious. Lisa picked up on the irony of it all, and in the next breath they all were laughing.

"You made my evening," Terri said. "All I've done the past few days is feel sorry for myself."

"Is it the professor from your university?" Ashley glanced at her girlfriends.

Terri brushed back a stray lock of hair. "As a matter of fact, it is." Without considering the matter another instant, Terri told the girls everything. "I'm not such a great person and certainly not a good role model for the three of you."

"But you're transparent," Tami said. "I wish I could so easily confess my mistakes."

"Thanks, but I'll feel a whole lot better when I can apologize to Ryan." She paused. "I've taken advantage of him too many times. Guess I got what I deserved." Terri shivered. "That's not a feel-sorry-for-me attitude; it's simply the truth."

"We'll keep praying for you," Tami said. She glanced at her friends. "We'd better go. I promised my parents I'd call, since tomorrow is our last day on Capri."

Terri reached over to take Tami's hand. "You've been a real blessing. And who knows? If you ever decide to attend Louisville University, you might want to take my Italian class."

After the trio left, Terri turned to Lisa. "You, too, off to your room. I'm fine, really. God's peace came in the way of my new friends."

"Tomorrow's our last day," Lisa said. "We need to make the most of it."

Terri picked up the tour schedule. "Free day. Sounds good. Think I'll take my own personal walking tour and review a few of the villas. Maybe soak up some sun at the pool."

"I have some last minute things to do before I conclude the tour."

"Please," Terri said. "I want us to keep in touch."

"By all means. We'll E-mail and maybe squeeze in a little visiting."

Terri hugged the young woman. "You've been my biggest blessing. Thanks for not allowing me to rot in self-pity, and thanks more for helping me see my faults."

"Absolutely. We're sisters now—just from opposite ends of the country. The next time we meet, we'll work on my head junk."

After tears and more hugs, Lisa left and Terri phoned the front desk to see if Ryan had left a message.

"I'm sorry. Mr. Stevens did call, but we're experiencing problems again."

For the first time, she didn't note the anxiousness. He had attempted to contact her again. His repeated efforts mattered more than anything. She'd make it through this, and if God so desired, the two could mend their relationship. No doubts festered in her heart; she loved Ryan. The thought of hearing his voice sent shivers up and down her arms, and the idea of seeing him again brought emotion to the surface.

I'm in a heavy-duty maintenance mode, God, but I know You will carry me through. A control freak who's out of control. She giggled.

The next morning, Terri took a taxi to the Punta Tragara, a magnificent hotel that some of the members of the tour had visited. After basking in the luscious vegetation along the road, she reached the hotel and its magnificent view of the

Faraglioni Rocks. At this height, she could see over their tips. Her mind wandered. The rocky cliffs were forever separated by the clear blue Mediterranean. Dare it not be the case with her and Ryan.

The taxi drove a precarious winding road down to the marina, where she strolled through the throngs of tourists, listening to the romance of the Italian tongue intermingled with the languages of the world. Everyone was in a hurry, impatient to maneuver their yachts into the sea. She observed all those around her. They were too hungry to wait for food; too many people stood in the way to snap the best picture; there weren't enough taxis to take them to their hotel; and there were too many crowded tourist shops. She wondered how long before they stopped to understand Capri's true beauty came in the sense of harmony with God and His nature.

In the moment between the cacophony of the busy crowd and a secret whisper breathing peace in her soul, Terri understood the meaning of Great-grandmother's letter. She also grasped God's purpose in bringing her here to this beautiful island—for Terri to abandon her fantasy world and to mature in her faith. Great-grandmother fulfilled her destiny in marrying a man who brought her to America. He loved her and their children. He took on the role of spiritual leader by becoming a servant to his God and family and establishing a legacy of truth and love. One didn't need an isle paradise to find those things; one only needed to wait for blessings by being obedient and allowing the heavenly Father to control the universe.

Leaving the busy dock, she contemplated a quiet walk with the thought of shortening her trip in Capri. The island's charm held her tightly, but Terri felt a hunger to return to life as she knew it.

"Terri."

At the sound of her name, she whirled around. The words caught in her throat. *Ryan.*

Chapter 8

Ryan saw the varying degrees of emotion pass over Terri's face: surprise, fear, and perhaps regret. He questioned her response. Did meeting him face-to-face cause that much despair?

"I won't take up much of your—"

"I know you've been trying to reach me." Her lips quivered. "Sorry, I didn't mean to interrupt."

He wondered if her abrupt reply was to shorten the conversation. Wouldn't be the first time. "I'm going to finish my vacation touring other parts of Italy, but before I leave I'd like to talk to you."

Terri's face paled. "When did you have in mind?"

"I know you're busy. I'm fairly flexible in my departure."

"Where have you been? I called every hotel, villa, and rental property in Capri."

Startled, he jammed his hands into his shorts pockets. "I was in Naples."

"I thought maybe you returned home."

"Is that what you wanted?"

Tears welled in her dark eyes. "I'm not sure. I don't think so."

"You must believe our relationship is over, which—"

"Ryan."

Frustration bit into his resolve. "Please, Terri, would you let me finish before you interrupt?" He took a breath. "Which is why I need to say a few things. Are you available to listen to what I have to say or not?"

She nodded and a large tear rolled down her cheek. He hadn't expected weeping; although occasionally she resorted to tears to manipulate his actions. This seemed different.

"I'm trying to control the situation, aren't I?"

Her admittance shocked him. "Most likely," he said.

"I can listen now or later. You name the time and place."

"Would you like to take a walk?" His heart picked up pace.

"Yes, and I promise not to interrupt."

He smiled. "You might have to change your heritage."

She returned a shaky smile. "I'll do whatever it takes, and when you're finished, I'd like to talk, too."

Terri's last words touched his heart. He hadn't been deceived; she was sincere. Without a word, the two strolled away from the crowd. "I've been doing a lot of thinking, and I owe you an apology for coming here like a love-struck kid." He expected a response, but she said nothing. "I told myself that I came because I'd planned a trip to Capri for us, and I didn't want the enthusiasm wasted. Truthfully, I chased your plane in hopes of persuading you to marry me. I should have realized you wouldn't have planned this trip without my prior knowledge unless you wanted to end our relationship. For the problems I caused, I am sorry."

He slipped a sideways look at her and saw more tears streaming down her face. Normally she used this opportunity to point out his mistakes. Terri reached inside her purse and pulled out a tissue. Dabbing at her eyes, she peered his way.

"I don't think you caused as much trouble as I did, but if you feel you need my forgiveness, then it's yours," she said.

"Thank you. Now, it's my turn to listen."

Her tears flowed freely, momentarily setting him back. "Terri, I've never seen you like this. Has something happened? Is your family okay?"

"What's happened is the realization of my selfish, controlling nature."

Ryan focused his attention not only on Terri's words but her body language. Could the woman he loved have grown in her relationship with the Lord? She combed her fingers through her hair, and he inwardly smiled.

"Since we started seeing each other, I've called the shots. Really, Ryan, I used the excuse of my Italian family's boisterous personalities to control you and everything we did." She paused and he waited for her to continue. "I feel horrible about this trip—treating you more like a disobedient puppy than a man."

"I'm interrupting here, but I allowed you to manage us. You can't take the responsibility for something when I share the blame."

She reached for another tissue. "I don't know how else to ask this. Are we finished?"

"Do you want to be?"

She burst into sobs. He couldn't bear not comforting her any longer. Gathering his beloved Terri into his arms, he laid her head against his shoulder. "I want another chance," she finally said. Her silky hair fell from the back of his hands; the touch and scent he thought he'd never enjoy again.

"So do I," he said. "I've prayed for this very thing."

She lifted her head. "Really?"

"That's why I kept trying to reach you."

She relaxed and snuggled against his chest—his Terri who never wanted any signs of affection displayed in public. "I will do my best to break my nasty habits."

He chuckled. "Some of them I liked. I do have a suggestion. Could we make our way to the Piazzetta? The church there, San Stefano, sounds like a great place to seek out God. I'd like for us to pray for guidance and His blessings."

"You've never initiated prayer before—other than meal times."

"I'm stepping up to the plate, Miss Donatelli."

She placed a hand on his cheek. "Then swing with all your might."

❧

An hour later, Terri floated on a grand cloud. She and Ryan walked to the Piazzetta and in the quietness of the old church, he prayed. He'd taken the attribute of assertiveness, not pushy or controlling, but one of gentle guidance. She treasured this spiritual side of him. Regret washed away and in its place stood anticipation for the future.

After a talkative lunch, they walked hand in hand through beautiful gardens and villas, although the magnificent structures, vivid colors, and choice greenery could not compare to the love in her heart for Ryan. At one point, she wanted to tell him of her feelings, but feared she might be controlling the moment. This new attitude would take time.

"Where are you staying?" she asked as late afternoon set in.

"The same hotel. I figured if I couldn't get to you by phone then I'd need to come there."

"I'm so glad."

He lifted a brow.

"Really. I missed you so much. Right from the start, everywhere I looked I saw your face."

"How about dinner tonight?" Ryan asked.

"Absolutely."

Soon afterwards, they took a taxi and a bus to the hotel. They visited Lisa by the pool where Tami, Heather, and Ashley sunned. Terri didn't have to explain a thing. Her friends could see the truth in her eyes. Terri and Ryan strolled the grounds, sometimes in silence and other times laughing and talking.

"Are you wanting to rest before this evening?" Ryan asked.

She gazed into his green eyes and watched the afternoon sun cast golden highlights into his amber hair. "I don't want to waste a single moment by being away from you."

"Do you have your great-grandmother's letter with you?"

She startled. "No, I have it memorized."

"Can we sit down? I want to go over everything she wrote."

Confused, Terri agreed. They found a secluded bench among the flowers. With her head on his shoulder, she recited the letter.

My darling Giovanni,

How foolish and wrong I've been. Please forgive me for the pain I've caused you. Believe me, I never meant to hurt you. You brought so much love and laughter into my life, a precious gift from heaven, and all I've offered in return is heartache. You gave me your heart and a promise of a lifetime of devotion. I gave you tears and pleadings for you to join me in Venice. Always I begged for my way until now I fear it is too late. My selfishness eats at my soul; my tears declare my guilt. My joy, my love, I pray you still have feelings for me.

I thought I couldn't leave my family, but God in His infinite wisdom has shown me I can do anything with Him. Giovanni, we can be together, forever as God intended. I love you more than life and I want to live out my days with you. I pray this is not too late.

Visions of Capri are before me. I remember the sound of the waves breaking against the shore, the salty scent of the blue Mediterranean, the cry of the seagulls, and the lure of the mountain peaks. Most of all, I remember your arms around me asking me to be your wife.

Oh, you have captivated me along with the beauty of the island. Please answer me, my Giovanni! I long to be with you. Tell me you still love me!

Feeling a little foolish, Terri couldn't meet his gaze. "I cannot believe I allowed a letter to rule my life for so long. Why did you want to hear it?"

"Ever wonder why the letter was returned?" He wrapped his arm around her shoulder.

"I used to. I really think he must not have loved her after all." She paused. "I will tell you what I think about my great-grandmother's life. She loved my great-grandfather and they had a wonderful marriage, which tells me that was the heart of God's plan."

Ryan kissed the top of her head, the first kiss of the day. "Capri is a beautiful place."

"Being in God's will is the most beautiful place," she said. "I want to go home when you do. Do you mind?"

"I planned to leave in four days."

"Do you mind if I make reservations at the same hotel? I'd love to see Italy with you."

"I wouldn't have it any other way."

Terri lifted her head and he slowly descended to brush a kiss across her lips. "I love you," he said barely above a whisper.

"And I love you."

❧

The food, music, and atmosphere at dinner seemed perfect, or perhaps it was the love in Ryan's eyes that made the evening memorable. The violinist sounded sweet, and when he sang at their table, she nearly wept.

"What are the words to the song?" Ryan asked.

Terri smiled, and as the words graced her ears, she softly translated. "I lost my love, my joy, my all. My heart cried out for peace. Return to me and say you will stay forever in my arms."

Ryan reached inside his jacket pocket. With the shy smile she'd learned to love, he opened a small, black velvet box. Her heart began to pound, and she gasped. He laid a diamond ring in the palm of his hand, the biggest she'd ever seen. In the candlelight, it shimmered.

"You're not translating," he said.

She took a breath and attempted to steady herself. "A life with you is all I ask, a chance to show my devotion. Tell me yes and ease my pain."

The singer stopped. Terri glanced up, and the man smiled. Her gaze swept to Ryan's face.

"Tell me yes and ease my pain," he said.

"Yes," she said, feeling emotion seize control of her heart and mind. "Yes. Yes. Yes."

Dear Readers,

When my son and daughter-in-law returned from a vacation in Italy, they told of their love for the island of Capri. They were captivated by the island's beauty and the warmth of the people as well as the century old structures. Soon, I found myself lost in the stories, the descriptions, the history, the romance of the language, and the photographs. I could smell the sea and feel the cold water of the Blue Grotto. My mouth watered at the thought of pasta and rich coffee. I want you to "visit" Capri. This is an invitation to curl up in your favorite chair and experience the adventure and grandeur of *The Lure of Capri*.

I have been blessed with several novels, novellas, short stories, articles, and devotions. My husband and I live in Houston, Texas where we are active in our church. My hours are filled with writing, speaking engagements, teaching Bible study, and church librarian. I'm looking forward to hearing from you!

Web site: www.diannmills.com

DiAnn Mills

To Florence with Love

by Melanie Panagiotopoulos

Dedication

With much love to my brothers,
Derek and Chris and their lovely families.
And with many thanks to Christina Nevada Caughlan
and David Maria Massei, who were friends to a stranger
when friends were needed the most.
God bless you all!

Therefore, as God's chosen people, holy and dearly loved,
clothe yourselves with compassion, kindness,
humility, gentleness and patience.
Bear with each other and forgive whatever grievances
you may have against one another.
Forgive as the Lord forgave you.
And over all these virtues put on love,
which binds them all together in perfect unity.
COLOSSIANS 3:12–14

Prologue

S
amantha Day breezed into the marble foyer of her elegant Fifth Avenue penthouse. She deposited a Barneys New York silver-lettered black shopping bag on the hall table, while tossing her heather gray cashmere sweater across the shoulder of the human-sized reproduction of Michelangelo's statue of David. She was probably one of the few people in the world who could buy a designer evening gown that cost more than most people made in a month of working and walk out of the store with it casually dropped into a bag without there being even the hint of a smile on her lips. But smiling was not something Samantha Day did often.

"Ms. Day." Her housekeeper addressed her, and while carefully removing the Oscar de la Renta sweater from the statue, the small woman dressed in an immaculate housekeeper's uniform motioned toward the library with its tastefully decorated, classical motif. "Several letters arrived for you this morning. One came by special delivery from Texas."

"Texas?" Samantha turned and cast her famous eyes, known most for their natural color, an amazing design of green encircled by two aquamarine rings, in the direction of her housekeeper. Whenever she played a psychopathic killer or a bitter housewife wanting to get even with her cheating husband or any other similar role, her eyes had been written up in movie reviews as being creepy, chilling, scary. They looked a bit that way now as she regarded her housekeeper.

"Yes, Ma'am." The woman nearly stammered, and with a regal nod of her head and its expertly dyed, blond hair, Samantha dismissed the older woman. Samantha coolly regarded her housekeeper as she all but scurried down the marble hall and out of sight. She hated the way the woman seemed almost afraid of her. But that was the problem with the roles she had played. Too many people confused who she really was with the acts she performed.

Sighing, she turned toward the letter that sat propped and waiting against the lamp on her glass-topped pediment desk. Her two-inch Manolo Blahnik heels, which gave her a height of five feet eleven inches, clicked across the marble floor toward it. Reaching down, she picked up the envelope.

For just a moment, as she regarded the strong and handsome penmanship belonging to the man who had raised her—her maternal grandfather, she felt a pang of guilt, of remorse even, for her actions or rather, lack thereof, toward him during the last ten years. But she knew very well that he disapproved of both her lifestyle and her work. A slight grimace crossed the fine line of her mouth. To be one of the most highly paid movie stars in Hollywood and a Golden Globe recipient were not considered great accomplishments by her grandfather.

She stared at the name on the address.

Samantha Day.

The fact that he called her Samantha Day and not by her

actual name of Florence Celini was something she often wondered about. It was true that everyone in the world knew her as Samantha Day. But it kind of confused her that her grandfather called her by that stage name, too. She had never requested he do so. If he had been a vindictive person, she might have understood his not addressing her by her actual name. She had left his home a decade earlier—after having lived with him for the same amount of time—and had never returned. But she knew that that couldn't be the reason. Her grandfather didn't have a spiteful bone in all of his six feet four inches of body.

Kicking off her shoes, she reached for the ivory and gold letter opener the director of her last film had brought back to her from Greece and neatly sliced open the sealed manila envelope.

Two pieces of mail slid from it. A loose, folded piece of binder paper and a sealed envelope made of quality stationery.

She reached first for the binder paper. She was certain that it would contain a short note from her grandfather. A high-school science teacher, he always had an abundant supply of notebook paper on hand.

> *Dear Samantha,*
> *This just arrived for you.*
> *I think that it might be important so I'm sending it on to you by special post.*
>
> > *All my love and prayers,*
> > *Grandpop*
>
> *P.S. Please let me know if you need anything, anything at all.*

That familiar pang that she was neglecting her grandfather—

the man she had affectionately called "Grandpop" when growing up and who she still thought of in that way—went through her like a flash. But, as is the nature of a flash, it disappeared just as quickly.

Sighing, she reached for the envelope, the reason for her grandfather sending this letter by special courier.

She turned it over, and as she did, the gasp that would have been recognized by moviegoers around the world came from between her lips.

Not only was it addressed to her grandfather's address in Texas, which was the only one the sender of this letter could possibly have had, but also, it was addressed to Florence Celini, the name that was to be found on her birth certificate.

And it was from Italy.

A letter from Italy. . .

And Samantha knew then that she had been expecting this letter—forever.

She looked carefully at the return address and a frown, the world-famous one people paid big dollars to see on screen, marred the perfect smoothness of her high forehead.

The name she had expected to see on it, that of her paternal grandfather, Lorenzo Celini, wasn't there. Rather the name of some unknown lawyer, Domenico Ferretti, and his law firm, was professionally and impersonally emblazoned across the upper left corner of the expensive envelope.

And that could mean only one thing.

Samantha's hand, with its long perfectly manicured and polished nails, started to quiver, which in turn made the envelope she was holding shake with a tremulous motion.

Her grandfather, her father's father, must have died.

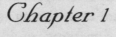

Chapter 1

An ache that was as unexpected as it was fierce throbbed through her. She had never met her Italian grandfather—had never had any desire to do so since he had been so mean to her parents—but now, with all the longing of an actress who liked happy endings more than the sad ones for which she was always cast, she knew that she had, in a secret place deep inside her heart, dreamed of a reunion with the man who had never accepted her mother as good enough for the lineage that belonged to his son.

Up until that moment in which she held the envelope that most likely told of her paternal grandfather's death, she had acted out in her mind at least a thousand times how she would first berate him for having so wronged her parents, while holding out her own success as an example of how mistaken he had been about his son's choice of a bride. Afterward, after he spent some time begging for her forgiveness, she would have grudgingly granted him a partial pardon and they would have lived, if not *happily* ever after, at least somewhat *peacefully* ever after. . . .

But now, with a sadness that seemed to envelop her entire being, she wasn't so sure that that was what she would do if she was lucky enough to meet him. At this moment all she wished for was the opportunity to forgive him totally and completely without him even having to beg for her forgiveness. Isn't that what her parents would have done? Isn't that what she—Florence Celini—would have done before she became Samantha Day?

She had received only one other letter from Italy: a letter of condolence from her grandfather a few days after her parents had died in a small plane crash when she was seven. That was a letter she had long since thrown away.

She wished she could throw this letter away, too.

For all that he had treated her parents badly, simply for the crime of having fallen in love with one another, she didn't want to hear about him dying.

As far as she knew he and her American grandpop, the man she had disappointed when she had turned her back on most of his Christian teachings, were her only living relatives. Neither her parents, nor she, had siblings.

She looked at the name of the lawyer again.

Domenico Ferretti.

She wished that she never had to open Mr. Ferretti's letter.

But she knew that she had to. And the sooner she did so, the better.

Using the same instrument to slice open this envelope with its fine Florentine stationery as she did the manila one, she swiftly cut into the fold, segregating it, and, without hesitation, pulled the letter from its envelope and read it.

Dear Ms. Celini:
I am writing on behalf of your paternal grandfather,

Lorenzo Celini, who greatly wishes that you might travel to Florence, Italy as soon as possible so that you might meet.

A gasp emanated from Samantha.

He was alive!

Her Italian grandfather was alive!

And he wanted to meet her!

Her knees went weak at the unexpected, but most welcomed, news, and feeling faint, she sank into the chair behind her as she continued reading the formal, and yet very friendly, letter.

> *He greatly regrets the years that have gone by without your having met and begs your indulgence and forgiveness.*
>
> *Please call this office—a collect phone call—so that arrangements can be made. Your fare, accommodations, and spending money will be taken care of while you are here.*
>
> *Yours very sincerely,*
> *Domenico Ferretti*

The letter slid from her fingers. Her paternal grandfather was still alive. Alive! And he wanted a reunion with her!

Like being given a second chance, she felt a sense of happiness fill her unlike anything she had felt since she had left her grandpop's home.

But, as so often happens when people make pledges when in distress, as she had done a moment earlier when she thought her paternal grandfather had died, it didn't last.

Even while still riding on a wave of delight, reality crashed down upon her, as all that made her the movie star, Samantha

Day, imperiously demanded of her the *reason* why she should forgive her Italian grandfather.

He had found her mother—without even giving the woman a chance to prove herself—to be unworthy, had consequently turned his back on his only son, then on his only grandchild. What sort of man did that?

A man whose personality Samantha Day's greatly resembles, a still small voice whispered to her soul, and a shudder rippled through her slender body.

She reached down and picked up her grandpop's handwritten note. She looked at it and whispered as if to the man himself, "Why couldn't I have been more like you, Grandpop? Life would have been so much easier, simpler."

You could be, that still, small voice whispered to her again. *You can be—or act—in any way you choose. It's all about volition.*

Her left eyebrow curved upward and irony glinted in her eyes. She was an actress. Who better aware of that truth than she? She made her living—and a very good one—*acting* in different roles.

Slowly, then more quickly, a plan formed in her head. She *would* go to Italy to meet her long lost grandfather. She looked down at the name on the envelope—her name—Florence Celini.

Evidently her Italian grandfather didn't know who she was now. But that was only as she expected it to be. Practically no one knew that Samantha Day and Florence Celini were one and the same.

In her usual decisive manner, she determined to keep it that way.

She would go to Florence to meet her grandfather but she

wouldn't go as Samantha Day, the movie star.

No.

She would go as Florence Celini, her parents' daughter—until it suited her to do otherwise.

Getting excited with the thought of playing *herself* in a role, she paused as it occurred to her that she didn't know *who* Florence Celini was anymore. Samantha Day—the cool, aloof, femme fatale—she knew and played perfectly. But Florence Celini, that was something entirely different.

Walking over to the picture window and its enviable view of Manhattan she contemplated who she might have been had the film star, Samantha Day, not intruded upon her life. That was a question for which she had few answers. Neither did she have a script nor a ready-made character profile on Florence Celini in which to read either. She considered that she probably would have still been working in her parents' former bookstore on Main Street in the gulf town in which her grandfather lived. Maybe she would have owned the store again by now. That had always been her dream: to buy back her parents' bookstore.

When had she forgotten that?

She shook her head. That wasn't the point right now. *Who* she would have been, was.

She looked in the direction of where her housekeeper could be heard preparing lunch. One thing was for sure; Florence Celini certainly wouldn't be a person who made others feel afraid of her. Of that she was certain.

But with her blue-green gaze scanning over the trees of Central Park she knew that she would find the answers.

She would.

Because to *play* the part of herself and to travel to Italy as Florence Celini excited her more than anything she had done in a good long time. She somehow knew that this was something she had to do before the strong personality of the movie star, Samantha Day, totally erased that of Florence Celini.

That brought her thoughts to a screeching halt.

Is that what was happening to her? Had she lost the actual person she was behind the persona of a Hollywood movie star?

She sighed irritably and touched her blond hair.

So much more had changed about her than just the color of her hair.

She had been blond from the beginning of her career. No one—except for her grandpop, hairdresser, and agent—knew that her actual color was chestnut brown. She would start there. She would cut it, too, cut the long locks of honey blond—her showbiz trademark—that cascaded down past her shoulder blades. Chin-length brown hair and a pair of studious-looking glasses in the place of her clear contact lenses would take care of a disguise. And if anyone asked what she now did she would say that she owned bookstores. It wasn't a lie. She loved bookstores and as a sort of hobby, and at the advice of her accountant who had been searching for tax breaks for her, she had invested in a chain of them. She owned seven shops now throughout the Northeast. Each personal and small, just like that one on Main Street where she had worked after high school most every day and where she had been when she had been discovered by the man who was still her agent.

She walked back to her desk and, picking up the lawyer's letter, ran her fingertips across the gold embossed name and address there.

Domenico Ferretti.

Now that was a good Italian name. She wondered what he looked like. A tall, dark, and handsome man who might be cast for the lead in a spy movie, perhaps? Would he have a strong chin, the classic Italian face that Michelangelo Buonarroti might have deemed worthy to immortalize in Carrara marble, but with the actual olive skin that was warm and smelled as good as it looked?

"Probably fat and bald with a paunch the size of a basketball," she mumbled as she reached for her phone and punched out his number.

As she listened to the beeps and hums of the connection going through on the phone lines, she turned her head and looked over her shoulder toward the Manhattan skyline. It was magnificent, vibrant. It was. . .New York.

And a smile—one almost of contentment—curved her perfect lips. New York in its entire twenty-first century splendor was beautiful—magnificent even. But she *was* looking forward to exchanging it for the Renaissance refinement of Brunelleschi's dome, Giotto's bell tower, and the medieval store-lined Ponte Vecchio—Old Bridge—in the river valley of the Arno. Florence was not only home to half her ancestors, but she somehow felt that it was a place for her future, too. A pilgrimage of sorts to discover whom Florence Celini might still be.

The call went through, and upon identifying herself to a secretary, Florence only had to wait a moment before a strong male voice broke through the line, startling her from her reverie.

"Good day, Ms. Celini. I'm Domenico Ferretti. I'm so happy that you called." The voice did not sound at all as if its owner possessed a fat tummy. In fact, if his voice was anything to go by, it sounded as if he was not only a perfect specimen of a classically handsome Italian—tall, dark, and extremely handsome—but also one with an Oxford flare. A distinctive British accent, spiced by an Italian upbringing, gave his voice a sonance that was as charming as it was unique. Being a voice person, Florence decided that this man's definitely had merit.

"I only just received your letter." She paused. "It came as a bit of a shock."

"As I wrote to you, your *nonno*—grandfather—greatly wishes to meet you." He was articulate and firm without being haughty. "He deeply regrets the years that have passed without him acting in the role of your grandfather."

Acting? She frowned. *Did* her grandfather and his lawyer, Domenico Ferretti, know something about her professional life. She would continue as if they didn't until she knew for sure. "I have another grandfather, one who has been very kind to me." *Much more so than I deserve,* that little voice of conscience whispered to her even as her antagonistic words came out.

"I'm glad to hear it. I know your *nonno* will be, too." He paused, then, when she remained silent, he asked, "When will you be able to travel to Florence?"

"I don't believe that I've said that I'm able to come." She didn't know what made her say that. Maybe the way he called her paternal grandfather *nonno?* Although she knew it was the Italian word for grandfather, it somehow seemed too familiar, too nice, too caring on the part of a man who had shown none of those characteristics. And in spite of her determination to travel to Italy, it rubbed her the wrong way.

"I hope that you are able to do so," Domenico Ferretti replied smoothly, totally unperturbed by her stand.

She remained silent. It was obviously his job to get her to travel to Florence. Samantha Day wouldn't make it easy for him.

"If getting leave from your work is the problem, I would be happy to talk to your employer." His voice seemed to fade a bit so she knew that he had taken his mouth away from the phone and was looking at something. "Caller ID indicates that you're at a number in New York City. Manhattan," he qualified. "Is that where you're living now?"

That answered her question about whether they knew of her as Samantha Day, the actress. If they had he wouldn't have needed Caller ID to tell him where she was calling from or, for that matter, he wouldn't have sent the letter to her grandpop's address. "I'm impressed, Signor Ferretti." She couldn't see him of course, but she was almost certain from the length of the pause that a smile had flickered across his lips. In the true spirit of her thespian soul she couldn't help musing what those lips looked like.

"The wonders of the computer age." *Yes, there was definitely a smile in his voice.* "The Medicis would have loved it."

She knew that he referred to the banking family of the fifteenth century that had been one of the major monetary influences responsible for the flowering of the intellectual and artistic life for which Florence was still famous. Her gaze went to the M section of her library. She had numerous books about the Medicis. "Their banks throughout Europe probably never would have run into mismanagement problems if Cosimo dé Medici or his progeny had had a Bill Gates among the contingent of brains that so added to the world during that time."

"Your knowledge of Florence's history impresses me."

She remained quiet. It was something she had learned to do

187

long ago when she wanted to unsettle someone. But Domenico Ferretti was not the unsettling kind.

"Then again, maybe not," he continued, not seeming to find anything awkward in the pause, as she had intended. "You *are* half Florentine, after all."

"Half Italian," she corrected him.

He laughed. Not chuckled, but laughed. A deep robust sound that came through the wires, making her feel just as disturbed as a man coming through her sixth floor library window would. It was an intrusion. No one had laughed at her. . . not to her face anyway. . .ever. "You're right, of course. A true Florentine would never make such a correction."

She ran her hand across the cool glass of her desk, trying to ward off the uneasy feeling that he had just turned her words back upon her. This time she remained quiet for want of what to say; a very unusual occurrence for her. She was the queen of comebacks.

"I do hope you are able to come to Firenze—Florence— soon. Your *nonno* really does want to meet you."

She decided then that not only she, but Hollywood, too, would love the way Domenico Ferretti enunciated his words. He had a persuasive voice, but at the same time a calming one, one that seemed to caress her soul and make her feel as if he spoke the truth, made her feel that her *nonno* really did want to meet her. But hadn't Tom Knight—the man she had almost married thirteen months ago—made her feel that way, too? And that relationship had turned out disastrously. She had been dating Tom for over a year and never, not once in that entire time, did she suspect that he had only been using her to further his own acting career. Not until she had overheard him talking to his agent. . . .

She had thought Tom to be her "knight in shining armor," come to save her from the fake world with which she had become an integral part, a major cog, actually. But he hadn't been her knight at all. Only a hanger-on and one of the worst kinds, one who had hung onto her heart and then tossed it away without a care.

"Miss Celini?"

With a decisive flick of her wrist, she tossed the blond locks that had fallen over her shoulder back behind her and, with a no-nonsense tone, answered the man with the intriguing voice. "Yes, Mr. Ferretti. I'll be able to come toward the beginning of next week. Monday or Tuesday would be fine." That would give her time to dye her hair back to its original chestnut brown, have it cut, buy a wardrobe Florence Celini— the bookstore owner—might wear, and take care of any other loose ends. She had a month before she started shooting her next film. The timing was perfect. Her grandpop would have said it was God's timing.

"Wonderful," Domenico Ferretti returned and Samantha couldn't help but feel as if her decision really did make him happy. It made something resembling the start of a smile touch upon her lips. "I'll ask my secretary to make all the travel arrangements and we'll get back to you in a couple of hours with them, if that is agreeable with you."

"That would be fine."

"Your *nonno* really is anxious to meet you, Signorina Celini." He paused, as if seeming to choose his next words with care. "He has many regrets. His treatment toward you is one of his greatest."

The lump that formed in her throat caught her off guard. Was she to finally act a part that had a happy ending? She shook her head. She couldn't let herself go soft. That would only lead to disappointment. And besides, her main reason for traveling to Italy wasn't to assuage an old man's conscience, but rather to give herself both the chance and the anonymity to discover who Florence Celini was, once again. She swallowed the lump and returned, "My, and it only took him twenty-seven years to come to that conclusion?"

"Don't be too hard on him, Miss Celini. He's an old man. And to forgive is easier than to hold on to anger and bitterness. Particularly since your *nonno* is *requesting* your forgiveness."

Blood rushed to Samantha's face as both the deep-seated anger and bitterness Domenico Ferretti referred to filled her. Even though she heard a caring quality in his tone, his words made her mad. *How dare the man preach to me!* "Thank you, Counselor. I'm sure your clients have to pay big money for that advice."

"No, Miss Celini," he spoke softly. "They only have to go to one of the many churches Florence has to offer to the people of the world to learn that."

Zap! Conviction like a burning fire spread through her at his words. They were exactly the ones she might have expected her grandpop to offer, were in fact, one of the reasons she had stayed away from her grandpop for so many years. And the real reason why she hadn't bought her parents' former bookstore located in the same town as Grandpop. She would have had to go there more often, had she owned it.

"My office will get back to you as soon as we can with the travel arrangements. Arrivederci," he said, and the line went dead.

Florence stood for a moment without moving. When she finally placed the phone in its cradle, her mouth quirked in a dry line. For some reason she was quite certain that Florence Celini—as opposed to Samantha Day—would probably agree with Domenico Ferretti that to forgive is better than to hold on to anger and bitterness. But how could she be sure?

How?

And other than being her paternal grandfather's lawyer, who was Domenico Ferretti?

Two questions for which she was anxious to find the answers.

Chapter 2

Domenico hung up the phone and, placing his elbows on his hand-carved mahogany desk, cupped his chin between the palms of his hands. His gaze sought the golden Tuscan countryside on the opposite side of the Fiume Arno—Arno River—outside the window directly in front of him.

It was a graceful land. The lilt of the green and rolling hill-sides, which hid the *pietra forté*—strong stones—of the earth that had built Firenze and was one of the agents that lent the city its famous golden color, was only enhanced by the deep masculine green of the reaching, soldier-like cypress trees and that of the soft and feminine silver-green olive trees that danced in the wind like a troop of ballerinas. Stone villas and domes of churches with their campaniles dotted the land but not in an intrusive way. The builders of Tuscany had been one with the earth around them and hadn't invaded the space as people so often do when they move in upon it, but rather had joined with it, a perfect marriage. Domenico thought that, other than the architectural wonders and magnificent artworks his city possessed, it was that harmony of the surrounding countryside that people from around the world sought when they traveled to the "city of the red lily," his home.

A deep sigh rumbled from his chest.

He only hoped that its charm might work its magic on his friend and client's granddaughter, Florence Celini. From their brief conversation, Domenico had decided that Florence Celini was one tough woman.

A smile edged his mouth. She kind of reminded him of how her *nonno,* his friend Lorenzo, used to be. Bitter, haughty, moody, difficult—all in all, not a very pleasant person to be around.

But the old man had changed: A true testament to the power of God's grace. Domenico hoped that that same grace might fill Lorenzo's granddaughter's heart and that she might soften toward Lorenzo. Because as things stood now, Domenico was certain that she harbored a great deal of enmity toward her *nonno.* And he didn't want her to hurt the old chap.

A year ago, their meanness would have been perfectly matched.

But not now. Lorenzo was finally a man after God's own heart, and he was using the time remaining him on earth to try and undo some of the harm he had done to his fellow humans during the seventy-nine years he had lived. And his granddaughter was high on his list of wrongs to make right.

"Dear Lord, please bring peace to Lorenzo's granddaughter, Florence. Your peace." Domenico whispered out his plea to the God he had loved, known, and trusted since he was a young boy. "And please bring about a reunion between grandfather and granddaughter that will make all the angels in your heaven sing."

Swiveling his chair around, Domenico looked at the view that he possessed from the window behind his desk. The dome of the *Duomo*—Cathedral—of Santa Maria del Fiore, seemed to float above the rooftops of Firenze. It was as inspiring to Domenico as the green earth he gazed at from his front window but in a different way. That beautiful structure—the fourth largest cathedral in the world—had been built in honor of the God who had been worshipped on this land from the middle of the third century when Greco-Syriac merchants had brought Christianity to Roman Florentia—the name by which Florence had then been known.

He suspected that for Florence Celini to find the truth it represented and proclaimed was probably the only way she would ever be able to "clothe" herself with the compassion, kindness, humility, gentleness, and patience that she would need in order to forgive the grievance—one Domenico could well understand—that she harbored against her *nonno*. To have ignored his only grandchild—and an orphaned one at that— was an unnatural response from a grandparent. But Lorenzo *had* changed.

A frown sliced across his face. Unlike Giovanna the previous year.

Giovanna Lazzareschi.

Domenico glanced at the calendar. Today would have been their first year wedding anniversary *if* she hadn't taken his heart, chewed it up, then spat it out again.

He sighed. To learn that the woman he had loved had been nothing more than a conniving fortune hunter hadn't been easy. But he had thanked God every single day since that he had found out that her love for him had all been an act to get what she had really been after in their relationship—his social standing and wealth—*before* they had married. He—both of them, so he'd thought—had wanted a child quickly. A shudder ripped through him and, closing his eyes, Domenico whispered out, "Thank you, Lord. Thank you for protecting me from such a wife. . .and the child we might have had from such a mother."

Reaching for his phone in order to instruct his secretary to make travel arrangements for Florence Celini, he paused before lifting it to add, "And please, Lord, protect Lorenzo from his granddaughter. Don't let her hurt him. Please fill her heart with Your love and Your grace. In Jesus' name I pray."

❧

Florence picked up her grandpop's handwritten note once again. She ran her fingertips over the strong letters, and as she did, she could just imagine him sitting at his desk by the window—with the weeping willows waving so softly in the breeze outside it—writing to her. Walking over to the white leather sofa she sat, but she didn't look out at the million-dollar view of Central Park or at Manhattan itself, but rather, she looked within herself.

Who would Florence Celini be now if the professional life of Samantha Day hadn't become so all-consuming, so all-demanding? What would she believe? Where would she be living now? How would she act on this trip to Florence—the city of her ancestors for which she had been named—to meet her long-estranged grandfather?

She sighed, that sound for which Samantha Day was so famous, a sound that really belonged to Florence Celini. She really had no idea who she would have been.

But what had the lawyer with that deep and caring voice said?

" 'To forgive is easier than to hold on to anger and bitterness. Particularly since your *nonno* is requesting your forgiveness,' " she repeated his words, but this time, using all her acting skills, she clamped down on the anger that wanted to erupt within the short-tempered person Samantha Day was. Closing her eyes she leaned her head back against the sofa and allowed his words to wash through her brain, to soak it. She had thought even when he had spoken them that they were words her grandpop would have said. But thinking back, way back into the fabric of her mind, she was almost certain that her mother and father would have said the same thing and, even more, that her parents would have accepted the olive branch that her Italian grandfather was extending. Accepted it with open arms.

Her mother and father. . .

She was sure that they would have been disappointed in the woman she had grown into. Not because she had chosen a career in acting, as she knew her grandpop was, but rather because she hadn't grown up to be the woman of faith that they would have wanted her to be.

"Woman of faith." Her eyes popped open and she jumped up. "Of course," she said, as she paced in front of the window. "Florence Celini, without the star, Samantha Day's intrusion, would have been a *woman of faith*." She clicked her fingers together like she always did when inspired. "A good Christian woman just like. . .her parents had been. . .who always went to church and. . .tried to help others as much as possible. . .and. . . who read. . .the Bible. . . ."

"Bible!" As if a light had been flicked on within her, her

whole face lit up. Skipping over to the B section of her extensive personal library she immediately spied the white bound volume with the words *Holy Bible* emblazoned across its spine. Since it was near the top of the case, she had to stand on her tiptoes to pull it down. She held it before her and blew on its upper edge. When no particles of dust flew free, a pang of guilt that it was dirt free only because of the thorough cleaning it received from her housekeeper, and not because of use, gave her that same burning feeling of conviction that she had felt when Domenico Ferretti had said that people only have to go into one of his city's churches to learn about forgiveness.

Shaking her head as if to clear it, she returned to her favorite spot on her sofa by the gold-plated reading lamp. For just a moment she held the Bible that her parents had given to her when she was a young girl and just looked at it. It was as new and glossy looking as it had been the day they had presented it to her.

Her lips twisted in the direction of a smile.

She remembered that day. It had been Easter, their last Easter together. She was wearing an Easter dress of soft pastel pink with a sash of pure Chinese silk. Her shoes had been shiny new Mary Janes, white, without a single scruff mark on them yet. And she had had a hat, an Easter bonnet of the same pink as her dress with white ribbons that hung all the way down to the middle of her back.

She had been so happy then. So happy.

She shook her head. That had been then. Twenty years earlier. This was now. Twenty years later. And what she had to do at this moment was to find out how Florence Celini might act on this trip to Italy.

She took a deep breath, and for the first time in more years than she could remember, she opened the Bible. She flipped to the first page, then to the second; but while turning to the next, something strange happened. The pages seemed to be stuck together.

Frowning she slid her long nail along the edge of the page. The second and third pages were definitely adhering, almost as if they had been glued together.

"Not even the publishers of Bibles can do a good job these days," she grumbled. But when she carefully pried the pages apart and a long inscription—a letter actually—greeted her eyes, she gasped.

Her gaze flew to the signature.

Both her parents had signed!

Florence blinked. Then she blinked again. She thought she was dreaming.

But she wasn't. Softly, lovingly she ran her fingertips over the words her mother's neat hand had penned. Feeling her hands start to shake Florence cupped them together as her gaze scanned across the words that had been written to her and placed within this book for safekeeping so that she would some-day find them.

To Florence, with love. . .

It began, and with the words of love that came through time to reach Florence at this moment she most needed her parents' advice, tears washed the corners of her eyes. But it was the words at the end of the letter that most captured Florence's attention.

. . .and should a letter ever arrive for you from Italy asking you to go meet your father's father, go and do so with a gracious heart, forgiving your grandfather for the estrangement. Life is too short not to forgive, dear Daughter, and it is a part of the Christian life when requested. A person can forgive and go on with life. Without forgiveness, however, a bitter hole remains within a person's soul: A hole that grows through the years like a cancer. . .

And never forget these wonderful verses:

"Therefore, as God's chosen people, holy and dearly loved, clothe yourselves with compassion, kindness, humility, gentleness and patience. Bear with each other and forgive whatever grievances you may have against one another. Forgive as the Lord forgave you. And over all these virtues put on love, which binds them all together in perfect unity." (Colossians 3:12–14)

With all our love and hope that you should never choose to "wear"—or act at—any life other than the life of virtue so directed by God in these verses, your loving mother and father,

Mary and Cosimo Celini

"Mamma. Babbo." Florence softly spoke as if in answer to her parents. "Is that who I would have been had you not left me? A woman who lived a life of virtue who 'wore' such characteristics? Compassion. Kindness. Humility. Gentleness. Patience. Forgiveness. Love." Florence shook her head and turned eyes that looked at but didn't see the view outside the window. Although she had always acted in a moralistic way even to the extent of having turned down a part that had nudity in it, and for which the actress who had taken the role won the much-coveted Academy Award, Florence knew that practically none of those characteristics described who she, as Samantha Day, had become.

She made a disagreeable sound. "What *practically?* None of them do," she admitted to the empty room.

She wasn't compassionate. . .except toward animals. She wasn't kind. Samantha Day didn't even know the meaning of the word humility. And gentleness, patience, and forgiveness may as well have been rocks on the moon rather than characteristics she could be "wearing."

And love?

That was where she was the biggest failure of all.

She had spurned all the love her grandpop had wanted to give her for years, and as far as a personal relationship with a man was concerned, well, if she were honest with herself, she knew that Tom Knight wasn't the only one at fault the previous year. She might not have been "using" him to further her career but she had used him.

She nodded her head affirmatively. She certainly had.

He had been her "whipping boy." Whatever bothered her in her work or life or the world in general, she had taken it out on him. Samantha Day's temper on the set was as legendary as was the yelling that accompanied it. Again, if she were truthful, she knew that she was little different at home, hence the real reason her housekeeper seemed afraid of her. Not because of the roles she played. She'd always wondered why Tom had stayed with her. Because of the same morals that had kept her from taking that Oscar-winning role, he hadn't even been privy to the physical closeness most men in the world in which they worked and lived expected from their fiancées.

Yes. She had wondered until that afternoon when she'd heard him talking to his agent. . . .

She looked back down at the loving letter her parents had sent to her, one that had been safeguarded within the pages of her Bible—and meant for her to find when she finally cared enough to take the book off the shelf, open it, and read it carefully.

Then she looked over at the lawyer's letter, and that of her grandpop's, lying on her desk.

"An afternoon for letters," she murmured but, sighing softly, continued with, "But nice ones." Letters that she felt might just change her life.

She ran her hand over the Bible. Her grandpop had always called the Bible *Letters from God.*

She smiled, a real smile.

The Bible was another letter and one she felt might somehow show her how to act as Florence Celini. And even, she considered as she flipped to Colossians so that she could find the verses her parents had written to her, how to live that life, too.

&

Normally Domenico let his secretary take care of calling clients about something as mundane as travel information. But because of her latent anger and antagonism, he felt that it was important that he call Florence Celini personally. He was taken aback when the phone was answered on the first ring.

"*Pronto.*" The friendly Italian salutation surprised him even more.

"Miss Celini?"

"That would be me."

He frowned. She was so chipper sounding, so different from the heavy haughtiness of before. "Domenico Ferretti here."

"Of course. I've been waiting for your call."

He hadn't thought she was the type to sit by the phone waiting for a phone call. But he accepted the friendly atmosphere with a grateful heart and was glad, too, that he'd returned the call himself. "That's good to hear."

"When can I expect to be landing at Amerigo Vespucci Airport?"

He frowned. "You know the name of Florence's airport?"

"I've been doing some reading."

From the complete turnabout in her tone, it sounded as if she had been doing more than just the normal tourist reading, though. Would it be too much to hope that she had maybe been reading her Bible, maybe praying, too? According to information Lorenzo had given to him when they talked an hour earlier, the grandfather who had raised her was supposed to be a very strong Christian, as her parents had been. So it was possible. She just seemed so different from before. Gone was the haughty autocrat that had him concerned, and in her place seemed to be a very nice young woman. For the first time, Domenico wondered if she was married.

"I neglected to ask you before. But if there is someone special that you would like to have travel with you, his expenses will be taken care of, as well." There. That would take care of both asking if she was married and finding out if she had a boyfriend with whom she was particularly close.

"No, there's no one. I'll be traveling alone."

Domenico couldn't help how much that information pleased

him. "How does arriving here at three o'clock Monday afternoon sound?"

"Wonderful. I'm looking forward to it."

Domenico blinked. *Wonderful? Looking forward to it?*

Either the woman was schizophrenic, or his prayers—and those of Lorenzo's—had done some good. She was acting totally different from before. Not just her friendly words but the tone of her voice, the way he was sure that smiles had to be touching upon her lips in between her words.

As much as it pleased him something seemed off.

He wished that he had insisted that Lorenzo allow an investigation of her before contacting her. Or maybe the shock of his letter telling about her *nonno's* wishes for reconciliation had thrown her before. But wouldn't the woman she seemed to be now have reacted differently? Whatever, it was too late to have her investigated. He could only trust that she was who she seemed to be.

But as he gave her her travel schedule, he knew that he would watch her carefully. Very carefully. He didn't want Lorenzo hurt.

"Do you have any other questions?" he asked, after giving her the arrangements.

"No. I think I've got it. Thank you."

Bright and cheery sounding again. And as much as he wanted to, he didn't trust it. Something just didn't ring right to him. His experience as a lawyer had taught him to trust his first impression of people. If adverse, it would take several encounters of a changed individual for him to alter it. "If you have any other questions, please feel free to call this office. Collect."

"Thank you."

"I'm looking forward to meeting you, Signorina Celini." That was an understatement. For good or bad, the woman intrigued him. Not only was she Lorenzo's granddaughter, but also something about her had captivated him in a way a woman hadn't done since. . .Giovanna Lazzareschi.

He frowned. Should that be a warning to him? He was normally a pretty good judge of character. Only Giovanna had managed to trick him. And she had captivated him, too. Was that what this woman was doing to him, too? But Giovanna's exceptional physical beauty had been primarily behind that and the way she had of *acting* the part of loving fiancée. He had no idea what Florence Celini looked like. And still, she fascinated him. He liked that. It made him feel less superficial.

"Me, too, Signor Ferretti. Ciao!"

"Ciao," he replied but waited for her to hang up before he did. He looked at his phone and shook his head. Maybe he would have an interesting week for a change. That would be nice. He was ready for. . .something.

As his gaze scanned over the green and golden Tuscan hillsides, he only wondered if that something might be Florence Celini.

Chapter 3

As the small plane landed at Amerigo Vespucci Airport, Florence looked out over the green and golden mountains surrounding the city of her father's birth and couldn't shake the feeling of somehow having come home. Although she had never visited Firenze in person, she had always felt a connection to the renaissance city because of her father. She probably had every coffee-table book ever published on the little city in her library.

She just hadn't given any of the books more than a casual glance until. . .receiving Domenico Ferretti's letter.

That letter had set in motion such changes in her life, changes that were as unexpected as the letter itself had been.

She pushed her bluntly cut shoulder-length chestnut-brown hair behind her right ear.

And she meant much greater alterations than just the cutting and coloring of her hair, the discarding of contacts and donning of glasses, and a modification of her wardrobe from Carolina Herrera and Oscar de la Renta to Gap and J. Crew.

Her gaze sought out her flight bag beneath the seat in front of her and the Bible that was in its front flap.

Bible. She made an amazed sound.

She had never traveled with a Bible before.

But this one, the one that contained the letter from her parents, was one she knew she would never leave home without again. Even though she had started out using the verses in Colossians as a guide for the character sketch that might belong to Florence Celini, the verses were becoming much more to her. An identity—one linked to her parents—she now *chose* to wear. And not just in acting but for real. The more she "wore" the virtues, the more comfortable they became. She felt that they went a long way in describing the person she would have been had the fake world of movie stardom not changed the path of her life.

"Wearing" the virtues of compassion, kindness, humility, gentleness, and patience was turning her into a person whose company she actually enjoyed. It felt really strange not to be angry or disillusioned or moody all the time, something Samantha Day had become without Florence's even understanding that it had happened or, even more, how.

But unusual, too, was how she had left her apartment in Manhattan unassisted, in a yellow city taxi rather than Samantha Day's normal limousine, had gone through all the check-in points at Kennedy Airport, and again at Rome's airport, had ridden on two airplanes, and hadn't been recognized by anyone. Not flight attendant, not gate agent, not fellow passenger. No one. On either continent or in the air in between them, either.

That was the first time since her acting career had exploded seven years earlier that that had happened. Normally she was inundated with well-wishers and celebrity-seekers.

And although it was something she had never really minded, had even liked on most occasions, it was a heady experience being a private individual again—something she was enjoying. For the moment, anyway, it gave her the time she needed to think, really think, about whom she was and what she believed for the first time in years and without the persona of Samantha Day intruding upon her thoughts.

And as she left the airplane and boarded the shuttle bus that was to take her to the terminal, she thought about her long-estranged grandfather—how he would act toward her, she toward him, and what he would look like—as well as the lawyer, Domenico Ferretti, who had said that he would be personally picking her up from the airport.

She was certain that that was something he normally didn't do. But as she left the bus and went through the doors of the terminal and scanned the small airport, she couldn't help but wonder again what Domenico Ferretti would look like. Would his body fit his voice? And his name? *Domenico Ferretti* had to be one of the nicer names she had ever heard.

She wouldn't mind if his body went together with his voice and name. She knew that to become acquainted with her grandfather was the reason she was in Firenze acting in the role of herself—private citizen, Florence Celini. But she couldn't help but wonder what meeting a man while in that role might be like. What sort of man would she, as plain old Florence Celini and not superstar Samantha Day, attract, and how might he treat her? One thing was certain: as Florence Celini, she could be sure no one would be after her to further their career, especially not a lawyer with a nice voice from Firenze.

"Signorina Celini." *That* voice spoke from behind her and

she spun around to meet its owner. The fine specimen of man she beheld through her clear glasses robbed her of her breath.

Paunch the size of a basketball? Bald? This man didn't have an extra ounce of fat on his athletic frame, and as for baldness, her fingers itched to reach out and touch the rich forest of dark hair that was styled in a classic way around his face. He had the refined features of a man of pure Italian bloodline, and he was tall, too. Much taller than she, and at five feet nine, that was something she always noticed. Hollywood would definitely love to train its cameras on him.

She licked her lips, which had suddenly gone dry. "Signor Ferretti?"

"Yes." He held out his hand, but as his gaze scanned over her face, a look of recognition, like someone discovering a secret, came upon his face. Dread washed through her.

He knows who I am! She was certain of it. Why? Why did the one person to recognize her during the last twenty hours have to be one of the two she didn't want to know that Samantha Day, the film star, and Florence Celini, the bookstore owner, were the same person? Domenico Ferretti had intrigued her when only talking to him by telephone. Seeing him face to face made him many times more appealing. His body definitely fit his voice. And then some.

He blinked. "I'm sorry. I don't mean to stare. But you look just like—"

"I know," she cut him off. "I've been told that before." She was going to try and bluff her way out. Act as if to be told she looked like Samantha Day was a normal occurrence. It was, after all.

He looked at her curiously. "You mean by your parents?

When you were little?"

"My parents?" What was he talking about?

"Is there anyone else who would know that you are the image of your *nonno?*"

Nonno! She nearly sagged in relief. He meant that she looked like her grandfather, her father's father, not like the movie star Samantha Day!

"No. I mean, yes. Yes, my parents did say that. When I was little." She motioned to her eyes, which were partially hidden behind her clear glasses. She thought it better to point out one of Samantha Day's most famous physical characteristics rather than to leave it to him to make a later comparison. The best defense being an offense, or some such thing. She'd learned that from playing numerous evil characters on the silver screen. "My father always told me that they were the same unusual color as his father's. Green with the same aquamarine rings." That was the reason, too, she hadn't bothered to get colored contacts to disguise the color of her eyes. She thought her father's father might have known that she had inherited his unusual eye coloring.

Domenico Ferretti's intelligent gaze looked past the lenses of her glasses and into them now. Deeply. She felt as if he were looking at much more than just their coloring. Trying to determine what sort of person she was, perhaps? "Yes, they are the same," he pronounced and took a step back, much as photographers do when trying to decide upon the picture they want to take. "But no. Not just your eyes. Everything. Your general look. Except for your height and gender, of course, you are the image of your *nonno.*"

And as Samantha Day she had probably inherited his

mean streak, too, she wanted to say, but of course, she didn't. Instead she kept to her physical appearance. "I inherited my height from my grandpop."

"Ah. . .your mother's father."

"That's right. The man who raised me. And you?" she asked, thinking it was time to turn the conversation away from her, something Samantha Day was an expert at doing.

His chin lifted a fraction of an inch in reaction to the unexpected question. "Me?"

She nodded. "Where did you get your height from?" She knew he had to know her history. She wanted to learn something about him. Actually, she wanted to learn a lot about him.

He smiled, a wide one that looked like it had laughter hiding right behind it. Real laughter, not a fake one brought forth upon the demand of a director. "My mother. She was actually taller than my father."

"Was?"

Sorrow pushed the humor out of his eyes. "I lost them both several years ago."

"I'm sorry." She tilted her head, and she couldn't have said what made her continue with, "So we're both orphans."

"Except I was blessed to be a man of thirty when my parents went to God's kingdom."

God's kingdom. Spoken just like her grandpop. That's where he'd always told her her parents had gone. It had always been something more substantial to her than when people tried to assure her with the cliché "They've gone to heaven, Dear." Even as a young girl, she had always been able to picture a place called God's kingdom. To say they were in heaven was too much like a fairy tale. It might be correct, theologically speaking, but it was too vague a place for her, unlearned about such things, to imagine. But God's kingdom, she could just see angels and believers living with God in that mighty place of joy and comfort. And no pain.

She shook her head. Reading her Bible had gotten her thinking about such things a lot during the last few days. More than she had in all the previous ten years put together. Unlike what she knew her grandpop thought, she had never renounced Christianity; she just hadn't been a practicing believer.

"You were. . .blessed," she agreed. *Blessed?* She hadn't used that word before. Not ever. But for some reason to say he was lucky just wouldn't have seemed correct.

He looked at her in a curious way, but in a manner that made her feel as if she had just passed a test. "They were great people. And so in love with one another."

A man who came from a loving family? She hadn't met one of those. . .in years. Most all the men she had known during the last decade had come from broken homes. "Tell me, when will I meet my grandfather?"

His square jaw lifted a fraction of an inch, alerting her to something being wrong. One thing acting had done was make her very aware of nonverbal communication. "It was to have been immediately, but there's been a slight. . .complication."

She tilted her head to the side. "What sort of complication? Is he ill?" She hoped not. Although she couldn't muster up much feeling for the old man—even while acting in the role of herself and with wearing the virtues of Colossians Three— she really did want to meet him. He was the man who had fathered her beloved *babbo*, her daddy. As much as she might not like it, she existed because of him. She was a direct descendent of his.

"No, no," he was quick to assure. "Quite unexpectedly he had to go out of town for a few days."

So, that's how much he was looking forward to meeting me! Samantha Day wanted to blurt out. She pressed her lips together to keep the antagonistic response from flying out of her mouth. She *had* to let God's virtues rule her mind and not allow the jaded actress, Samantha Day, to have that place. Samantha wanted to assume the worse. But patience was a virtue she was sure she would be "wearing" had she not let Samantha Day become anything more than just her profession. And compassion, too. Two things she, as Samantha, had forgotten how to practice. She had to give Signore Ferretti the chance to explain.

"He greatly regrets it, but—"

"Seems to me, that my grandfather has a lot of regrets," she cut in, remembering the letter this man had sent to her and his writing how her grandfather had "greatly regretted the years that had gone by without them having met." She couldn't help the words from coming out, but was glad that the tone was the compassionate one Florence might use and not the haughty angry one with which Samantha would definitely speak.

"He does." Domenico Ferretti surprised her by answering in the affirmative, a direct response that didn't mince words. He took a deep breath, and looking at her squarely, his dark gaze settled on hers. She felt her heart pick up its rhythm in response. "Signorina, your *nonno* has asked me not to say too much about him to you. But as it is public knowledge, this I can say: He was for many years a very difficult man.'"

"The way he treated my parents tells me everything. I think he was more than just difficult."

Domenico Ferretti acknowledged the truth of that with a lift of his Ferragamo-clad shoulder. "But he has changed. Through the grace of God, he's much different from before, and he's now trying very hard to set right many of the wrongs for which he is responsible."

She tilted her head. "Sounds something like Charles Dickens's character, Ebenezer Scrooge, in *A Christmas Carol.*"

A quick smile turned Domenico Ferretti's full, but perfect lips, upward. "Yes, but without the ghosts. Unless we're talking about the Holy Ghost moving in his heart."

Again something Grandpop would say. It was amazing, but Domenico Ferretti and her grandpop were so similar. She hadn't thought anybody in the world believed as her grandpop did.

And couldn't she of all people understand about a person changing? Wasn't that what she was in the process of doing, herself? She had let her Hollywood personality intrude upon the woman she should have been. Had her *babbo's* father done something similar? Had her grandfather's work, like her own, turned him into a person he didn't like? She thought it must be much more than just that, though, for him to have turned his back on his only child. Although she wanted to ask more questions, she respected the lawyer-client relationship that Domenico Ferretti was bound to follow and didn't. She would meet her grandfather when the time was right. Patience seemed to be a virtue she was learning. Samantha would have demanded more information.

"So." She smiled, but not the brilliant one movie goers around the world would recognize as belonging to Samantha Day, rather the soft one that had been curving Florence Celini's lips the last few days. "I guess I get to play tourist in your fine city until my grandfather returns." She shrugged her shoulders. "I can think of about twenty billion worse things to do."

She saw something like a mixture of relief and admiration come into his deep shiny eyes, but esteem, not over her appearance as had always been the case with Samantha Day, rather, because of a high regard for her character. It was a heady experience and one she hadn't had in years. She knew that most considered Samantha Day spoiled, supercilious, and rather unpleasant and only had anything to do with her because her beauty sold box office tickets. A lot of tickets.

"It would be my pleasure if you would allow me to show you around."

Allow him? His pleasure? Had the man looked in the mirror recently? What mirror? He only had to notice all the admiring glances he'd been getting from the women in the terminal. She'd noticed them. Add to that a character of dignity that seemed more and more to remind her of her grandpop, and Florence thought he had to be just about perfect. Was this the type of man she as herself, as Florence, attracted? If so, then she had played the role Samantha Day for far too long.

"That would be great." *Great? It would be fantastic, wonderful, perfect!* "But do you have the time? To take off from your work, I mean?" That was something Samantha would never have asked. She would have just assumed it to be so.

His lips curved in an indulging way, and she knew that

there was a lot more to this man than just being a lawyer or good looking or a man with Christian character.

Christian character? That thought brought all her others to a jarring stop. She really *was* changing. She had never thought of that as being an attribute before. For her grandpop, maybe, and her *babbo*. But not for a man her age whom she might be interested in getting to know better. *Interested?* That was an understatement. She was more attracted to this man than any other since the varsity football team's star quarterback when she was a freshman in high school.

"As unexpectedly as your *nonno* had to go out of town, I have found my calendar cleared. This next week I am your most willing guide. But how about if we get your bags now and get you settled. You must be tired." He started directing her toward the baggage claim area.

Even though she hadn't slept in a day, she wasn't sleepy at all. "Where will I be staying?" she asked, as she pointed out the two Louis Vuitton bags that belonged to her. She had thought to leave them behind and get nondesigner bags, regular ones. But even had she only been a bookstore owner she would have bought these bags. She loved them.

With a seemingly effortless movement, he removed her luggage from the conveyer belt and started walking in the direction of the exit. "Your *nonno* has an apartment in town that he thought you would enjoy for the days he's gone so that you can easily get into the city."

"That sounds great."

He turned to her and, with amusement glinting in his dark eyes, asked, "Are you always so easygoing?"

She laughed. She couldn't help it, but his question was

proof that she was wearing the virtues found in Colossians, and "wearing" them well. "No. Not always." What an understatement!

As he directed her toward his Range Rover he said, "I must admit, when we talked the second time by phone, you seemed to be a different person from the first time."

"Really?" He had noticed the change and in only one conversation? But why not? She had felt the change in herself almost immediately upon making the decision to act differently by using the wise words found in the letter from her parents and the "letters from God," the Bible. Why shouldn't an observant person have noticed a change? Part of a lawyer's training was to "read" people after all.

But she didn't want to share all that had happened to her since receiving his letter—that would mean explaining about her professional life, her stage name, and her acting career—and she didn't want to do that. Not yet.

As they got into the car and he started driving off, she motioned toward the rear section that had what was obviously a dog fence separating it from the rest of the vehicle. "What type of dog do you have?"

"German shepherd," he replied, as he paid the parking ticket.

"They're beautiful dogs."

"None better than Michelangelo," he agreed, as he directed the car onto the roadway.

She laughed. "Do you think the actual man, Michelangelo, would appreciate your naming your dog after him?"

"As long as I let him sculpt my dog in marble, I doubt that he would mind."

"I don't know," she bantered back, with a challenging tilt of her chin. "He was supposed to have had a fiery temper."

A deep laughter rumbled from his chest. "He was both an artist and Italian. What else could one expect?"

"Oh, but Fra Angelico was both those, too. And he was called Beato Angelico—Blessed Angelico—because he was so sweet natured."

He took his eyes off the roadway long enough to look at her with a quizzical frown. "You know about Fra Angelico?"

She nodded. "One of my favorite painters. Last year I sent out Christmas cards that had his painting of *The Annunciation* on them. I can't wait to see his work at the convent of San Marco's."

"We'll go there one day this week if you like. He's one of my favorites, too."

"It's a date."

He shook his head. "Who would have known?" he asked, as he switched lanes.

She looked at him and couldn't help the quizzical frown that cut across her face. "Known what?"

He took his eyes off the road long enough to glance in her direction. "That all this time Lorenzo had such a sweet and interesting granddaughter growing up in America."

Florence's eyelids rose and her lips formed a perfect O.

Sweet? Interesting? Yes, who would have known? Certainly not her. As she turned to look out the window toward the foothills of the mountains to the north of the city, she considered that the Italian air must be good for her. She slanted her eyes toward Domenico Ferretti, who was weaving his way through traffic that would have done Manhattan proud. Or maybe it was just being in the right company. This man's company. His letter had been the impetus behind her finding her parents' letter and, in turn, God's "letters" as given in the Bible. She glanced down at it still in the pocket of her flight bag. Still close to her.

The more she was with this man who had inadvertently so changed the path of her life, the easier she found it to wear the virtues of Colossians Three.

And the easier she found it to be herself—Florence Celini.

It was proving to be a much nicer way in which to live life than that of Samantha Day's.

Chapter 4

Less than half an hour later, Domenico watched her as she stood by the window in the living room of her grandfather's penthouse. She seemed to want to soak the city of her ancestors into her very pores.

Domenico thought her the most intriguing woman he had met. . . .ever. Not only had her physical beauty nearly taken his breath away when he'd first beheld her, but her spirit—so sweet and calm—seemed to mesh with his, to communicate and mold together in a web he hadn't wanted to get loose of. Her body was long and graceful with gentle curves in all the right places, while her unblemished face was as creamy and smooth as a marble statue. His fingers begged to reach out and touch her cheek. But what he felt for her went beyond the physical. It went to the very center of him that seemed to know that this woman was one he could look at every day for the rest of his life; this was a woman with whom he could share a friendship, a romance, a love as great as that which his parents had been blessed to have.

She was so totally different from what he had expected. He had thought that she would be angry when she found out about her *nonno* being gone—the reason why he and Lorenzo had decided it would be best if he took off the week in order to spend time with her. But she had handled the situation with a refined decorum that was so seldom to be found in such exceptionally beautiful women. At least from those of Domenico's experience.

But best of all, she seemed guileless.

After the deception of Giovanna, that was one of the most important characteristics in a woman to Domenico. He had to know that a woman was honest and frank with him from the first. He didn't like surprises. Didn't want to ever give his heart away to a woman again only to discover afterwards that her agenda for marriage was based on different attributes from those of his own.

He wanted a woman to love. A woman to be his companion, his helper, his friend: a woman with whom he could share the joys of parenthood. A woman who would never be anything but truthful with him about what she believed, who she was, and what she felt. And vise versa.

He had acted like an adolescent—staring at her with a gapped-mouth expression—when she'd turned around in the airport, and he had gotten a real good look at her. He was only glad that he had been able to cover up his reaction by telling her that she looked like Lorenzo. She did. But that fact didn't have anything to do with making him stare at her in that star-struck fashion. Rather, it had everything to do with Cupid's arrow shooting him through his heart.

At this moment Domenico couldn't be happier that Lorenzo had had to leave town. Another case of God taking a situation that at first glance seemed all wrong but with the passing of time—and just a little bit of it—showed itself to be absolutely perfect. If Lorenzo hadn't had to go to Milan, then Domenico would not have had the chance to get to know his granddaughter personally and closely. Now he had a whole week.

A smile touched upon his lips as he watched the tall woman who so intrigued him breathe in deeply of the panoramic view of Firenze. She clasped her hands tightly together upon her chest. He knew what she was feeling.

Firenze's magic.

The magic of a city that probably had more artwork executed in honor of Jesus Christ than any other city in the world. From architecture, to paintings, to sculpture, to stained glass windows, Firenze had it all. And from the masters.

That was something everybody felt upon coming here, one of the city's innate charms and something that helped to make it one of the most romantic cities in the world. So many people fell in love after spending just a week together in Firenze.

His smile deepened. It had been long enough for his grandparents to fall in love—and they had been married for sixty years—and long enough too for his parents who had spent nearly fifty years together.

Domenico knew that a week would do for him. Do perfectly.

He was already enamored of her.

And she had used the word *blessed*, not *lucky*, when she'd agreed that to be orphaned at thirty, as he had been, and not seven, like she, was the better of the two. And she liked the work of Fra Angelico. Such little things, but things that were so important. Showed a character he liked.

A Christian character.

"I love it here," she spoke out suddenly and swiveled away from the view. Her shiny brown hair danced around her chin like strands of pure Chinese silk. His mouth went dry. She was intoxicated by the view and seemed to glow with pleasure. He understood. He felt the same way about her. She motioned with her arm to the city. "It's like a little jewel with church domes and spires and bell towers sticking up everywhere." She looked back out. "And the color. It's golden. I mean it really is. I always thought it was the photographers' lenses that gave it that hue." She pointed down to the Arno River, which was moving right below them along its ancient course on its way to the sea. "Even the river seems golden in the afternoon sunlight."

"That's Tuscany. Only this land can take a brown, rather dirty river and turn it to gold."

She sighed. "I can't wait to go out and walk around the city."

"Whenever you want."

Whenever I want? "Now."

"Now?"

"Now!" She not only didn't want to waste a moment in seeing the city but also, as long as this man was here with her, she wanted to see it with him.

"You aren't tired from your trip across the Atlantic?"

Tired? After having spent as much as eighteen to twenty hours on movie sets in the past, to sit on a plane and fly across six time zones was easy for her. But she didn't disclose that. Since he hadn't figured out her stage persona she wanted to keep it that way. She wanted to give Florence Celini the chance to grow without the persona of Samantha Day intruding. "I'll sleep early tonight then be on Firenze's time zone."

That's what she always did when she traveled far from New York. "So if you are indeed free, Signor Ferretti, I'd love to take a walk with you around your enchanting city."

He tipped his head to one side, and she was perplexed when he frowned. "I'm afraid that's impossible."

Impossible? What game was he playing? "But I thought you just said—"

"I can't walk around my city with a pretty lady by my side who calls me Signor. Now if that lady were to call me Domenico. . ."

Handsome and humorous, too. She could get used to that. "Domenico." The name rolled off her lips. "Such a nice name. Musical sounding. Is it a family name?"

She was surprised when he shook his head negatively. "Meaning 'of the Lord.' I was born on Sunday—the day of the Lord—so that's the name my parents gave to me."

"And are you? Of the Lord, I mean?" She didn't know what made her ask that. But since reading her Bible and now with looking out the window at the many churches that made up the city's distinctive skyline, it just seemed natural. And she really was interested, even though she was almost certain of the answer. He was too much like her grandpop not to be "of the Lord."

"I have been ever since I was a young boy and I started to understand the meaning behind the crucifixes that I saw hanging in the churches all over the city. With that supreme act of sacrifice, God won for me—for all of us—life everlasting. And not just that, but life as it is meant to be lived here and now, too. A life with Him in it, a part of my very own."

Yes, he believed just like Grandpop. And her parents. People from so many different backgrounds, different lands, and yet all believing the same thing. She smiled. "That's beautiful." It really was. She knew her grandpop would have called it a testimony.

"And you?"

Fear clutched at her. She should have anticipated his question but she hadn't. She wished now that she hadn't brought the subject up. How was she to answer? *Truthfully*, that voice of conscience that she had heard more and more lately spoke to her. *Truthfully*. "I. . .I was raised a Christian, first by my parents then by my grandpop. And even though I'm a Christian—I do believe that Jesus is God's son and that He saved humankind when He hung on that cross." She paused. This was the hard part. "I must admit, however, to have lost both Him and my faith somewhere along the way."

"Firenze, with all its artwork, is definitely the place to rediscover both Him. . .and your faith." His voice was deep and gravelly. So encouraging. So masculine. . .

She smiled up at him.

He smiled down at her.

That connection she had felt even through the phone line shot between them like an electric charge.

She licked her lips as he softly continued with that voice, that beautiful voice of his. "Maybe other than meeting your *nonno*, that's one of the reasons you had to come here. To give you the time to find the woman of faith that the girl of faith should have grown into."

She stopped breathing. How did he know? That was exactly what she felt like she was doing. What *felt*? She was doing. She started breathing again. But at his next words she again stopped.

"I prayed for you after our first conversation."

"What?" A week ago that would have offended her, affronted the cold, hard heart of the woman she had been. But not now. Now it left her almost dumbfounded. But in a way that made her feel warm and tingly all over. This man, who she hadn't even known, had been praying for her. *Praying for her.* Maybe prayers really did work. "What do you mean?"

"To be honest, after talking, I was afraid that you might come here and hurt Lorenzo—your *nonno*. And even though Lorenzo was a very"—he seemed to search around for the correct words—"shall we say, unpleasant man for most of his adult life, he has, because of the grace of God, changed. I prayed that the Lord might bring peace to your heart—His peace—just as he did to your *nonno* and that there might be a reunion between you and your *nonno* that will make all the angels in heaven sing." As silence reigned, he softly said, "I hope this doesn't offend you."

She shook her head. "To be honest, it would have before, but many things are changing in my life. And now, no, I'm not offended. Not at all. In fact," she smiled, a brilliant smile that came straight from Florence Celini's heart, "if you could help me rediscover how to pray, I would be grateful. It's something else I seemed to have lost the ability to do during the last ten years."

"I'd like that." He looked at her curiously, and his eyes narrowed a bit at their corners.

She shook her head. "What?"

"I'm sorry. But you looked so familiar to me when you smiled like that."

Her stage smile! She nearly groaned. She was almost as famous for it as she was for her sigh. But it hadn't come because the director had called for it. Rather, for the first time in years, that smile that had been written up as "brilliant, luminous, sparkling" had been a true reflection of how she was actually feeling.

"You said I look like my grandfather," she reminded him, hoping that would be enough. She wasn't ready to tell him about Samantha Day. Not yet. Not until she was better acquainted with Florence Celini.

"I don't know." She could tell from the way he looked at her with his intelligent eyes narrowed at their corners that he wasn't entirely convinced that that was it. She remained quiet and was glad she did when he shook his head as if to clear it from all the possibilities that were running through his mind. He finally said, "You're right, of course, that must be it."

"Now, shall we go see the city?" She was anxious to do that, but even more to get away from the subject of whom she reminded him.

He glanced at his watch. "I just have to take Michelangelo out for a walk first."

"Why don't you bring him with us."

He looked at her curiously. "You wouldn't mind."

"Of course not. I love dogs." She really did. Even as Samantha Day, she loved animals.

"And he loves nothing more than long walks around the city and is, in fact, a canine expert at waiting for me whenever I go into places he can't. Thanks. I'll get him and be back in a moment," he said and started to walk toward the door.

She frowned. "Do you live so close?"

He stopped and pointed down to the floor. "Right below this apartment."

"Really?"

He nodded. "I redid the apartment right after Lorenzo finished with this one. That was three years ago. And how we became acquainted personally."

For the first time, she looked around at her surroundings, noticing the artistry that could have only come from a very good interior designer. "Who would have expected such a modern apartment in such an old building? It's beautiful." It was. She had only had eyes for the view when she first walked in, but now she let her gaze wander around the airy penthouse. It was bathed in light with open spaces that easily filled up with the golden Tuscan sunlight. A pair of Italian sling chairs set the tone in the living area. Contemporary and simple. Nothing dark. Silk covered the sofa. Only blinds were on the windows, no curtains to hinder the view or shut out the light. And there was no clutter.

He nodded. "I liked it so much I had mine designed by the same person."

"So your apartment looks just like this one?"

"Except that it's not on three levels and there's a bit more clutter. And plants." He smiled sheepishly. "And dog hair that my housekeeper is always chasing."

"Just sounds lived-in to me." As beautiful as this apartment was, it didn't have that feeling. It looked like it was ready for a magazine crew to come in and take pictures of it. She reached for her purse. "I'll come with you. I can't wait to meet your dog and get out into that city."

Domenico laughed, a sound that came from low in his throat. "I have a feeling that they both can't wait to meet you, either."

Chapter 5

Firenze was everything and more than what Florence had expected. It was large squares filled with people, medieval churches filled with people, arched bridges filled with people, large and small museums filled with people, long streets filled with people, quaint alleyways filled with people, beautiful restaurants filled with people, and stores of all kinds—both designer and Ma and Pa—filled with people: people from around the world and not one of whom recognized Florence as being Samantha Day.

And Florence loved it, loved the anonymity, and loved hearing all the different languages being spoken as she walked over the Ponto Vecchio—aptly named Old Bridge since the bridge as it was in its present form had stood from 1345. And she loved ambling down the Piazza d'Uffizi with its outdoor gallery of nineteenth century statues of Firenze's famous citizens in niches built into the Galleria degli Uffizi—Uffizi Art Gallery—on her way to the Piazza della Signoria—the traditional center and political hub of the city. The fourteenth century *loggia*—porch—located across from the Palazzo Vecchio was an outdoor art gallery with original artwork from as far back as the fourth century B.C.

But spying Brunelleschi's enormous fifteenth century dome that topped the *duomo*—cathedral—as she and Domenico walked the many roads and alleys of the city stirred her heart and made her catch her breath each time she caught a glimpse of it. At least half a football field in length and more than an entire field in height, it seemed to almost be floating above the city, like a vision from heaven. And if the *duomo* wasn't visible, then the elegant lines of its bell tower, designed by Giotto in the early 1300s with its iridescent marble covering, was. The structures were magnificent, and each time she saw them from yet another angle between the golden tones of the city's buildings, whom they were built to glorify—Jesus Christ—somehow seemed to sink deeper and deeper into her soul. The reaction she was having to being in this city of churches and Christian artwork was continuing the chain of events that had started when she first received Domenico's letter. Combined with her daily Bible reading time—the last thing she did each night before falling to sleep—the change it was bringing to her was all a bit mind-boggling.

But something else that boggled her mind was walking through the quaint medieval city with Domenico Ferretti by her side.

That first afternoon started a trend that they continued for each succeeding day of the week. And the more time they spent together walking the streets of their ancestors and sharing noon meals together at outdoor cafés in the city's piazzas and at candlelit restaurants filled with Tuscan ambiance at night, the more they grew to both like and respect one another. In a very short time, Domenico Ferretti became Florence's very best friend.

Florence's first thought that he was very similar to her grandpop proved to be correct. He was a man who lived his life according to the precepts of the Bible. And as they were standing before the eastern doors of the octagonal Baptistry—the oldest building in the city—looking at Old Testament scenes that Ghiberti had masterly sculpted in bas-reliefs from gilded bronze, Florence realized that that had become something very important to her. She suspected that Domenico was a man in the way God meant for boys to grow into men: like her grandpop and beloved *babbo,* one who always had God in the center of his heart. It had been a long time since Florence had been around such a complete man. Ten years.

"It took Ghiberti twenty-eight years to complete these doors," Domenico said from her side, startling her from her reverie.

"Twenty-eight! That's longer then I've been alive by one year."

Domenico nodded. "Michelangelo—the man I mean," he qualified and looked down at his dog, who sat by their feet, and smiled, "stood right here before the original ones—which are now in the Museo dell'Opera del Duomo—the Cathedral Museum—for protection—and said, 'They are so fine that they might fittingly stand as the Porta del Paradiso.' "

" 'The Gates of Paradise,' " she murmured.

He squeezed her hand. They had been holding hands for the past four days, something that felt perfect and right, like an extension of her own self. "Very good, *carissima.* Your ability to pick up Italian so quickly amazes me."

She beamed and tilted her head toward his. "I've had a good teacher." He had been helping her add to her smattering of

Italian all week. But other than that, she knew that she was only incorporating the same technique to learn the language as she did when studying scripts. She looked toward the door again and its ten panels, most of which were subdivided into several subjects. "I can see why Michelangelo would say that. These are so moving." She pointed to the first panel in the upper left corner of the huge door that depicted the creation of Adam and Eve. "Even if I didn't know the story, I could understand what is going on here. It's almost like a children's picture book."

He chuckled. "I like that. Ghiberti's golden doors compared to a picture book."

She was afraid she had offended him. In a city of artwork, she knew that these doors were one of its most prized. "I mean no disrespect."

"None taken. Honestly. I like the analogy." He indicated the doors. "It was Renaissance man's answer to the value of teaching through pictures. All people, both young and old, saw them. In a day when books were scarce, they learned Bible stories this way."

"Exactly." She was glad that he understood what she meant. She indicated the lower left corner of the panel and recited the verses she had read just the previous night in Genesis. " 'The Lord God formed the man from the dust of the ground and breathed into his nostrils the breath of life, and the man became a living being.' " She paused for a moment and gazed at the work that showed Adam being literally raised from the dust of the earth by God. "That is so obviously what is happening here. Makes me wonder why people have a problem with evolution and the Bible's story of creation. It's so obvious here. Man was finely sculpted just as God wanted him to be and could now receive the breath of life."

He looked at her and, with awe in his voice, said, "I've never thought of it like that." He shook his head. "You told me the day you arrived in Firenze that you had lost both God and your faith somewhere along the way. But after all these days we've spent together, you haven't seemed that way to me at all."

She grimaced. "I've changed. . .a lot, Domenico, since coming to Firenze." She shrugged her shoulders and wondered if now was the time to tell him everything about her, including the Samantha Day part. She decided not. As with other times, it just didn't seem to fit in with the moment. "Something about this city"—she waved her arm out in an all-encompassing way—"its churches, its beautiful works of art, all seem to guide my thoughts in a God-centered way, one it hasn't traveled in many years. That so many people—smart, talented people—like Signor Ghiberti who believed so greatly in God above and in His redemptive work through Jesus Christ that he spent twenty-eight years making these panels that visually tell the Bible stories"—she pointed back to Ghiberti's masterpiece—"makes me think. Think about God."

"I know what you mean, although a lot of the work you see around the city wasn't necessarily done because of faith. As much as I—as a Florentine—might not want to admit it, a great deal was commissioned just so that the rich of the city could show off to the world their wealth." He shrugged. "It was good for business. Not in every case, of course, and I'm not referring to Ghiberti, whose knowledge about the Bible stories had to have been extensive to have created this, but often."

"How cynical."

"Artists created what was asked of them because they had to

eat." He smiled and, looking at his watch, started guiding her and Michelangelo away from the doors. "Come on." He looked up at the overcast sky. "I'll take you to see the work of a man for whom there is absolutely no doubt about his love of God."

✍

"It's more wonderful in person than any card or poster could ever depict." She spoke a few minutes later, as they stood in the southern corridor on the upper floor of the convent of San Marco—now a museum devoted to the fifteenth century painter Fra Angelico—looking with awe at the fresco entitled *The Annunciation*.

"I knew you would like seeing it in person."

"Like it? I stand in awe of it. I can almost feel Mary's joy, surprise, fright, and amazement that an angel should visit her and with such amazing news. It's so serene and filled with diaphanous light. And Gabriel's wings seem to be made up of rainbows from the sky."

"The rainbow of God's promise, perhaps?"

She pulled her gaze away from the painting, not an easy thing to do, and turned to him. "The promise He made to Noah after he flooded the world? Telling that he would never flood the earth again?"

"Maybe."

She nodded and he could tell from the way she rearranged her glasses and pursed her lips that she was really thinking about it. That was something she often did. And it was something he loved about her. Giovanna had claimed to be a Christian, and yet she had always shied away from talking about deeper theological topics. He liked how a love of discussing things of God was something he and Florence seemed to share.

But that wasn't all he loved about Florence.

He loved how open and truthful she was about everything, but mostly about her search to rediscover the faith of her childhood. She didn't know it, but she and her *nonno* were so similar. He was only certain that Florence had never been as mean to people as Lorenzo had been.

"Yes, maybe," she continued after a moment and turned back to the painting. Holding her hand out as if to touch the colors of the wings, but of course not doing so, she said, "I don't claim to be an expert, but I've never seen an angel's wings painted like the rainbow before."

"And yet, according to the Bible, angels are fantastically beautiful creatures. Why not colors?"

"Why indeed? Fra Angelico must have been a very special Christian to think about that."

"The art historian, painter, and architect Giorgio Vasari, who was born just a little more than half a century after Fra Angelico, wrote that he was 'a simple and most holy man.' "

She motioned to the paintings that surrounded them. "Even though Fra Angelico has been gone for more than five hundred years, his work lets us know him. His soul was definitely at peace. No disturbing or agitating elements could have been in the man he was." She waved her hand in front of her in a dismissing way. "I don't mean that living the life of a medieval monk he didn't have problems—everyone on earth has problems of one sort or another—but he seemed to let God take charge of those problems. He would have had to, in order to execute works that seem so God-inspired, so much a part of heaven, works that seem to be not just for the glorification of God but also for the edification of his fellow humans, something to help us in our. . ." She paused and frowned, the frown whereby fine lines crinkled her forehead and made her seem so familiar to him. Sometimes when she smiled he had that impression, too. And he didn't mean just because of her *nonno*. "I don't know," she continued, bringing his thoughts back to their conversation. "Something to help us see God?"

"Exactly. That's the reason he painted the monks' bedrooms, their cells, and the walls of these corridors: To help his brothers in their devotions."

She walked over to cell number one. "Imagine having *Noli me Tangere*"—she indicated the painting depicting Jesus appearing to Mary Magdalene outside of the tomb on Easter morning—"to help you in your devotions?"

"Would you like a copy of it"— he indicated the direction of the corridor—"or of *The Annunciation?*"

She gasped, a sound that once again seemed so known to him. But the way she looked at him, as if the idea that she could own a copy of such a work of art had never occurred to her, was only as familiar as their days together had been. "I would. I really would."

"Which one would you like?"

"You choose." She took his hand and squeezed it, and Domenico felt his blood pound through his veins. It felt so right, so good, to make Florence happy. She was so grateful for the littlest of things. "But you don't have to go to all that trouble, Domenico. I'll look for a print."

"No, I want to." What he had in mind was far more than just a print bought from the museum's store. But he wanted that to be a surprise. "Besides, that's what dear Fra Angelico would have wanted. Even after five hundred years, his artwork is still helping his brothers and sisters in the Lord."

Emotion gathered in her eyes in the form of tears. She could only nod in agreement. At this moment Florence didn't know how she had lived the last ten years without the faith that was becoming so much a part of her since first receiving Domenico's letter or. . .how she had lived without Domenico.

Both having faith and Domenico by her side brought out the very best in her. And she was beginning to realize that the very best in her was. . .Florence Celini.

"Thank you. I'd like that," she said, when she could find her voice. She would replace the Pablo Picasso she had in the bedroom of her Manhattan apartment with the print Domenico would give to her. That print would be far more valuable to her than that original work of art by the twentieth century artist. First because it would be a gift from Domenico and second because she would, as Fra Angelico had intended for all who looked upon his work, be edified by it in her devotions. It would always help her remember what was important in life.

Compassion, kindness, humility, gentleness, patience, forgiveness, love. . .

Love. . .

She slanted her eyes up to Domenico as they walked arm in arm under the arched porticos of the convent turned museum toward the exit.

Love. . .

She *loved* this man.

She didn't know how it was possible to love a man she

hadn't known even existed two weeks earlier, but in her heart—the heart that had, only the previous night, welcomed God to be a part of it again after an eviction of ten years—she knew that she did.

But she knew, too, that before she told Domenico anything—even about her life-changing decision of the previous night—she had to tell him about Samantha Day. And finally answer the question of recognition that she had so often seen in his eyes. Even a few minutes earlier when Samantha Day's world famous gasp had escaped her lips.

She owed him the total truth before she could declare her love. Because love was based on truth, and without total honesty between them, there could never be a future. And a future with Domenico in it was what she wanted.

She slanted her eyes over at him.

Such a future seemed like pure Tuscan gold to her.

Chapter 6

The next day Florence awoke to a sky that was ominous. But unlike when the persona of Samantha Day had ruled her life, and not God, it didn't bother her in the least. Her soul was sunny. She was in love with a wonderful man, and they were going out on the best "date" Florence could now imagine: they were going to Sunday morning church service together.

Since it looked like the Tuscan sky was going to pour some of its ample supply of rain upon the land, Domenico decided to drive them.

"How can you decide which church to go to in this city of churches?" Florence asked as they drove over the Amerigo Vespucci Bridge just as the first drops of rain started to fall from the windy autumn sky. The surface of the Arno River was dancing with the big fat drops of liquid. Florence decided then that she liked Firenze in the rain just as much as she did in the sunshine. It was cozy.

"Today it was an easy choice. St James is the American church at Firenze." He flashed her his smile. "I want you to be able to understand everything, so it's the only choice, really."

"The service is in English?" She hadn't expected that. It thrilled her that after her decision of two nights earlier, she was going to hear a sermon she could understand. She was almost craving it.

Amusement glinted in his eyes. "Totally."

But what else she hadn't anticipated was how the pastor's sermon seemed to speak directly to her heart. It was all about forgiveness. What stunned Florence the most, however, was that she didn't sit in the congregation as he spoke about forgiveness and consider whether she would forgive her paternal grandfather for the estrangement as much as whether her *maternal* grandfather—her beloved grandpop—could forgive *her* for spurning all his love, prayers, and advice throughout the last ten years. The dear man had given her nothing but love, and she had returned it by giving him only obligatory phone calls a few times a year while pursuing a lifestyle that was, if not exactly harmful, not good for her, either.

"Grandpop," she mouthed out and fished around in her purse for a tissue, as conviction over her behavior washed through her like the rain outside did the city streets. She wished she could hug the dear old man right this minute and beg his pardon. She glanced at her watch. She would call him as soon as it was morning in Texas.

Domenico leaned close to her and, with his eyes full of compassionate concern, offered her a linen handkerchief from his pocket. It only made her tears fall faster. She remembered how her grandpop always had a supply of fresh linen handkerchiefs to offer crying souls touched by worship service on Sunday mornings, too.

With a tremulous smile, she took it. She held it to her nose and inhaled its special aroma, a blend of Domenico's after-shave and that fresh laundry smell, before she lifted it to her eyes and dabbed at their corners. The service ended shortly afterward, and it was with a grateful heart that she let Domenico lead her back to the car and with even more relief that he drove through the rain-soaked streets without saying a word.

Guilt over having mistreated her grandpop still swept through her. Her grandpop had never given her anything but love. He had taken her in when she was orphaned and had never made her feel as if she were intruding in his life. Not once. And since her grandma had died about the time her parents had married, that meant all the care for a seven year old had fallen upon him. And how had she repaid him? By not only turning her back on the unconditional love he had given to her but on the faith of their common ancestors, one that had produced such wonderful people as he and his daughter—Florence's mother.

"Do you want to tell me about it?" Domenico asked with that kind, gentle voice that musically caressed her soul. It was only then she realized that he had stopped the car and that they were parked near the old bridge, the Ponte Vecchio.

She nodded. She did want to tell him. Everything. It was time to tell all. About her grandpop and how she had behaved toward him, but even more. . .about her career and stage persona, Samantha Day. She nodded and pointed out at the gray September day. "It's not raining now. Can we walk onto the bridge?" The Ponte Vecchio, with its jewelry shops from the Middle Ages, had become one of her favorite "thinking spots" in Firenze. She loved standing in the middle of it and gazing out at the Fiume Arno below as the river wended its way under the many arched bridges on its inexorable way to the sea.

He smiled. "Just what I had in mind. We'll probably find it deserted, too, since the combination of rain and it being Sunday morning will keep most people inside."

He came around and opened her door for her. Stepping out of the car, she gave a slight shiver as the rain-cooled air touched her hot skin. She fastened her wine-colored cable knit cardigan sweater closer around her body. "It's chilly."

Putting his arm around her shoulder, he gently pulled her close to him. His warmth enveloped her like a down comforter might, and yet, in a comforting human way that was a million times better. "How's that?"

She leaned against him as naturally as breathing. "Perfect." Of its own volition her arm went around his waist, and she smiled up at him. They walked past the Mannelli Tower, which had been built in medieval days to defend the bridge, before walking beside the shops that both lined, and, with the use of support timber brackets, overhung most of the bridge.

"I'm glad the butchers were evicted from the bridge back in Duke Ferdinando's days," he said. "One of the wiser things for a ruler to have done." There was a dry humor in Domenico's voice as he motioned to the mostly still-shuttered windows of the goldsmith and jewelry stores that were old-world, unaffected ambiance at its best.

"These shops *are* much more pleasant," she agreed.

They walked over to the center of the bridge just below the middle arch that supported the Vasari Corridor—that private walkway that had allowed members of the Medici family to move about between their various residences without having to walk onto the streets below and mix with the crowds.

Since it still wasn't raining, only slightly misting, they moved to the uncovered opposite side and, with their arms around one another, they gazed out past the ducks that were paddling around on the surface of the river to the Ponte Santa Trinita, the closest bridge to the west of Ponte Vecchio. The three other western bridges could be seen off beyond it, all lined up like dominoes.

"Did you know that Ponte Vecchio was the only bridge not destroyed by the retreating Germans during World War II?"

She gasped and pointed to Ponte Santa Trinita. "You mean that bridge is new?" With its elegant lines and elegant statues situated at each end, it seemed to have been built during Renaissance days.

"In a way. After the original bridge—dating from 1562— was blown up in 1944, the Florentines decided to rebuild it exactly as it had been. Engineers used copies of sixteenth century tools and stone from the Boboli quarry, and the bridge was again reopened in 1958. Michelangelo was credited with having designed the original, the one this emulates."

She slanted her eyes up to him and quipped, "Your dog? What an amazing beast."

"Right," he chuckled.

She looked back at the bridge. "Michelangelo Buonarroti. . . no wonder it's so beautiful."

He nodded. "The statues of the four seasons are the original ones. They were dredged up from the river."

The pastor's sermon about forgiveness came back to her. "Living really is all about forgiveness, isn't it?"

"Are you talking about the people of this city forgiving the

Germans for destroying their bridges—works of art all of them," he qualified in the manner of a true Florentine who had been very hurt by the bridges' destruction, "or are you referring to your having to forgive your *nonno*?"

Her mouth crooked in a wry line. "Actually neither. I'm thinking about whether my grandpop—the man who raised me from the age of seven—will ever be able to forgive *me*," she touched her hand to her chest, "for spurning both his careful Christian counsel and the unconditional love he has always offered to me."

His gaze narrowed with wary censure. "I didn't know you had problems with your grandpop."

She stiffened at the challenging statement. "I don't. I mean," she shrugged and tried to explain. "I hurt him when I didn't pursue the life of faith he had raised me to follow. I know that he never approved of my moving to New York and of, well, my lifestyle. And because of that, I have been kind of avoiding him. It's just that. . .I always feel so guilty whenever I'm around him. I know he disapproves."

She was glad when he seemed to understand. Tipping his head to one side he said, "A very wise man once taught a prayer. Part of it went like this, " 'Forgive us our debts, as we also have forgiven our debtors. . .' "

She remembered that one. She had prayed it every night when a little girl. With her grandpop sitting by her side. "The Lord's prayer," she murmured.

He nodded. "God wants to forgive us all. But He will not forgive the guilt of those who knowingly refuse to admit their sin. Like the pastor pointed out in today's teaching, the key to forgiveness is that a person asks to be forgiven. Your *nonno* has asked that you forgive him; the Germans asked that the people of the city of Firenze forgive them; you want to ask your grandpop to forgive you; but the greatest example, of course, is the original one: people can ask God to forgive them their sins in Jesus' name, and because of what Jesus did when He hung on that cross, God does. Forgive us, I mean. Forgiveness begins with people asking for it, asking of God and asking of one another. That's when the healing process can begin."

His words reminded her of the verses her parents had written to her in their letter. She knew them by heart now, so she recited them. " 'Bear with each other and forgive whatever grievances you may have against one another. Forgive as the Lord forgave you.' "

He looked at her curiously. "You know, after our first phone conversation I thought about you and your situation with your *nonno* in terms of those verses."

Her parents' verses? Her heart seemed to skip a beat. "What do you mean?"

He guided her out into the center of the bridge where the dome of the *duomo*—a beacon to Christianity—rose above the narrow city streets and golden buildings into the Tuscan sky. It was as striking and awe inspiring on this rainy day as it was on the sunniest. "I was looking out my office window at that and considered that the only way that you would ever be able to forgive your *nonno* was if you were to "clothe" yourself with the virtues of compassion, kindness, humility, and patience talked about by St. Paul in the verse preceding the one you just spoke."

She squeezed her eyes shut at the feeling of destiny that swept through her. "My grandpop would say, Domenico, that this is a. . .'God thing.' " Funny how she remembered that expression after all these years. But her grandpop had a way of making everything simple.

"What do you mean?"

She explained. "After talking to you, I had some decisions to make. Not only about whether I would come here but," she bit her lower lip, "about other things, too." She would tell him about Samantha Day, just not right now. She didn't want Samantha Day to intrude upon this moment. Now it was more important to tell him about finding her parents' letter in the Bible and the verses. She did. "So you see now why it's a God thing?"

After a thoughtful moment, he nodded. "God was using the same exact verses to speak to our hearts even though we were so far away from each other and really didn't even know one another." He looked at her as if a piece of a puzzle had just fallen into place. "And that's why you seemed to have changed from the first conversation to the next."

She nodded, but could only hope that when she told him about what else had happened during that time—that she had decided to come to Firenze as Florence Celini and to leave Samantha Day behind—that he would "wear" the virtues, too. . . and forgive her not telling him sooner. *Is now the time to tell him, Lord, now that we are talking about forgiveness?*

But when he suddenly turned and walked over to the edge of the bridge to look out toward Ponte Santa Trinita again, she knew that it wasn't. He obviously had something on his mind that he wanted to tell her.

She went to stand next to him.

"Last year, Florence, I almost married."

Her eyes widened. That was the last thing she had expected him to say. If he had told her that he was going to swim across the Atlantic, she wouldn't have been any more surprised. A slight tremor went through her. She couldn't help it. But to have met a *married* Domenico Ferretti at the airport the previous week would have been a tragedy to her.

An ironic smile twisted his full lips. "I fancied myself very much in love." His face turned as stormy looking as the sky that looked as if it were ready to soon let loose with more rain.

She slightly shook her head. Why was he telling her this? And why now?

Interpreting her question he put his hand up in a lawyer way that said he had a point to make. To bear with him. She did. "The woman I loved was not who she seemed to be. She had only been acting as if she loved me. When in fact what she loved was the lifestyle she hoped to marry upon 'catching' me." He turned to fully face her, and the pain from that time was still visible in the deepness of his eyes, in the tautness of his stance. "She had deceived me. Acting a role in order to catch herself a husband of old Florentine lineage."

Florence's blood seemed to stop running. *Acting a role?* Thank God—and she meant it literally—she hadn't said anything to him about Samantha Day. What would he think of her when he found out about her stage persona?

But it was different.

Totally.

She wasn't trying to "catch" him. The fact that she had fallen in love with him had had nothing to do with her having spurned the persona of Samantha Day while in Firenze. But why was he telling her this now? What was his point?

She forced herself to listen as he continued. "But do you know what the worst part about her entire deception was?" She knew it was a rhetorical question so she waited for him to continue even though all she wanted to do was shout out, "What, what?"

"She never, not once, asked for my forgiveness. She acted as if she hadn't done anything wrong. In fact," his voice lowered, and she could hear the pain in it, "she turned everything around to make it sound as if *I* was the one who had hurt *her*."

Now she understood his point. It was all about the process of forgiveness. She was glad that he had shared it with her. Placing her arms around his neck she hugged him tightly to her, wishing she could hug all the pain away. Into his ear she said, "I'm so sorry, Domenico."

She felt her heart flutter like leaves falling from a tree, and he hugged her back tightly and yet with control. It was as if he had found his home in her arms, the one woman in the world who he knew would always be there for him. It made her feel special in a way she had never experienced before. She hoped that he always felt that way. She wanted to be that woman, *his* woman. For always.

As she pressed her nose into the softly scented skin of his masculine neck, she knew that she felt the same way. It was his arms she would always seek for comfort, for support, for love. Combined with everything else about him, his sense of dignity, his faith, his arms just felt so right to her. They fit together.

When he released her and took half a step back, a poignant smile lifted the corners of his mouth, and reaching up, he ran his fingers in a caressing way down her cheek. His fingertips felt like cotton against her cool skin. "She never even said that much."

Florence squeezed her eyes together. For the pain he had experienced the previous year, for the pain she was afraid he would feel upon learning about her, well, kind of deception. *Dear Lord*, she prayed within herself, *please Lord, help him to forgive me. Help him to understand that I love him not for anything temporal that he can give me but for who he is. . .and that. . .I had to leave Samantha Day behind in order to find Florence Celini. Please, Lord.*

Exhilaration flowed through her when she understood what she was doing. Praying. . . She realized that her mouth had dropped open when he looked at her curiously.

"What is it?"

"I. . ." She let out a sound that was a cross between laughter and amazement and shook her head vaguely. "I was just praying. . .and. . .I did a few moments earlier, too. I haven't done that in. . .years."

"Praying?" He smiled, his eyes crinkling at their corners in a pleased way. "About what?"

"Us," she whispered.

"Umm. . ." His husky voice was like a caress. "I like the way that sounds." And slowly, as slowly as little drops of rain now fell from the sky, he lowered his lips to hers, and the magic, the wonder, of knowing that those lips belonged to the man she loved filled Florence. In her work she had kissed many men—some of the most sought-after men in the world today—but those kisses had been like kissing cardboard compared to the joy, the delight, the overwhelming feeling of having found her home, as Domenico's lips moved against hers in a dance of oneness that was as ancient as that probably experienced by Adam and Eve. And Florence knew as they stood on the bridge that her ancestors had walked over for generations upon generations that she had indeed found her home, her place in this world. It was by Domenico's side.

Domenico lifted his lips just far enough from hers to say those three most giving words, "I love you."

"I love you back," she whispered, knowing that she had never spoken any more truthfully.

Bells started ringing all around the ancient city of Firenze, with the *duomo's* huge bell leading them all. Looking around, Florence and Domenico laughed together.

"Do you think that's a sign?"

"Not even Hollywood could have orchestrated that timing better."

"No," he agreed. "This is God's timing." He paused, then said, "And I have something else to tell you."

"What could be better than 'I love you'?" she asked, still feeling the warm touch of his lips upon her own.

He kissed the tip of her nose. "I didn't say it was better. But it *is* good. Your *nonno* is going to be back tomorrow."

She nodded. "It really is God's timing, Domenico." She paused and explained. "Even yesterday, I wouldn't have been ready to meet him. But today, after listening to that sermon and talking to you and knowing that it is up to me to ask my grandpop to forgive me, I know exactly what I will do with my. . .*nonno*."

With a slight catch to his voice that matched the twist of his head he said, "That's the first time you've called him *Nonno*."

She knew it was true. "I couldn't before. He didn't seem

like a *nonno* to me. But now, having lived in his apartment and walked his city, I feel privileged to know that there is a man to whom I'm related who wants to meet me. He made a mistake." She shrugged her shoulders. "I've made mistakes, too. With my grandpop, and well," she sighed out deeply, "with many other things."

"So will you forgive him?" She could tell from the hopeful sound in his voice how much he really loved the old man.

"No." At the sight of the disappointment that sliced across his classical features, she quickly explained. "Since, through your letter, he's already *asked* that I forgive him, I already have. It's not something I have to do in the future—tomorrow—when I meet him. It's done. My forgiveness is his. Now I just want to get to know him."

With that voice, that deep husky voice that did nothing but get better sounding to her ears, Domenico repeated, "I love you, Florence."

"I love you, too, Domenico." She did. More than anything or anyone in the world she loved this man. And she thanked God for the letter from her parents that had taught her to "wear" the virtues of compassion, kindness, gentleness and patience, forgiveness and love, which had in turn taught her how to be a woman of faith again—one who Domenico Ferretti could love.

Chapter 7

Florence called her grandpop the minute the clock showed that it was seven in the morning in Texas. When she heard his dear voice on the phone with its sweet Texan drawl, she nearly started crying. But pulling once again on her training, she managed to keep her decorum and to tell him all that had happened to her since receiving his manila envelope with the letter from Italy enclosed. When she told him that she had, somewhere among finding her parents' letter, reading her Bible, walking the streets of Florence with all its artwork glorifying Jesus on the arm of a man who reminded her of him in belief, finally become the woman of faith he had raised her to be, he called her by her name, Florence. It was the first time he had since she had taken on the name of Samantha Day.

"I always knew my Florence would return someday," he said, his voice deep and gravelly with age and sentiment, but filled, too, with all the love for which a granddaughter could ever ask.

"Grandpop. . .can you ever forgive me for. . .everything. . .?"

"How can I not forgive you when my Lord has forgiven me

251

for so much more? Of course I forgive you. Especially since you ask me to do so. Thank you for that."

There it was again. . .the asking of another's forgiveness. . . just as the pastor and Domenico had said yesterday. "Oh, Grandpop. . .I've missed you." She had, more than she ever even realized.

"You know, Little Darling," he called her by his pet name for her, making the tears that had been swimming in her eyes brim over and ride down her cheeks. "I never minded your pursuing a career in acting. What I didn't like was how you let acting change you. There are many fine actors working in Hollywood and in New York who don't let the job change them—change their belief and their faith in God. You did, though. That's what I didn't like. Acting is a career. It's not your life. You are Florence Celini. Not Samantha Day."

"I know that now, Grandpop."

"I love you, Little Darling."

"I love you, too, Grandpop."

"Come and visit me soon?"

She knew what it took for him to ask that of her. She loved him even more for the giving of that gift. This was a man—a man after God's own heart—one who would never hold a grudge. "I will. And. . .I might even bring someone special with me."

"He's like me in his faith, you say?" She could hear the smile in her grandpop's voice, could just imagine the soft crinkles around his eyes, the way his lips turned down, not up, in his own special way of smiling. "Who says God doesn't answer prayers?"

"Not me, Grandpop. Not me." And as she hung up the

phone she knew that she would never question that again.

⁂

Domenico drove her through the fragrant hills above Florence to the *palazzo*—palace—in which her father had grown up and where her Italian grandfather now waited for her. Located on forty acres in the Tuscan Apennines, the villa, built in the sixteenth century, was surrounded by groves of olive trees and vineyards on terraced fields, with reaching cypress trees lining the long drive leading up to the grand entrance. With its arched porticoes and numerous Renaissance fountains, this *palazzo* made her Central Park apartment in Manhattan seem like a trailer home.

She eyed what could only be a drawbridge that connected the main entrance hall to a stone bridge that led to the front garden and frowned as bits of misty memory mixed with the feelings she was getting from this actual place to move together within her mind. "I've. . .seen. . .this house before," she whispered to Domenico.

She felt him glance over at her. "What do you mean?"

Sitting up closer to the windshield she said, "Not with my eyes, but with my mind. My father. . .he always told me stories about a young princess who lived in a house that was filled with all the good and wonderful things any little girl could want. It was huge but friendly, had a red-tiled roof with a tower," she said, pointing to the highest point of the house—a tower that sat in the middle above three arched porticoes, "a draw bridge, and a garden that had the most wonderful maze made of tall, thick bushes."

"There is a maze here," he motioned to the back and side of the house. "Over there. It's very old. Centuries."

She felt ready to jump out of her skin. *Of course there was!* "And there is a room on the second floor with a portrait of a famous ancestor on horseback and"—she held up her hand as if moving it over what she saw in her mind's eye—"an elaborate grisaille fresco frieze with scrolls crowning the brocade-covered walls and a Renaissance-style ceiling. It's called the grand reception room but my *babbo* always said it was really the throne room where the little princess used to hide behind the velvet curtains and listen to all the events affecting her world take place."

"That describes the room on the second floor perfectly." There was the same amazement in his voice now that had been in hers a moment before. "Your father told you about his home? Through storytelling?"

She swallowed the lump that had formed in her throat. "I. . .didn't know he was describing *his* childhood home. I thought it was a magic fairy land filled with everything good and pure and right."

"I think perhaps that's what he hoped it might one day become for you."

She nodded. "But he knew that until his father changed, that it could never be so." She reached over for his hand. "Please, Domenico, pray with me about this reunion."

Pulling the car to a stop in the shade of a four-story-high cypress tree, Domenico turned to her and to the sound of birds and insects singing all around them and to the wind softly blowing its melodious tune over the sun-drenched ancient land he wrapped her hands in his own and they prayed. They were one in spirit as God intended man and woman to be when they came to Him. . .together. "Dear Father, please bless this reunion between Florence and her *nonno*, Lorenzo. Let it be the very reunion that Cosimo had been praying for even when his daughter, Florence, was just a little girl. A reconciliation that is full of your light and grace and love, one that brings all the good Cosimo dreamed might someday come to this land where his little princess—his daughter—might be happy among its walls. In Jesus' precious name we pray. Amen."

Florence squeezed his hands. "That is really just what my *babbo* was hoping," she whispered. "That someday I would come here and find it the happy place he described in his storytelling."

"And that could only have happen if your *nonno* changed."

"God's grace," she murmured. Then, looking up at the imposing lines of the *palazzo* she said, "And God's timing. It took many years but Nonno has changed. And I have, too. And now I'm here in this house that my father must have loved very much." She flashed him her brightest smile, not even caring when that look of question crossed over his face. Samantha Day wasn't even important any longer. Loving Domenico and meeting the ancestor who waited for her in that storybook palace was all that presently mattered. "I'm ready."

❧

The big, but compact, man who welcomed her with opened arms and with tears of remorse in his eyes, begging over and over for her forgiveness, was not at all the person she had expected her *nonno* to be. She had expected a frail, autocratic man with pinched lips who had to, in spite of God's work in his heart, swallow his pride in order to ask for her forgiveness. Instead, she was introduced to a man she was thrilled to call her second grandfather. She liked him immediately.

"What you see in me, *mia cara*, is a work only God could

have performed. I was a bitter, hateful, unforgiving man consumed with materialistic pursuits. Until all the prayers offered up for my salvation and all the churches and artwork in Firenze glorifying God converged with that still small voice in my soul to speak to my heart." His handsome head, with its full covering of white hair, hung down, and he spoke with so much emotion that between it and his strong Italian accent, Florence almost couldn't understand him. But the fact that everything he described had also touched her heart helped her to understand. "I only wish I had comprehended what Cosimo was trying to tell me all those years ago. So much pain could have been avoided. So much harm. . .all caused by me."

Florence's gaze sought that of Domenico's. She could tell how much he hated seeing his friend like this. She understood. Even though this was the man who had been so mean to her mother and father, she felt the same way.

She tentatively reached out to softly place her hand on her grandfather's arm. "Nonno—"

She jumped at how suddenly he looked up at her. Was even more startled when among the sorrowful lines a smile split across his face. It was like the sun cutting through clouds on a dark wintry day. "That is the first time anyone has ever called me that. Nonno. . . Thank you for forgiving me enough to do so. I know I don't deserve the honor the title bestows."

Tears pricked at her eyes and made her throat close up. "But you are my *nonno*. And because of that . . . because. . .you gave life to my *babbo*. . .I love you."

He shook his head. "I don't deserve your love."

"How many of us ever deserve the love another wants to give us, Nonno?"

"But I am the most undeserving of all."

"I think St. Peter might have felt that way after he disowned the Lord three times the night Jesus was betrayed. And look what Peter went on to do."

He looked at her deeply, but she knew he wasn't seeing her face, but rather searching for bits and pieces of the young man he had disowned so long ago, his son. "You sounded just like Cosimo when you said that. He always knew about things of God, too."

She had to set him straight about how she had been living her life and the part he had played in her changing it. "Nonno, until I received Domenico's letter,"—she motioned toward Domenico—"telling me about your wanting me in your life. . . and that you had changed. . .I was a very different person, too. More like you had been than my father had been, actually."

Incredulity entered his eyes, eyes that she had immediately noticed were indeed a mirror of her own, the exact same green with aquamarine outer circles. Looking at them she could finally understand why people sometimes considered her own scary. Her *nonno's* eyes were intense in a soul-piercing way. She had to assume that hers were the same. "I don't believe it," he finally said.

She nodded. "Domenico's letter reminded me about the Bible my parents had given to me when I was a little girl. I found it and a letter they had written to me which had verses from Colossians—"

She stopped speaking when he held up his hand. He had a commanding way of doing it that she considered had probably always made people pause. "Wait a minute. They gave me a Bible, too. One I had forgotten about until two months ago when my housekeeper found it and brought it to me. It, too, had verses from Colossians written in it."

Another God thing! She looked up at Domenico, and understanding what she was thinking, he put his hand on her shoulder and, with a soft smile, nodded his head. Turning back to her *nonno,* she slowly recited the verses she had found in her Bible. Before she was done speaking them, she knew from the tears that were streaming down the lines time—and his having spent most of it in anger—had wrought in her *nonno's* face that they were the exact same words.

"My Cosimo and," he paused and heaved a deep sigh full of remorse, "the good woman he loved—Mary, your dear mother—have reached down from heaven to lead us both down the correct path, the one whereby we walk with God."

"Yes, Nonno." A faint tremor quivered through Florence. "They most definitely have."

❧

To say that the next hour was wonderful would be to take something away from the time the three of them spent together. It was a time of deepening love and understanding and one of bonding that they all knew could only be achieved through the grace of God.

Florence didn't think anything in the world could ever encroach on her happiness that day.

But when her *nonno's* housekeeper walked in with a tray laden with refreshments and, upon taking one look at her, blurted out, "You're Samantha Day!" she learned how tenuous happiness was, even with God's grace hovering around. People's emotions, and in this case that of Domenico's, could always be counted upon to impose upon it.

With three sets of eyes trained upon her, Florence could only nod her head.

"I knew it. I knew it," the housekeeper blubbered out, as enthusiastic as the best of fans and almost dropping the silver tray in the process. "I go to all your movies. All of them. Did you think changing the color of your hair or wearing glasses could hide who you really are? You are the best. The very best actress in the world."

But right now, with Domenico looking at her as if she had just sprouted horns, Florence felt anything but the best. She felt rather like a heel.

"Samantha Day, eh?" Nonno said, as he autocratically waved the housekeeper out of the room, giving Florence just a small taste of how he must have acted before. "Yes, we really were alike, weren't we?"

Florence cringed. But in truth again she could only nod. "That's why I told you. . .your letter changed my life, Nonno. I had forgotten how to be myself. I was always acting in the role of Samantha Day and. . ." she looked up at Domenico, and with her eyes begging him to understand, said, "I had forgotten not only how to be myself but had forgotten. . .God."

But from the way Domenico's pulse pounded in his temple and the way his lips had turned almost white, Florence knew that he was mad, very mad, and that not telling him about Samantha Day sooner had been the wrong thing to do. She hadn't wanted Samantha Day to intrude in their relationship but, in spite of her desire, that was exactly what she was doing.

"You lied to me," Domenico ground out. "By omission, you lied." She gasped, but when his lips curled in recognition now of the famous sound as he finally understood why she had always seemed so familiar to him she wished that she could have prevented doing so. "Why? Why didn't you tell me?" he snarled out. "You knew I wondered at times if I had met you before or why you seemed so familiar to me. Why didn't you tell me?"

"I'm so sorry, Domenico. I see now that I should have, but I didn't want you to love Samantha Day the movie star," she blurted out the truth. "I wanted you to love me." She patted her chest. "Florence Celini."

He shook his head, and she cringed at the disgust she saw in his dark eyes. "I don't know who you are."

"But you see, I do now. I'm Florence Celini, the woman you have gotten to know while walking around this city. Who I have been while with you is who I actually am. The only thing I'm guilty of is not telling you about my professional life."

"You told me you own bookstores," he reminded her.

She had told him on their second day around the city. She had almost told him about being an actress then. She wished now that she had. "That's not a lie. I do. Several."

"You know, however, that they are secondary to your career as a world-famous movie star." He made a disgusted sound. "Most likely you own them at your accountant's advice. A tax break."

She couldn't honestly deny that, so she remained quiet.

"You have made a fool of me." He admitted to what really bothered him. "You have deceived me just like Giovanna did last year."

She shook her head back and forth, denying it. "Domenico. . .no. This is nothing like that. Giovanna acted falsely toward you because she wanted something from you—your name, wealth, social standing." She motioned around the lavish *palazzo* in which they now sat. "Do I need any of that? Even with my own profession, I have all of that. Could I possibly be after you for any of what you might have? I don't know what your background is, but I seriously doubt that it could match mine."

"It does," Nonno spoke from her side. "Sorry, my dear. But Domenico's lineage is even older than our own and his *palazzo* makes this one seem like a small country home. Oh, and he's a duke, too."

She jumped out of her chair. "A duke!"

"We aren't royalty," Nonno grimaced. "We would have been had your father married the woman I wanted him to marry. . . ."

"A duke," she repeated and tapped her foot, something she did when about to make a point. "Wait a minute." She swiveled to face Domenico. "You're accusing me of not having told you about my career. What about your keeping being a duke from me?"

His lips curled in a very autocratic way, a very ducal way, actually. "Most women aren't upset when they discover I'm a duke."

"And do you think most men are upset to have Hollywood 'royalty' love them?"

Clapping his hands upon his thighs, Nonno stood suddenly and spoke. "I'm going to leave you two love birds to sort this out, but I think you two might want to 'wear' the virtues found in Colossians right now. To 'bear with each other and forgive whatever grievances you may have against one another,' might be a good thing, too." He started walking toward the door. "Oh," he turned back to them, "and I think I should tell you. It was *your* mother, Domenico, who I wanted my son, Cosimo, to marry. She would have made my family royal and. . .you would have been my grandson." He looked over at Florence and winked. "But for some reason I think he will soon be my grandson anyway. God really does have His way with us. . .if only we trust. . . ." He walked out of the room with laughter trailing behind him.

Florence looked at Domenico.

Domenico looked at her.

And before they even took another breath, they were in one another's arms; then their lips met in a kiss of forgiveness and love, which did indeed bind all the virtues of compassion, kindness, humility, gentleness, and patience together in perfect unity.

After a moment with the deep rumble of a chuckle in his voice Domenico said, "Samantha Day, huh?"

"A duke, huh?" she replied.

And then they laughed, a glorious sound that filled the walls of the *palazzo* in exactly the way Florence's *babbo* had told her in his stories the palace always sounded.

It was the music of love.

And for the first time Samantha Day as Florence Celini was finally cast in a role that had a happy ending.

She didn't think she would ever want to star in any other.

Epilogue

One Year Later

Florence sat speechless when Domenico unveiled the huge painting he had bought for her. She gasped when *The Annunciation* by Fra Angelico, was before her. They had seen it together a year earlier when she had first come to Firenze to meet her *nonno*.

"I thought you had forgotten." He had told her the first time they had visited St. Marco's and seen the painting that he would buy a print of either it or the *Noli me Tangere* for her. She reached out to lightly touch its corner. "It's so beautiful. But. . .it isn't a print."

"No. That's why it took so long to get it for you. I had it specially commissioned by one of the foremost painters in Florence today."

"It looks just like the fresco. It's even the same size." She threw her arms around his neck. "I love it."

"And I love you."

Even though they had been married for six months now,

Florence knew that she would never tire of hearing his wonderful voice speak those words to her. "It's the best present you could possibly give me. Especially now."

His eyes narrowed quizzically. "What do you mean, especially now?"

Reaching down she placed her hand over her flat tummy. "Because, dear husband, I have an 'announcement' to give to you. It might not be one along the same magnitude of that which the angel gave to Mary but—"

"We're going to have a child," he shouted out. It wasn't a question but a certainty.

She nodded. "In about eight months."

Tears came to his eyes. They didn't fall; they just made the dark orbs shine like jet. He pulled her close to him. "That is the best 'announcement,'" he said, chuckling, "you could ever give to me. I love you so much." He put his hand over her tummy and looked down at it with all the wonder of husbands throughout the ages who have longed to be fathers shining over his face. "Our child. . ." then, "But what about the movie? It's supposed to start shooting next week."

During the six months of their marriage she had been touched over and over again by how supportive he had been of her career. And the amazing thing was, now that she had shed the persona of Samantha Day and married her duke she had become even more sought after in Hollywood and for roles for which even her grandpop approved. The only problem was she didn't want to work as much anymore, especially now that a bambino was on the way. This movie was going to be the last she did for awhile. She wanted to spend time with her husband and child and *Nonno* and Grandpop. Her two grandfathers had become the best of friends and now that her grandpop had retired, he spent more time at the *palazzo* with them all than he did at his home in Texas.

"It will be fine. My part will be completed before I start to show, and after the babe is born, I'll take a break for awhile."

He nodded, accepting in his normal supportive way anything having to do with her work. "Who would have known?" he asked, after a dreamy moment of hugs and kisses and laughter.

"Known what?"

"What one letter asking for forgiveness could do. It started events that a year and a half later will even bring a new human into the world."

"Hmm," she agreed. "But it wasn't really just one letter, Darling. Along with *Nonno's*, there was yours and Grandpop's notes, which in turn led me to my parents' letter, which then guided me to the letters from God." She looked over at the white Bible that her parents had given to her when she was a girl of seven. The binding was crinkly now and its pages a bit worn—a much "happier" Bible than a year earlier, when it had sat on her shelf forgotten and unused.

Seeing where her gaze was, Domenico reached for it. He opened it to her parent's letter. And he read:

To Florence, with love. . .

He turned his gaze away from that which they knew by heart and asked, "How could they have known?"

"Known?"

"That you would one day travel to Florence with love in

your heart and not only heal a deep family wound but bring love to this Florentine man's heart?"

She smiled, that bright open happy smile for which Florence Celini-Ferretti was becoming well known. And putting her arms around her husband's shoulders, she said, "It's a God thing, my love. A God thing."

Dear Reader,

Living in Athens, Greece with my family (husband, daughter, son, cat, and dog) one might think that a short trip to Florence would be easy. But it's been more than a year since I last visited the city.

But with the writing of this novella it was as if I was once again walking the streets of this amazing little city. But this time I visited it through the eyes of my character, Florence Celini. I stood with her when she first soaked in the view of this city of churches, and I was with her as she stood before Ghiberti's golden doors, and again while on the Ponte Vecchio looking out at the Arno river as it ran its timeless course to the sea far beyond. And it felt good, really good to be back in Firenze.

Real life for me is one of taking care of my family, getting together with friends, sitting at my desk weaving stories, going out and doing hands-on research, studying, praying, etc, etc. But in spite of all this I strive to keep my life as simple as possible. To make time to just be—to subtract the "busy-ness"—is one of my daily goals. Sometimes not attainable but still, much sought after!

I hope you enjoyed reading *To Florence, With Love*. I delighted in writing it and as always, I thank God for His help in doing so. Without Him, I'm certain that I would still be on page one!

Many blessings to you!
Melanie Panagiotopoulos

Roman Holiday

by Lois Richer

Prologue

"One day you'll wear my wedding dress, Dear." Emily Cain let her fingers trail across the thick ivory satin one last time before refolding the delicate layers into the old cedar trunk. Maybe she would—one day. But until that happened, what was she to do with her life?

"God will light your path if you let Him, Emmy."

Her grandmother's words brought a sad little smile to Emily's lips. Dear Gran. How she missed that tiny woman and her snippets of encouragement. Especially now.

Two months ago Tad had called off their wedding and left town. The pain had eased a little since then. But what was she to do now? Emily couldn't help speculating on what was to become of her life.

"Be too busy for sin to overtake you."

Right now another of Gran's homilies sounded like very good advice. Emily closed the lid of the velvet-lined trunk, blocking the glossy sheen of bridal satin from view, just as she'd buried her hopes and dreams for the future. She shoved the trunk back into the closet, shut the door, then hurried out of the room. It was time to get on with her life.

But to do what?

Emily picked up the dog-eared syllabus off her desk and flipped through it. Perhaps it was time to return to her studies. She'd left college to be with Gran when the pneumonia had drained her tiny body, leaving her weak and needy. After the funeral, Tad proposed. Believing she would be moving as soon as they were married, Emily hadn't reenrolled.

The general arts courses held little interest now. Even the language studies her grandmother had encouraged seemed a useless waste of study. To whom would she speak Italian?

The doorbell rang, rousing her from wistful dreams.

"Special delivery, Miss. Sign here, please."

Emily signed for the letter, glancing at the return address. Nick Fellini. That name—Fellini. It seemed familiar, but she didn't know any Nick. She closed the door, slit the envelope, and tugged out a single sheet of paper.

My dear Miss Cain:

I extend to you sincere felicitations on the passing of your grandmother. I regret that only recently did we learn of her death, which, I'm sure, affects you deeply. I apologize for my tardy response. Though Mrs. Cain wrote to us some time ago, my own grandmother has been quite ill and has only recently recovered sufficiently to respond to Mrs. Cain's request.

In that regard, we would be pleased to have you visit us at your convenience. May I suggest you time your arrival soon to take advantage of our spring season, certainly the most beautiful time to see Rome? My grandmother is anxious to make the acquaintance of the

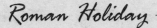

*namesake of her dear friend. Apparently some years ago,
the two formed a pact to meet again, yet neither was able
to keep the agreement. Perhaps you will visit instead?*

*In closing, may I encourage you to forward details of
your journey as soon as possible. My grandmother dearly
wishes to meet you.*

Most sincerely,
Nick Fellini

Surprise and confusion vied for supremacy. *Go to Rome?
Now?*

A longing flickered inside. To get away from here, just for
awhile—if only she could. Emily reread the letter, pausing to
reflect on each phrase, each undertone. His grandmother
wanted her to visit, but what about this Nick? Did he live with
her? He'd suggested she see Rome in the spring—which would
be about now.

Apparently Gran had requested this family be her host,
though she'd never told Emily of such a letter. But Gran had
often mentioned her friend Cecelia, her Italian roommate for
two years while she'd studied art in Rome. Cece Fellini. How
many times had she noticed that name scratched on the thin
blue sheets of airmail paper her grandmother had anticipated
with such pleasure?

Emily trembled with excitement. *Italy.* She'd never been.
But her entire childhood had been filled with Gran's stories
about the eternal city. The fountains, the catacombs, the sculptures. Emily had spent her teenage years dreaming about the
seven hills of Rome, imagined herself one day strolling through
the Tivoli Gardens.

Perhaps a short trip would shed some light on the future, on her next step. There was nothing to hold her here. She'd quit her job when Tad said they'd be moving to Seattle and hadn't yet found new employment. Leaving now was no hardship. Escaping Chicago's slush and chilly spring winds would be wonderful.

Emily squeezed her eyes closed. *Is this my answer, Lord?*

If she was frugal, she could close up the apartment, travel for a few weeks, and return home refreshed, ready to focus on the future. Maybe then God would show her the next step. Emily inhaled deeply, her mind made up. A step of faith, Gran called it. She sat down to compose a telegram.

A week later, on a cold Midwest morning, Emily boarded the wide-body jet that would whisk her away from the past, to a city Gran had loved.

Chapter 1

I t's beyond anything I could ever have imagined." Emily whispered the words, unable to tear her eyes away from the window.

"Sì. Roma is a beautiful city." Nicolo Fellini seemed content to weave his way in and out of traffic while she stared.

"Is it always this busy?" Emily asked as the car zigged left, then right, in a crazy-quilt pattern that confused her sense of direction.

He nodded.

"Sì. Always. Many Americans have heard the saying that all roads lead to Rome. Perhaps this is true. Unfortunately, we have not so many roads to accommodate all those who arrive."

That short terse sentence didn't begin to answer the questions that bubbled inside her curious heart. In fact, it sounded as if Nick felt certain visitors should have stayed away! Emily wondered if she'd made a mistake coming here, believing they wanted her.

But surely a visit to Rome could never be a mistake. She would just have to ignore Nick's grumpy attitude and savor every bit of pleasure from this trip.

As the car wound through an older, magnificently main-tained suburb of the city, Emily pinched herself to make sure she was really here. Blossom-covered bougainvillea filled the air with perfume that danced on the breeze. Everywhere she looked it was green, lush, inviting. Expectation sent her stomach on a roller coaster ride as she peered ahead. The car turned into a cir-cular driveway and stopped beneath a portico supported by white marble columns. The Fellinis lived in a villa?

And such a villa—small but exquisite. On either side of the entrance, flowers cascaded from baskets, burst from planters, and curved themselves up and over wrought-iron gates. To the right, behind the gates, a fountain cascaded sparkling water from a marble statue of a child holding an urn.

"*Bene*. This is the home of *mia nonna*. Welcome." Nick stood beside her open car door, waiting rather impatiently, if the truth were told.

Emily slid out of the car, absorbing her new surroundings.

"Your grandmother's home is lovely," she murmured, slightly unnerved by his compelling hand beneath her elbow. "You must love to share it with her."

He waited for her to precede him into the marble foyer, then stood silent, stern faced, as a young boy appeared with her two bags.

"To the blue room, Martino," he ordered.

The boy nodded, hurrying up the stairs. Suddenly the silence in the high-arched entry unnerved her. She was glad when Nick finally spoke, though the timbre of his words chilled her.

"It is my grandmother I love. Not her home, Miss Cain." He turned, motioning. "This way, please."

Emily opened her mouth to explain, then closed it. What was the point? For some unknown reason, he seemed determined to think the worst of her. But why was a mystery.

He marched down the corridor, stopped, pushed open a heavy door. The change in his tone amazed Emily.

"Nonna, I present to you Miss Emily Cain. Miss Cain, this is my grandmother, Cecelia Fellini."

A petite white-haired woman rose from her chair and held out her arms.

"*Buon pomeriggio!* Ah, my dear. It is so good to see you at last." She drew Emily into her arms and held on for a few moments, then gently moved her away, staring into her face as tears rolled down her cheeks. "*Mi scusi.* You have the look of your grandmother," she murmured softly. "I miss her yet."

Emily's heart spurted a warm tide of relief through her body. She'd been so afraid Mrs. Fellini would be stiff and formal, like her grandson. Instead she was warm, welcoming, every bit as lovely as Gran had said.

"It was very kind of you to invite me, Signora," she murmured in Italian.

"Bah! What is a visit between friends?" Mrs. Fellini waved a hand, indicating they should sit. "It is a time to enjoy each other. And you must call me Cece. Or Nonna, if you prefer."

One look at Nick's sour countenance told Emily all she needed to know about that suggestion. Fortunately he seemed to have little say in the matter.

"Gran spoke about you so often, I almost feel I know you. I would love to call you Cece, if you think it isn't improper." Emily sank onto the edge of a small velvet love seat, her gaze on the huge tray a woman placed in front of Cece.

"Cece is perfect. This wonderful woman is Maria. She has been with us many years. You must ask her if you need anything." Cece patted the woman's hand and waited till she'd smiled at Emily and pattered from the room before lifting her teacup. "Now we must have tea. I'm sure you are very tired from your flight."

She wasn't tired at all. Rather, Emily felt invigorated, eager to explore everything, all at once. But she accepted the cup of English tea and a delicate sandwich when offered by Nick and murmured her thanks. She didn't dare risk a glance at his face.

"I understand you were to be married, Miss Cain," he murmured as she took the first bite.

Emily almost choked. How dare he! She swallowed, setting her sandwich on the edge of her saucer.

"Yes, I was," she told him, glaring across the room. "Unfortunately things didn't work out."

"Ah."

What a wealth of condemnation could fill that simple word. Emily tamped down her irritation and concentrated on the tea.

"I, too, am so sorry about your broken engagement, Emily. It is a hard thing to endure, but sometimes it works out for the good." Cece's dark brown eyes conveyed her sympathy. A moment later they sparked with life.

"We must do everything we can to cheer her up, Nicolo. Which is why I have made a schedule." She reached into the pocket of her elegant linen dress and pulled out a sheet of paper. "You will have enough time this afternoon for a drive—just to get a feeling of the city. Roma is very beautiful in spring."

"I think it must be very beautiful all the time, but—"

"I'm sorry, Nonna, but I will not be available to escort Miss Cain today."

Not ever, if Emily understood the frost in his voice.

"But I had planned—"

"*Scusi, per favore*, Signor, Signora." Emily shifted uncomfortably when both heads turned toward her, but nothing could stem the words she felt compelled to say. "I never expected anyone to take time off to show me around. In fact, I'm looking forward to exploring Rome on my own. Please don't alter your routines for me."

Nick looked relieved. Cece looked put out.

"But I so wanted you two to get to know each other."

"I have my classes, Nonna. You know that." Nick set down his cup. "In fact, I must be off even now." He turned toward Emily, executed a slight bow, his face implacable. "Maria will show you to your room. Please feel welcome. Arrivederci." Then he walked out of the room. A second later the front door thudded closed.

"Please to excuse Nicolo." Cece's alabaster skin wrinkled in a frown. "He does not mean to be rude. He has much to do at his school."

"He's still going to school?" Emily blinked, trying to imagine Nick at her college.

Cece burst into delighted giggles. "No, no, my dear. He is a professor. Of history. His classes are most sought after and always he tries to make them interesting for his students. Nicolo is very serious about his school."

"I see." Emily listened to her chitchat as she sipped the tea and munched on sandwiches. Fifteen minutes later Maria returned. Emily decided it was now or never.

"I am sure la signora should rest for awhile, Maria. And while she does, I shall hire a taxi to take me on a tour. Per favore, would you show me the telephone?"

In rapid fire Italian, Maria tossed away the taxi idea and offered her grandson as a chauffeur. Twenty minutes later Emily was seated beside Martino and they were rushing toward the center of the city.

"So you are *la fidanzata*," he said loudly, grinding gears so she could get a better look at the Colosseum.

Emily frowned, searched her vocabulary. Fiancée?

"Oh, no," she gasped, her cheeks burning with embarrassment. "You must have me mixed up with someone else. I'm just visiting."

Martino grinned, his white teeth flashing in the sun.

"Oh, no, I hear," he told her in labored English. "La signora says the *fidanzata* of Signor Nicolo arrives today."

He slammed on the brakes, screamed something in rapid Italian, then zipped them back into traffic. Emily had no time to be frightened. Besides, in the back of her mind, she was remembering a comment her grandmother had made long ago.

"Cece and I promised each other we'd get our children together, watch them fall in love, and be doting grandmothers."

Was that why Signora Fellini had invited Emily to Rome? As a prospective bride for her grandson?

A light clicked on inside her brain.

No wonder Nick seemed hostile!

Chapter 2

W elcome to the Piazza di Spagna—the so-called Spanish steps, which lead to the Church of Trinita dei Monti," Nick waved a hand. "I'm sure you can't help but notice the azaleas. It is a springtime tradition in Rome to decorate the steps with them. If you'd like to take a break, we will gather together at the top in fifteen minutes to discuss the obelisk."

He couldn't help but notice her sitting there.

The polished gold of Emily Cain's long hair spun round her shoulders like a cape as she peered at the book in her lap. Her clothes were not the pricey designer brands of the American students who'd paid to attend his lecture series. She wore a simple green skirt that brushed her ankles, a sleeveless cotton top of pale pink that matched the flowers in her skirt, and a pair of open-toed sandals. Yet she looked like a queen holding court.

Was that what irritated him whenever he looked at her—her demeanor? How petty was that?

Nick climbed the steps to where she sat framed by the azaleas.

"*Ciao*," he murmured.

She glanced up, her green eyes wide with surprise. A moment later the light dimmed.

"Oh, hello." She thrust one finger in her book, then closed it. Though her gaze remained on him, she volunteered nothing further.

"Are you having a good day of sightseeing?" he asked, wishing he hadn't bothered her. But that would have been churlish, and only this morning he'd promised Nonna he would be kinder to Miss Cain.

"Lovely."

Clearly she intended to volunteer nothing. In fact, her whole body had stiffened, as if prepared to repel him. A pinch of regret flicked his conscience. He deserved her ire. She'd done nothing to merit the brunt of his anger. Nothing but accept his grandmother's invitation to come here.

"Why are you here, Nick?"

The question surprised him.

"What do you mean?"

She waved a hand. "I'm sure there's nothing here that you haven't seen before. Why are you here?"

"I have a class of students. From America, actually. I make it a point for them to get out of the tour bus and climb the steps, to relax a bit before we continue with our studies." Did she suspect him of following her?

"Where are they now?" She glanced around.

He pointed. "No one can come to Piazza di Spagna and not enjoy a cup of—" he frowned, pretended to search for the English word.

"Cappuccino?" she supplied.

He nodded, then realized it had not been the right thing

to say. Emily Cain was not enjoying such a treat. In fact, as far as he could ascertain from his grandmother, she was on a very strict budget. Which was another reason he'd avoided her. He felt guilty every time he looked at her.

"Would you like one?" he offered belatedly.

She wrinkled her nose, then shook her head, blond hair dancing in the sunlight.

"No, thanks. I had one the other day. It's too strong. I prefer my water." She pointed to the bag near her feet, then glanced back up the steps, her gaze wistful.

"You have already been up there?"

The blond hair danced its little jig once more as she shook her head.

"Oh, but this is necessary." He glanced upward, unable to stem the words that came so naturally. "The church of Trinita dei Monti was built in 1495 for the use of French Catholics. Today it houses a most famous fresco entitled *Descent from the Cross.*"

"I know."

"But you will not go there?" Something was wrong and he didn't understand what it was. Concern flooded him. "Are you all right?"

"Not really." She did glance up at him then. Her green eyes were turbulent with unspoken emotion. "I've just come from the Colosseum. It—bothered me."

"Ah." This, at least, Nick understood. He sank down on the step beside her. "The atmosphere can be a little overwhelming."

"Overwhelming?" She tipped up her head, her eyes blazing. "It's—disgusting!" She swallowed, but her chin remained thrust out. "I suppose it's not nice to say such a thing to you, since this is your country, but I can't help it. Feeding people to lions for their beliefs—it's barbaric."

"Yes, it is. But some historians do not believe that is true, Emily," he murmured gently. "Though, of course, no one can say for sure. We do know that the *Ludi Circenses* became favorite shows of the Romans because they were invented to develop the war-like spirit that made Romans the conquerors of the world. This is the origin of the gladiators—professionals trained to fight to the death against many wild animals."

He paused, gauged her response as interested, then continued.

"In the early fifth century, a monk named Telemachus, who had come from the east, one day entered the arena and tried to place himself between the gladiators while he begged the people to stop the horrible shows. The people protested, in fact, they stoned him to death. But from that day, the shows ended."

Emily sat silent while she considered his comments.

"Perhaps," she sighed. "I don't know. But I do know that Christians died for their faith. Many of them in Rome. Your talk of stoning makes me think of Stephen. He prayed, at the end. Do you remember?" She cocked her head like a curious bird. "How could he forgive them? How could he?"

Nick knew his class waited, that he had to go. But how could he leave Emily like this? Something more than the deaths of the early Christians bothered her.

"It isn't easy to understand," he murmured. "But many of those who died were men and women who knew Jesus, who'd lived with him, talked to him. Perhaps they felt it was worth anything to be with Him again."

"Perhaps." She stared at him, her green eyes swirling with

glints of something he couldn't understand.

"I must go now." Nick rose, dusting the seat of his pants. "My class, you understand. I promised them a full day."

He stood there, looking down at her, loathe to leave, but afraid to stay. Something about her outburst had touched him, in spite of his resolve not to get involved. Emily Cain was turning out to be anything but the spoiled brat he'd expected.

She smiled, not the radiant one he'd glimpsed before. This was merely a polite tipping of her lips.

"Thanks for stopping. I guess I'd better get on, too." She rose, stowed her book inside her bag and slung the handle over one shoulder. "Perhaps I'll see you at dinner. Good-bye."

"*Ciao*, Emily."

She smiled a real smile then. "Ciao," she repeated, then danced down the steps where she paused to study the Fountain of the Barcaccia by Bernini for a few short minutes before veering right into the Piazza Mignanelli.

Nick found himself hoping she'd stop in front of the Progaganda Fide Palace to study the column of the Immaculate Conception. For some reason he wanted her to see all of Rome's history, not just the ugly parts. Though why that should matter to him wasn't immediately clear.

He had no intention of marrying anyone, let alone Emily Cain, no matter how high his Nonna's hopes. Alexandra's death three years ago had taught him that hard lesson. He'd accepted that love, marriage, and the family that inevitably went with it were not to be his.

Which was why he'd chosen the orphanage and the children. At least while he was with them, he didn't feel so alone.

Chapter 3

Today would have been her wedding day, if Tad hadn't deserted her.

Emily slipped from her room and padded down the staircase to the front door, her bag with its full water bottle slung over one shoulder. The taxi she'd called for waited outside. She climbed in quickly, giving her directions. Thankfully, traffic was still light, as light as traffic here ever got, and she arrived at the Vatican in good time, well before Nick.

He didn't know she would be there, of course. She'd revealed her plans to no one. But last night, after she'd heard him tell Maria he had to leave early to take his students through the Papal Palace and would not be in for dinner, she'd made her decision.

She'd been in Rome for a week. Hopping on and off the trundling shuttle buses that offered headphones and an ongoing tour of the highlights every tourist should see had become a simple matter.

But it wasn't enough. Emily found herself longing to know more about the early church, about its founders and their deep commitment to a faith that willingly gave up family and friends, even life.

Today, as she watched young lovers linger beside fountains, she thought about Tad. How could he have dumped her like that—without warning? Had he ever loved her? Though she'd tried to pretend otherwise, Emily was well aware of the kernel of bitterness that lodged deep inside her heart and stopped her from forgiving him. Maybe if she could understand how others had handled betrayal, she would understand how God could have let this happen to her.

Nick Fellini was a bottomless pit of knowledge. She'd heard him yesterday when she'd been sipping her water and admiring the elegant hotels and coffeehouses on the Via Vittorio Veneto. She'd been so intrigued by his comments about Bernini's fountain of the Bees, that she'd tagged along to listen to him speak about the Capuchin Church. She'd even accompanied his group as they visited the Baths of Diocletian. Her nervousness about being seen had disappeared the longer he spoke. He had a knack of bringing the past alive, of drawing word pictures that helped her visualize Rome's history in Technicolor.

"I see you intend to accompany us again today." Nick stood behind her, his mouth drawn in a tight line.

Emily flushed.

"I don't want to bother you," she murmured, praying he'd let her stay. "Really I don't. And I've tried to keep out of your way. But you are so knowledgeable about everything. Listening to you is far better than trying to decipher those headphones."

He blinked, then a crooked smile pulled up the corners of his mouth.

"I guess one might take that for flattery."

"Oh, I wasn't flattering you. It's the truth. I learned so much about the baths yesterday. Why don't they put those details in the books?" Emily saw the group of students beyond him, and realized they were waiting. "I'm sorry, I've kept you from your work. But would it really be too much to allow me to tag along? I promise I won't get in the way or ask any questions. I just want to learn."

"I noticed how intent you were yesterday. Our history seems important to you. Why is that?" he asked, his frown rippling his smooth olive forehead.

Emily knew her cheeks were red, but she didn't look away from his scrutiny.

"I want to understand how the first church grew and developed. Besides," she grinned, "If I'm hanging around with your group, you won't have to keep sidestepping your grandmother's questions about showing me the city."

It was probably the wrong thing to say. His already dark eyes deepened to bittersweet-chocolate. But after a moment, he tossed back his curly head and chuckled.

"Tag along for as much of the tour as you can tolerate, Emily Cain. I hope you find the answers you look for." He turned to the group. "Is everyone ready? Then—*Benvenuto a Piazza San Pietro*. Welcome to St. Peter's Square."

The morning was filled with wonder for Emily as Nick explained the history behind the Vatican, beginning with the Egyptian obelisk in the center of the square. Centuries before people just like her had created and inscribed this stone. Amazing!

"We move now to take a better look at the Porta Santa, the Holy Door. It is opened only every twenty-five years, on Christmas Eve." Nick continued his descriptions, leading them through the Vatican's splendor while he drew graphic images of days gone by.

Tantalized by his recounting, Emily found herself weeping as he described the apostle Peter's death and his wish to be crucified upside down because he wasn't worthy to die as Christ had. How, she wondered, as she stared at the celebrated bronze statue of St. Peter, how could he have forgiven his Roman persecutors when she couldn't forgive Tad for making a mistake?

It seemed only minutes until the tour was completed and the rest of the students departed on a bus for a field trip. Freed of their chatter and with plenty of time left, Emily wandered back through the basilica until she stood in the first chapel of the right aisle and once more beheld Michelangelo's *Pietà*.

"I thought perhaps I'd find you here." Nick's quiet voice sounded neither impatient nor irritated.

"You did?" Emily twisted to peer into his face. "Why?"

He nodded and returned his gaze to the statue.

"I noticed earlier that you seemed drawn to this work. More so than many of my students. What particularly attracts you?"

"It doesn't attract me," she murmured, staring at the marble Mary holding her dead son. "It—puzzles me, confuses me. Mostly it makes me angry. Why isn't she upset? Why does she look so—resigned? I just can't figure it out."

"Well, if you're looking to understand grace, I'm not sure anyone can." He tilted back on his heels, surveying the marble. "Grace, true grace, is freely granted, without strings. Perhaps that's why the artist chiseled her head bowed in that manner. She accepted God's will when she first heard Gabriel's words, continued to accept it, even though it cost her a son. I believe she realized that the price outweighed her sacrifice."

"Perhaps." Suddenly Emily wanted to be outside, to feel

the warmth of the sun on her skin, to smell the flowers and forget about Tad and everything that could have been. "You don't have to stay," she told Nick. "I don't want to take up your afternoon. Thank you for letting me listen to the lecture."

She turned and walked through the basilica and out the door, shame nipping at her as she realized how close she was to tears. Angrily she scrubbed her eyes, drawing in deep breaths of control. Nicolo Fellini didn't need to hear about her petty disappointments.

"As it happens, I'm free this afternoon. Would you like to share lunch with me?" He matched her step for step until Emily reached the avenue.

"Look," Emily muttered, twisting to glare at him. He felt sorry for her, and she didn't want that. "You've made it more than obvious that you have no desire to shunt me around Rome. Fine. I'm happy to potter about on my own, anyway. You can go on back to your college, or wherever you disappear to each night, with a clear conscience."

His eyes widened. "Where I disappear—"

"I've seen you slip out when you think your grandmother is safely tucked up in her room. I've heard you come back, sometimes after midnight." She saw the color leave his cheeks and wondered what he was doing in those hours. "Don't worry, I haven't said anything. It's none of my business who you hang out with."

Nick's forehead furrowed, but his gaze never left hers. Finally he huffed out a huge sigh.

"I'm sorry, Emily. I owe you an apology. This situation is not of your creating. I've been rude and ungracious, and my grandmother would tear a strip off me if she knew. This is not how she raised her grandson to behave."

"Your grandmother raised you?" That explained the bond between them.

"We can't stand on the street talking." He stepped out of the way of a group of schoolgirls in navy-and-white uniforms and waited until they'd passed. "Let me buy you lunch. I know the perfect *trattoria*."

In less than five minutes Nick had maneuvered her down a tiny street and seated her at a table that offered a perfect view of the Vatican.

"May I order for you? I promise you will like their food." His dark eyes sparkled with excitement. Emily could do little but nod and listen as he conversed with their waiter in Italian too rapid for her to follow.

"So, shortly our meal will arrive." He took a sip of his cappuccino. "Where were we?"

"You were telling me that your grandmother raised you." For the first time Emily felt a connection with Nick as he described his parents' death in a plane crash when he was just eight. "I was a very active child," he admitted. "But Nonna never tried to hold me back or keep me from trying things. I had a wonderful childhood."

"I'm glad. It's rather like my story," she murmured, remembering the short months after her mother had died when her father seemed to lose his own will to battle the cancer filling his body. "I was older than you, a very angry teen. But Gran was patient, and we got along famously. I still miss her."

"I'm sure." He reached across the table and squeezed her fingers. "How sad to lose everyone you love. I don't know what I shall do when—" The unspoken words hung between them.

"Perhaps you'll be married with your own family by then," she offered quietly, trying to imagine stiff and formal Nick unbending enough to play with his own children. The image did not compute.

"I shall never marry."

Emily stared. He sounded so certain. She opened her mouth to ask why and then realized that would be prying. But he saw her reaction and smiled, albeit a sad, tired smile.

"Sooner or later my grandmother will tell you. I suppose I might as well give you my version first." He sighed, staring down the street. "Three years ago I was engaged to be married. But before the wedding could take place, *ma fidanzata* was injured in a car accident. She died later."

"Oh, but surely, given enough time, you'll meet someone else. . . ." The words died a silent death when she saw his head shake.

"I don't believe God intends for me to marry." He glanced at her, lips curved in a wry smile. "Hence my sour attitude. My *nonna* wishes to keep her pact with your grandmother and would have the two of us marry immediately."

"Yes, I'd heard something about that plan from Martino." She smiled, trying to show she hadn't taken it seriously. "But if that was your fear, you needn't have worried. I'm not prepared to be engaged to anyone. Once was more than enough."

Nick waited until the waiter had set steaming bowls of pasta redolent with robust tomato sauce, spicy peppers, and fresh basil before them. Once the basket of rolls was in place and the waiter had left, he asked the question she didn't want to answer.

"What happened to your bridegroom?"

Emily lifted her fork and pushed at the thick noodles, her appetite diminished.

"He left." She glanced up, saw the questions in his expressive eyes and sighed. Might as well get it over with. "He claimed he didn't love me, that he'd made a mistake. And then he called it off. As a matter of fact, today would have been our wedding day."

"I'm so sorry, *Carissa*. But surely you are relieved that this happened—"

Emily held up her hand.

"Please don't say it's for the best, or it would have been worse if he'd found out later. I've heard it all a thousand times before, told myself the same things." She felt the bitterness creep into her voice. "It doesn't help much."

"This feeling, I know it well." He grinned. "Smashing something, that would help, sì? Perhaps the urn of flowers would soothe the sting."

She giggled.

"Well, I don't know that I'd go that far. But I do get ticked that he didn't think it through before he proposed and I'd made all those plans."

"Ticked?" Nick frowned. "I do not know this word."

"Angry. Upset. Frustrated."

"*Quanti anni hai, Emily?*" How old are you?

"Twenty-two. What's that got to do with it?" She bit into her pasta and found it surpassed anything she'd ever tasted. "Does it hurt any less if you get dumped when you're older?"

"No. But you are very young. You have time to meet other people, to choose what you will do with your life. Marriage is not all there is."

"This coming from an Italian," she teased, but her smile quickly drooped. "That's just it, don't you see? I thought I had my life mapped out, that I knew where God wanted me. Now everything is all upset and I haven't the faintest idea where to go from here. This is a lovely holiday and I'm grateful for it," she hurried on, anxious to make him understand. "But after it's over and I'm back at home—then what do I do?"

"I don't know. But I don't think it is a problem for God. He will reveal His wishes at the right time. It's the waiting that is so difficult." He tasted his own meal.

They put all conversation on hold as they ate, savoring each bite of this most Italian of meals. At last Nick pushed away his empty dish, stretched out his arms.

"No one knows the future, Emily. But in the meantime, you are in Roma. That is not too hard to bear, is it?"

"No." As she stared into his handsome face, Emily realized that being here wasn't a hardship at all. Nick was good company, someday he might even be a friend. And when she was back in Chicago, she would take out the memory of these days and be glad she'd been able to experience this eternal city.

"So what shall we do this afternoon? I am at your disposal until this evening."

"And then what?" she asked, knowing that this was one of the nights he disappeared. "Have you something special planned for this evening?"

"Just some work," he told her, but he kept his face averted, pretending to fiddle with his chair. "Are you ready to go?"

"Go where?" Emily rose, anticipation rising in spite of herself.

"I think it is time to broaden your horizons, Miss Cain.

We shall visit the forum."

As she'd deliberately left this visit off her previous itinerary, hoping to arrange a personal tour, Emily could barely contain her excitement.

"And will you explain it all to me?" she demanded. "Every detail? You won't leave anything out?"

Nick laughed, looped her arm through his, and led her down the street.

"This is a dangerous thing to say to an historian, Emily. I promise I will regale you with so many details that you will beg me to be quiet."

Emily hid her smile as she walked beside him, aware of the curious glances they drew. She still didn't understand what God had planned for her, but an afternoon at the forum was a perfect way to wait. Especially when Nick was in such a jolly mood.

Maybe they would become good friends.

Someday.

Chapter 4

Nick slipped into his grandmother's villa, trying to cause as little noise as possible. It was late enough that everyone should be asleep, but just in case, he took off his shoes before climbing the stairs, trying to ensure the taped gauze pad stayed in place until he reached his own bathroom. He almost made it.

But he'd forgotten the big urn his grandmother had recently ordered to be placed outside Emily's door and filled with the fragrant pink roses grown in the villa's gardens.

"Ow!" he yelped, then swallowed the rest of his words as pain radiated from his big toe, up his leg. One shoe clunked to the floor, cracking through the silent house like thunder on a stormy night.

Unfortunately, Emily's door opened before he could get inside his room.

"Nick? What's the matter?" She was swathed from neck to tiptoe in a sprigged cotton robe tied securely around her waist. Her trademark blond hair cascaded over her narrow shoulders. She immediately saw his injury. "What happened?"

"Just a scratch. Nothing more." He tried to hold the saturated gauze in place, but a trickle of blood betrayed him.

"A scratch doesn't bleed like that." She glanced around the landing, then pointed to the staircase. "Let's go to the kitchen so we don't disturb your grandmother. I'll clean that for you."

"It doesn't matter. I can do it." Frustrated by his inability to stop the bleeding, he grabbed his handkerchief and wrapped it around his arm, realizing he'd reopened the cut.

"Go downstairs or I will alert your grandmother about your injury at breakfast tomorrow," Emily ordered, the light of battle gleaming in her emerald eyes.

Nick glared at her, assessing her intent as he studied her freshly scrubbed face. She meant it. But if Emily told Nonna, she'd insist on knowing where he'd received the injury. He couldn't lie to his grandmother. Even if she didn't know immediately, and she would, he'd never lied to her in all these years. He'd have to explain. Then the truth about his clandestine activities would be out. He didn't want that.

"All right." He nodded, motioning for her to go first. "On one condition. You tell my grandmother nothing about this."

Emily stopped so abruptly, he almost bumped into her. She twisted, stared at him, a frown marring the smoothness of her forehead.

"Is it something bad? Are you in trouble?"

"No, of course not." He motioned for her to go, then followed her into the kitchen. Once she'd flicked the light on, he moved to the sink and lifted the first-aid kit from under the counter before removing the gauze pad and throwing it in the garbage. Perhaps if she kept busy, she'd forget her questions.

"Oh, my goodness! What did you do?" Emily didn't wait for his response, but removed a sterile pad and immediately began swabbing the area with antiseptic cleaner.

"I was trying to fix something. The tool slipped and. . ." He shrugged.

"I think, for your own health, you might consider hiring someone to do whatever repairs you require. History seems more your forte." She grinned at him, obviously enjoying the flush of red that burned his cheeks.

"You're calling me an—what is the term? Egghead?" It was fun to joke and tease with someone. The evening visits he made three times a week sometimes left him awake for hours afterward, wondering why there wasn't more he could do.

"A very knowledgeable egghead," she murmured, then bit her bottom lip in concentration as she pressed the plasters holding his bandage into place. "But not, I think, about tools. Is that too tight? Have I made it worse?"

"It's fine. Thank you." He flexed his hand, felt relief that the stiffness was abating already. "I'm glad you insisted on doing this, Emily. I don't know how I would have managed with one hand. Where did you learn to dress wounds?"

"I nursed Gran a lot." Emily rinsed the sink and washed down the counters as she spoke. "Sometimes she was a bit awkward, because of her walking stick, and would injure herself." Her voice dropped and he knew she was remembering. "I got a lot of practice patching her up, but I never minded. It was the least I could do." She turned off the tap, wiped the sink dry, and hung up the towel. "Well, if there's nothing else?"

He didn't want to leave her, not yet. He wanted her to stay, to talk to him. Which was not a good idea. He ignored his brain's warning.

"Could you put on the kettle?" he asked quietly. "I think I'd like a cup of tea. Suddenly I'm wide awake."

"Of course." She moved around the kitchen easily as if

she'd been in here, done this a hundred times before. Perhaps she had.

Nick was ashamed to realize he'd never wondered what Emily did with her evenings. His pulse did a double step as he imagined her with the children. How would she handle them? Did she like children?

"Where do you go after dinner?" she asked, lifting the teapot from the shelf where Maria kept it. "It's quite late by the time we finish dinner."

"Quite late?" He blinked, then realized that she probably did find their dinner hour unusual. "What time do you eat dinner in Chicago?"

"Around six. Seven if I'm really late." She held up two tea choices and waited till he'd pointed at one. "Earl Grey. I might have known."

"Is there something wrong with this tea?"

She giggled at him.

"Of course not. I've had it quite often." She swished boiling water into the pot, let it heat the china, then dumped it out and refilled the delicate blue pot. "How do you say 'herb tea' in Italian?"

He stared at her shining swath of hair, while his mind worked to decipher her meaning.

"Herb? This is a name for another kind of tea? Named for a famous person perhaps?"

Emily's giggles echoed around the old stone kitchen, brightening the terra-cotta walls and sending a shaft of warmth through him.

"What is funny?" he asked, enjoying the sight of her beautiful face glowing pinkly from her extended afternoon in the sun. Her jade eyes sparkled and danced with mirth.

"You are. Herb tea," she repeated. "Herbs. You know, like parsley and peppermint, sage and basil. Herbs. You make tea out of them."

"You are telling me that Americans drink basil tea?" He screwed up his face. "I do not think you will find such a thing in Rome, Emily."

"Spice." She tried again. "How about orange spice tea?"

He shook his head. "I don't know about this tea. I will have to ask Maria. Perhaps she will take you to the market and you may find it there." He picked up the teapot in his good hand. "Shall we drink this ordinary tea on the patio?"

"Oh, yes, please." Emily placed two cups, the sugar bowl, and a spoon on a tray and carried them out to the little wrought-iron table that sat just beyond the kitchen door. "This is the most wonderful place at night. Look at that sky. Inky black." She set the tray down and tilted her head back to stare upward. "So beautiful," she whispered.

He wanted to agree, but it wasn't the sky he was looking at, it was she. Here in the garden, with only the fountain light to illuminate, she resembled one of Michelangelo's sculptures. Her blond hair cascaded over her shoulders and down her back like spun gold, her pure clear profile as beautiful as any finely sculpted marble in all of Rome.

Then she spun around on her toes, and the mirage was broken. She wasn't chilly marble on display, never to be touched. Emily was real, alive. She plopped down into her chair and poured the tea.

"Are you going to tell me where you were tonight or not?" she demanded, thrusting a steaming cup toward him.

"Not," Nick answered quickly. Too quickly. One golden eyebrow arched upward.

"Why? Is it a secret?"

"No." He busied himself sipping his tea, wishing he could think of a way to avoid her questions. She looked small and delicate, but he was beginning to realize that quiet beauty only served to hide her resolve and tenaciousness.

"I don't think you return to your school," she murmured, her eyes fixed on the fountain beyond as she mused on the problem. "Who would go there at night when there are so many sights to see in the city by starlight?" She twisted around, surveying him once more. "But if you were chauffeuring students to see the sights, how did you hurt yourself? Did your car break down?"

Amused by her mistaken deductions, Nick contented himself with studying the view in his grandmother's garden, including the woman across from him.

"You're not going to tell me?" she asked when she'd run out of *what ifs.*

"And ruin your fun?" He shook his head. "No. I won't do that."

"Then I shall have to find out for myself. Good night."

Before he'd managed to scramble to his feet, she'd pranced across the flagstones and inside the house, her long housecoat flapping at her legs.

"Good night," he murmured, knowing she wouldn't hear him.

He sat in the garden a long time, thinking, dreaming of something he'd never have. At last he rose, gathered up the tea things, and took them to the kitchen.

But by the time he was lying in bed, Nick had come to only one conclusion. He'd have to be very careful when next he left the villa for a visit.

❧

Emily kept to the shadows as she followed Nick's tall figure down the darkened street two nights later. A sense of unease tiptoed up her spine, but she refused to acknowledge it. This was a section of Rome she'd never visited, but she needed no guidebook to tell her it was a slum. These old buildings had no one lovingly restoring their finish. Cracked windows, peeling walls, and uneven walkways broadcast that few people cared what happened in this neighborhood.

It was such a change from Cece's neighborhood and from the carefully maintained tourist sights. What was Nick doing here?

She stopped, suddenly realizing that he'd disappeared. The taxi driver had warned her to be careful, but he was long gone and now she was alone. She had to keep going.

"Curiosity killed the cat," Gran had often reminded her. Emily refused to dwell on that.

"Where did he go?" she muttered, edging past another storefront. Two men ogled her. Suddenly the sound of children's voices drew her on. She walked quickly toward the sound and soon arrived at a doorway, opened wide to let in a night breeze.

Conscious that the two men had followed her, Emily slipped inside and moved to one corner, behind a plant, certain that this must be the place Nick disappeared to so often.

The walls had been whitewashed over patches of peeling plaster that, in spite of the garish light from overhead fluorescent lights, lent a fresh clean appearance to the inside of the old building. The stone floor bore more than its share of cracks, nicks, and dents, but it was clean and tidy. A long table ran almost the entire length of the front room with benches on either side.

As Emily stared, children poured in through a door in the rear, wiggling and jiggling into their seats with giggles that echoed against the high ceiling and tumbled back down on their black shiny heads. Though obviously poor, evidenced by tattered clothing that drooped off the shoulders of most of them, none of the children seemed unhappy. They folded their hands, bowed their heads, and quietly waited while a tall woman with white hair said grace, then eagerly awaited their bowl full of what looked to be stew.

So engrossed was she in them that she failed to notice someone had discovered her.

"*Come si chiama?*" What is your name?

Emily jerked to attention, bumped her forehead on the huge azalea bush and blinked the tiny boy before her into view.

"Ah, Emily," she mumbled, without thinking.

"*Piacere di conoscerla.*"

So the little sprite was pleased to see her. Emily grinned, hunkered down, and held out one hand and asked him his name.

"Mario," she repeated. "*Ma, dove abiti?*"

He stared at her as if she were slightly addlepated, then motioned around him. Here, she realized. Mario lived here.

"*Buon compleanno, Mario.*" Nick's voice echoed around the room.

"*Grazie!*" Mario was all smiles, even favoring the crowd with a little bow.

It was the child's birthday? Realizing that all eyes were also upon her, Emily slipped from her hiding place and repeated the congratulations, which Mario graciously accepted. He then wrapped his hand around her arm and pulled until she was forced to follow him to Nick who then introduced her to the entire assembly. The children greeted her, then turned back to devour their food. Several moments later another woman carried in a huge birthday cake, which she placed in front of Mario while everyone sang to him.

"I might have known you'd follow me."

"What is this place?" she whispered to Nick, hoping he wouldn't chastise her here, in front of everyone. "An orphanage?"

"Sort of. More like a mission. *La Dolce Vita*. The good sisters try to give these children a home, a school, and some much-needed mothering." He paused, then glanced down at her. "I help out whenever I can."

She opened her mouth, but a loud clapping stopped her response. One of the sisters told the group Mario would now receive his birthday gift. From behind a door she wheeled a very old bicycle that had been cleaned and polished as much as it would stand. Mario's brown eyes grew even larger, and he didn't move until one of the children pushed him forward.

Reverently he touched the handlebars, accepting the bike with several murmured *grazie's*. At everyone's urging he climbed on and pedaled furiously until Nick stopped him and suggested he try it outside in the yard. Everyone rushed to watch. Emily moved to follow, but Nick's hand on her arm stopped her. She glanced up, surprised by the frown on his face.

"Why are you here? Did my grandmother send you?"

"No. I told you I would find out where you disappear to at night. But I never expected this. I wish you'd told me." She thought of the many evenings she'd spent alone, lonely for the sound of another human voice. She could have come here, shared this.

"You do?" He frowned. "Why?"

"Because I would have enjoyed coming. I love kids."

"You must go now, Emily. It isn't safe here at night." His

dark eyes flashed with temper. "I wish you hadn't come here."

"But I did. And if it's so dangerous, then I can't go home by myself, can I?" She began stacking the dishes. "So I'll leave when you do. In the meantime, I can help." Suddenly his injury made sense. "You were fixing that bike, weren't you? That's how you hurt yourself."

His expression didn't change, but Emily caught the flicker through his eyes and knew she was right. He'd been working on a birthday gift for Mario.

"Why don't you serve the sisters their coffee outside while I deal with these? I'm sure they'd appreciate a break," she murmured, her heart swelling.

He looked about to argue, then shrugged and walked through the rear door. Above the sink was a huge window, open to the evening. As she scrubbed and scoured, Emily could both see and hear the children dashing about in a series of games. She'd almost finished the last dish by the time they all trooped back in to enjoy Mario's cake.

"You didn't have to do that." Nick peered down at her, eyes fixed on her reddened hands. "The sisters didn't expect it."

"Of course they didn't. I just wanted to help. What happens now? They seem far too excited to sleep. Where do they sleep, by the way?" She glanced around, reminded that the building had looked too narrow from the outside to offer enough space for beds for everyone.

"They sleep upstairs." He took her arm. "Come on. This is a special time. Everyone listens while one of the sisters tells a story."

Curious, Emily walked beside him into the room where they'd eaten. Now the benches were pushed under the table, and the children were sitting cross-legged on what looked like old quilts. Nick guided her to a seat, but before they could sit down, the older of the sisters approached them and whispered in Nick's ear.

"She'd like to know if you'd tell them a Bible story." He studied her face. "You can say no if you want to. I'll tell her your Italian isn't up to it."

"Actually I—I'd like to. If you think my Italian is up to it. I used to have a Sunday school class. They remind me of it." She held her breath, waiting for his approval, then wondered why it seemed so important to tell a story. One glance at the children's shining faces told her why. For them.

"There's nothing wrong with your Italian, but even if there were, they'd just laugh. They love stories and visitors." Nick squinted. "You're sure?"

She nodded and a few minutes later she, too, sat cross-legged, surrounded by the children. Mario had managed to assume the pride of position at her left side, and he shushed the group before grinning at her.

The only story that came to mind was the one about Noah, and she was a little hesitant to name animals she couldn't describe. Gran was right, vocabulary lessons were more important than she'd ever imagined. Still, it was thanks to Gran that she was able to speak to these little ones at all.

When Sister glanced at her watch, Emily quickly concluded the story and thanked them for listening. Mario reached out and shook her hand with his little one, his smile spread across his face.

"*Mi dispiace, ma non parlo l'italiano molto bene.* Sorry, I don't speak Italian well," she apologized.

"*Non fa niente. La capisco benissimo.* That's all right. I understand you very well." Mario thanked her for coming to his birthday party. Then, en masse, the group wished her *buona sera*.

"Come. We must leave now. Some tired children need their rest." Nick offered a hand to draw her to her feet, then waved at the children. *Buona notte.* "Good night."

Amidst the responses, he quickly ushered her out of the building and down the street to his car. Once inside they sped away, leaving behind the poverty to reenter the world she took for granted. A world filled with everything she needed. The children made do with broken-down toys, rusted swing sets, and stew for dinner, yet they laughed and enjoyed life more than many wealthy American children.

"Promise me you will not go back, Emily. It isn't safe for you to be there. Some people do not like the mission and would like to see it gone." His hands gripped the wheel, knuckles white, his voice stern. "Promise."

"You could take me with you when you go," she murmured, knowing he'd refuse.

"It is too dangerous. Do not go there."

But something about the mission drew her. She could help out, she knew she could. Oh, she didn't have huge sums of money to help, but she could hold the babies, tell stories to the older ones, that kind of thing. And she wanted to. She couldn't resist that warm, generous friendship they offered. For the first time since Gran had died, she no longer felt alone. The children had made her part of the group.

Perhaps that's why God had guided her to Rome, to do whatever she could for these little ones.

But what could she do? Emily mused on that all the way home. Then the answer burst upon her brain.

Cece—she might help.

Chapter 5

"Y ou are off to the mission again?" Cece watched as Emily filled her water bottle. "It takes a lot of your time."

"I know. And I feel dreadful leaving you once more." Impossible to believe she'd been here over a month. Cece was now as much a part of her life as Gran had been, listening, probing, and always offering sage advice.

"You know, I've changed my mind. I think I'll stay in this afternoon." She twisted the cap off the bottle, tipped it so the water ran out, feeling guilty that she'd even considered going.

"No, Emily. That would be foolish indeed, for I intend to relax for several hours. *Siesta* is my custom, you understand. I can't imagine running around as you do, in the midday heat." She wagged a hand to cool her red cheeks.

"But I thought the siesta time was mostly in summer." Cece looked flushed, but these lovely Italian spring days certainly were not overly hot.

"Ah. You have caught me in my fable," Cece smiled. "Now I will tell you the truth. It is not so much the heat that bothers me, dear Emmy. It is simply that I am old and weary and must rest to recover my strength." She shrugged in the familiar Latin gesture so common here.

"I'm afraid having me here has been too much for you," Emily murmured, wondering if she should have her ticket changed and go home. But home to what? She still had no idea what came next. But here, in Rome, she could at least help out at the mission.

"It has been my delight and pleasure to have you here. And I think you have benefited also. The young man, you don't think of him with sadness any longer, eh?"

Emily blinked as she realized it was true. She hadn't thought of Tad in days, hadn't wondered if he'd found someone else, hadn't stuffed down the twinge of hurt that he'd left her alone.

"*Si.* I did not think so. Rome has been good for you." Cece's wise blue eyes shone with compassion. "Somehow my beautiful city puts things into perspective, yes?"

"It's true," Emily agreed, musing on the past days spent in the eternal city. "When I walk among the monuments or look at the sculptures, I feel a sense of timelessness, as if I'm but one of many who's trod these stone paths wondering about the future. My petty problems, what do they matter in the course of history?"

"In history, I know not. But to God they matter very much. He cares for you, Emily. He wants your life to be filled with purpose and meaning. He always has a plan." Cece hugged her, then brushed her arthritic hand over Emily's head. "You just have to discover what it is. Perhaps the mission will help you to know what that may be."

"It already has." She tried to put into words what she'd only begun to understand. "True happiness doesn't come from what is around you. Those children—they have nothing. But they are truly happy. They know how to find joy in life, and it bubbles out of them onto me. I thought Tad would make me happy, but he couldn't. Tad wasn't in charge of my happiness."

What was the passage she'd read this morning—the Apostle Paul's words, weren't they? *I've learned whatever state I'm in, to be content.* She'd found contentment in working with the children. If only Nick could understand that.

"I don't like going behind his back," she murmured, as Cece walked her to the front door, where the car she'd hired waited. "And I don't like coercing you, either."

"*Pfui!* I have a friend who has a grandson who likes to drive. It is no hardship for him to take you to the mission when Martino cannot. And I know that you are safe. Nicolo is being unreasonable."

"Maybe." Emily leaned down to brush her lips over the parchment cheek. "Please rest well, Cece. I don't want to wear out my welcome."

"This is not possible. Your welcome is permanent." Cece stood leaning against one of the portico columns, waving as Emily rode away.

There was a mound of things to be done at the mission. Three of the children were ill with a virus that demanded cool pads on their foreheads and plenty of stories to keep their attention until sleep claimed them. Emily was glad to take over, freeing one of the sisters to help with the other children.

Once all three were asleep, she went downstairs to find others working on a craft. Soon there were many little boats made out of sponges, floating in a tub of water outside. Pestered to tell a story about water, Emily spoke of the disciples' fishing escapades. She was lifting the boats out of the water while the children did their homework when Nicolo found her.

"Emily, I asked you not to come here. It is not a safe place for someone like you to be." He looked angry as he glanced around, his eyes resting on the pictures Mario and some other boys had chalked onto the sidewalk. They claimed it was she, and with the bright yellow hair, it was hard to deny it. "You've been here before."

"Yes, and it was perfectly safe. I got a ride here, and the sisters phoned for a taxi to take me back. I was in no danger, Nick."

His lips pinched tight.

"Please try to understand. I enjoy it here so much." She stood her ground, staring up at him, willing him to hear what she needed to say. "I've been all alone since Gran's death. Being around these children is like food for a starving man. I can't *not* come here. Surely you of all people can understand that."

He studied her for a long time. Finally his chest heaved with a sigh and he gave just the slightest nod.

"Promise me you will take extra care. There are always thugs lurking in the side streets in this area. I do not want you to be hurt."

"I won't be." She couldn't contain her grin. "Thank you, Nick. Do you want to see what I brought?" Without waiting for an answer, she grabbed his arm and led him inside, where she'd stashed a small box. "Look."

She held up three of the puppets that she'd bought at the market.

"Aren't they cute? Tonight we are going to have a puppet show. Want to help?"

At first it seemed as though he'd refuse. But finally he nodded.

"What story are we to perform?" he asked, his smile widening when she produced a huge whale. "Ah, Jonah."

Emily didn't understand the odd look that passed over his face as she explained her plan for the story. Nor could she decipher the peculiar glint that sparkled in his dark eyes. She certainly couldn't decode the meaning of his murmured words. "You're an unusual woman, Emily Cain."

But she accepted that he approved of her efforts, and that sent an arrow of warmth straight to her heart. Which was silly. Why did it matter whether Nick approved or not?

"Do you know what I learned today?" she asked, waiting for his dark head to shake. "Mario told me the legend of Romulus and Remus. How could I have heard so much about Rome and missed that?"

"The Capitoline's she-wolf is an unusual symbol for a city to have." Nick smiled at her nod. "But I'm not sure Mario's version is accurate. Legend has it that Romulus and Remus, the sons of Mars, were tossed into a river by their jealous uncle. The she-wolf dragged them to safety and nursed them. According to the story, Romulus founded Rome on the twenty-first of April in 753 B.C."

"Oh." Emily frowned. "Mario's version was—different."

"I can imagine. He's a born actor." Nick's lips pulled into a crooked smile. "He's certainly taken a liking to you." He brushed his fingertip over her nose. "You've been touched by the sun again. Where were you today?"

"Piazza Navona," she told him, unable to suppress her grin. "I think I'm becoming Italian. I'm starting to use the piazzas as Italians do, like a big living room. I read a book, fed the pigeons, and had my picture done."

"Ah, a portrait. May I see it?"

"Sure." She lifted the page from her bag and held it out. "He was a caricaturist, so it's not exactly me."

Nick studied the drawing for several long moments, then lifted his gaze to her face.

"He was a clever artist, this man. He expressed exactly those things that make you who you are."

Emily stared, surprised by the softness of his voice. "Wh–what do you mean?" she murmured.

"The eyes. It's all there in the eyes. Compassion. Loneliness. Gentleness." Suddenly he blinked, shifted, as if he realized he'd shown her a side of himself she hadn't known existed. "It's a very good picture, Emily." He handed it back.

"Thank you." She tucked it back in her bag, then requested his help to build a temporary stage for the puppets, all the while fully conscious of the stare that remained focused on her when he thought she didn't see. That evening, for the first time since she'd met him, Nick seemed to lose the air of reserve he'd clung to and joined wholeheartedly into the puppet show.

"You are very good with children," she murmured later, as he drove her home. "They seem very comfortable with you. How long have you been going there?"

"Three years."

Three years—just after his fiancée had died, she guessed.

"Did it help?" she murmured, then wondered if she should have asked.

Nick took his time before responding.

"Not at first. But gradually, bit by bit, I found myself

313

thankful that I was alive, able to enjoy them. The wonderful thing about children is they accept you however you arrive, no questions asked."

"Mmm." The quiet that fell between them was not uncomfortable, but rather that of two companions who'd shared something enjoyable. Emily relaxed fully, her eyes on their surroundings. "This isn't the way back," she murmured.

"No, I thought we'd stop by the Trevi. There's nothing more wonderful than Rome at night. And *la fontana* is very beautiful. Did you throw your coin in already?"

"Oh, yes. More than one." Emily caught her breath as they neared the Colosseum, floodlit from below to emphasize its many arches. "Fantastic, even if it did give me the willies at first."

"More fantastic is the Villa d'Este. The hundred fountains are beautiful at night, even more so than during the day."

"I haven't been," she murmured, wishing she had months—no, years—to see everything Rome—no, Italy—offered.

Nick found a parking space along the crowded streets. Soon they were ambling down the Via delle Muratte to stand at the edge of the most sumptuous fountain in Rome. Water gushed from every part of the statues and from the bas-reliefs perched on heaps of rocks.

"Trevi was once celebrated for its excellent water." Nick's hand lay warm against her elbow, his words soft among those of the many tourists who stood staring. "Would you like to hear the story?"

"Oh, yes. Please." Would she ever tire of listening to Nick's voice?

"Agrippa brought the water to Rome by means of an

aqueduct. It is said that the soldiers of Agrippa, looking for water in the Via Collatina in the country, met a maiden who showed them the source of this pure water. Look there, to the right, that is what is depicted. The bas-relief on the left shows Agrippa explaining to Augustus the plan to bring this water to Rome. All of this was built in 1762."

"So long ago, and yet how well it stands the test of time, still spouting its waters." She tugged a coin from her bag and lifted her arm to throw it.

"Oh, no, not like that. And not just one coin." Nick's fingers wrapped around hers. "The first coin is a gift. The second is to assure your return to Rome, but you must turn around and throw it over your shoulder. A silly superstition, some say. But it has become a tradition with tourists." His white teeth gleamed in the darkness. "We must keep up with tradition. Yes?"

Return to Rome. The thought whispered through her like silk. How lovely to come back, again and again, to spend time with Nick the way he'd been tonight, lighthearted, teasing. Most of all, she delighted in the way he could surprise her— like bringing her here to see the fountain at night. He must have seen it a hundred times before, yet for her he made the experience seem new and exciting.

"Oh, yes. By all means, we must uphold tradition. You know what they say, *when in Rome—*"

"*Do as the Romans,*" he finished. "Never more apropos than now."

For one long moment, Emily couldn't tear her gaze away from him. Her breath caught, and to regain her calm, she turned her back to the fountain, closed her eyes, and tossed the coin over one shoulder, praying that God would allow her to come back here one day—soon.

"You must see more of Rome by moonlight, but next time we will go to the Piazza Navona to see the fountain of the four rivers. You will think you are having a dream of Aesop's fables."

He was going to take her? Emily couldn't stop the shiver of anticipation that rippled up the arm he held.

"You are chilly. Come, let us go." His fingers threaded through hers automatically as they ambled down the street. She wanted to make the moments last as he spoke of his city's history and she dreamed of being a part of this world.

Back in the car, Nick flicked the heat on low, then took a strange path through a plethora of back roads that seemed almost sinister in their darkness. But before she knew it, they were rolling up the drive in front of Cece's.

"I'm sorry." She reached for the door handle. "I must have fallen asleep." Embarrassment sent a hot flush to her cheeks at Nick's curious smile.

"Yes, you did. But don't worry, you are as beautiful asleep as awake."

"Thank you," she murmured, wondering how to take the compliment.

He seemed about to say more when the door burst open. Maria stood there wringing her hands, her words spilling over themselves in her haste.

Cece had been taken to the hospital.

Chapter 6

Three days later Emily sat at Cece's bedside, realizing, as she held the frail, parchment-lined hand, how precious this woman had become to her.

"You look so serious, *Carissima*. What troubles you?"

"Nothing." She dredged up a smile, smoothing the blankets with her free hand, but she could tell from Cece's expression that the questions would persist. "I was just thinking what a wonderful time I've had, thanks to Nick and you. I can never thank you enough for inviting me to Rome."

"That sounds as though you are leaving us. Surely your time here is not yet finished?" A troubled frown marred the older woman's face, her lips drew down. "I thought you were intending to stay longer. At least two weeks more, you said yesterday. I had so hoped—"

She closed her eyes, leaning her head back. A tear squeezed out to dance at the end of her lashes, then tumbled down her paper-white cheek.

"Oh, Cece. What's wrong? Are you in pain?" Emily whispered, her heart aching at the older woman's distress. "Please tell me. Perhaps I can help."

"I wish—I wish you would never leave us, Emmy."

The forceful whisper shocked her. Not leave Rome? Emily could only imagine it. To live here always, to revisit history whenever she wanted—such a thing was far beyond anything she'd even dared to dream. But what would she do, how would she live? She was still in the dark about God's reason for bringing her to Rome. How could she possibly stay, especially now, with Cece like this?

"It's kind of you to say that, but I think my being here is the reason you've ended up in this hospital." She caught Cece's sidelong glance at the water jug. "You've overdone when you should have been resting, because of me," she murmured, pouring a glass of water. Tenderly she lifted the thin frail shoulders so her friend could sip. "It's my fault you're ill."

"No! This is not true." Cece lay back against her pillows, her breath short and shallow. "Because of you, Nicolo laughs again. He has lost that dull bored look and begun to take new interest in life, has he not?"

"Well—" Remembering their puppet show, Emily couldn't suppress her grin. "He does love the mission."

"Exactly. But never before would he share it with me. Since Alexandra died and he began to go there, he has not asked, even once, for toys for the little ones. Yet after one puppet show with you, he scours the villa, chuckling like a boy who's found pirate's treasure when he unearths his old playthings. That is because of you, Emmy. You have brought joy to Nico."

"I only suggested there might be some old toys lying around." And spent hours stitching tattered rabbit ears and securing floppy tails while she waited to know how Cece would fare. "I was glad to help. It felt good to be needed."

"Yes, but you also feel a deep compassion for this mission, no?"

"Yes. What I do is so little, but they act as if I'm really contributing. Being there—it fills my heart," she explained simply.

"Do you think God might be telling you something, my dear Emmy?" Cecelia's sharp eyes probed as deeply as her words. "You care for Nico, don't you? The old love has passed away, the pain has disappeared. And in its place sprouts a fresh, new joy. Not only for the children, I think." She winked.

Emily laughed, then grew sober, thinking. She liked Nick, but—more?

"At first I found him standoffish. I knew what you and Gran had planned. He knew, too. It made things awkward between us. But now. . ." She closed her eyes. "I don't know, Cece. I've been so confused about the next step, about where God is directing me. I've prayed over and over to be shown what God would have me do, but going back to college somehow doesn't feel right. I'm tired of studying moldy books. I want to *do* something."

"And you shall have your chance." Nico walked through the door, kissed his grandmother's cheek, then grinned at Emily, looking every bit the carefree man his grandmother had suggested he'd become. "Sister Claudia telephoned me this afternoon. Children keep showing up at the mission, asking about your next puppet show. Apparently you've become famous."

"They liked it that much?" Sheer delight sent her spirits soaring. "I'm so glad. I've been working on a new show, you know. It's about the battle of Jericho. I even made some tiny trumpets for the puppets."

"This is another reason why you cannot go yet, Emmy. What about the children? They've come to expect your shows." Cece turned to her grandson. "Tell her, Nico. Tell her she cannot go yet. Tell her that she is not to blame for my silly illness or for my presence in the hospital."

"Is that what you think, Emily?" Nick's dark gaze brimmed with compassion. "That is foolish. Nonna had her heart disease long before you arrived. You must not blame yourself. She loves having you here, even though we've not fallen in with our grandmothers' plans." He winked at Cece. "You thought I didn't know what you were up to? But, of course, I couldn't *not* know. You are too obvious, *Bellissima*."

He flicked a gentle finger against her pale, thin cheek, his voice tender but firm.

"Emily and I are adults, Nonna; we make our own decisions. I understand her need to return to her home and so must you. She is no doubt lonely for her friends. A few more days, then her holiday is over and her life goes on."

Emily couldn't have uttered a word, even if her throat hadn't been choked. Lonely? Since Gran's death, she'd never been less lonely than she was right here. But it was obvious that Nick thought of her as nothing more than a guest, a tourist to chauffeur around when the mood struck. That hurt. Why?

Because she loved him.

The truth hit her hard and she blinked, hoping no one had noticed. Nick's attention remained on his grandmother, but Cece's gaze was on her, soft, compassionate. She gave a slight nod.

"Off you go, Nico. Offer your daily ranting about my welfare to the doctors, or they will think you are ill. When you finish, you shall take Emily to present her puppets." She shooed him from the room, waited until the door closed, then held out her arms. "Oh, *poverina*. I am so sorry. My so smart grandson is as blind as a bat where you're concerned."

"It's all right." Nonetheless, Emily sank into the embrace, relishing the gentle touch and soft words. "I–I didn't realize, you see. We'd become friends. I don't know when—"

"The heart doesn't always follow orders from the head. And my Nico is a most charming man, when he isn't brooding. Don't you think so?" She winked, then chuckled at Emily's blush.

"Most charming. But what I think doesn't matter, Cece. Nick sees me as nothing more than a guest, a tourist who visits for a short time. He doesn't care for me—that way." She drew away, dabbed at her eyes, anxious that Nick notice nothing when he returned.

Cece remained silent for a few minutes, her bright eyes only hinting at the thoughts inside her silver head. Finally she patted the side of her bed.

"Tell me, Emily, have you been to the Pantheon?" She frowned, then nodded. "Yes, I remember you said you'd visited. When you were there, did they tell you that the Pantheon is the most perfect of buildings? The height and diameter of the interior are equal, you see. This is unusual."

"Yes, and light and air enter through an opening in the center of the dome." Emily bit her lip to stem her impatience. "What are you trying to tell me, Cece?" What had the Pantheon to do with Nick?

"The workmanship is superb. Did you know that the best time to view the interior is not while the sun shines, but during a thunderstorm when lightening flashes, illuminating the shadows and the treasures they hide?" She waited a moment, then smiled. "But for that hole in the ceiling, we might never see them."

There was meaning to her words. Emily just had to figure out what that meaning was. Right now, illumination eluded her. Finally Cece spoke, her voice quiet.

"Nicolo has only recently let the light back into his life. Give him time to let it seek out the shadows and illuminate his fears. I think you will find your patience rewarded." Her bright eyes flickered, certainty in their depths. "God did not bring you here to us without a reason. We have only to wait and see what that reason might be. Search your heart, Emily. Ask Him."

"Are you ready to leave, Emily?" Nick glanced from one to the other warily. "What are you two talking about?"

"The Pantheon. Your grandmother was explaining the dome."

"Was she?" He walked across the room, kissed Cece's cheek, then straightened. His voice softened, gentled. "Remind me to question what she told you. History is not her forte. In fact, she always gets the dates wrong."

"Oh, she wasn't talking about dates. And I'm quite sure that, in this particular case, she is exactly right. At least, I hope so." Emily gathered up her bag, kissed Cece good night, then followed him out of the room.

But at the door she paused, glancing over one shoulder. Was Cece right? Did God have something special in store, something Emily hadn't imagined when she'd left Chicago? Something that would fill her future with hope and promise?

These thoughts and a thousand others occupied her mind until Nick stopped the car in front of Cece's gorgeous home.

"I have to get something upstairs and make a phone call," he told her. "I'll only be a few moments."

Left alone, Emily abandoned the car to wander in Cece's garden. She sank onto the smooth hardness of a garden bench, her attention drawn by the riot of colors and blooms that spilled out of containers, climbed up the walls and crept across the flagstones, each petal, each stem individually created for a specific reason by the Creator.

Consider the lilies of the field. They neither sow nor reap. Yet Solomon, in all his glory, was not arrayed like one of these.

She closed her eyes. *God, I'm so confused. I believe you sent me to Rome for some reason I don't yet understand. I love the children, I want to help them, yet I have no money to give and I must soon leave this place. But, Lord, my heart longs to stay here, with Nick. I don't understand these feelings. Are they just me, or did You plan it all along? Please show me your way. In Jesus' name. Amen.*

The thump of Nick's footsteps down the stairs echoed through the house, and Emily knew it was time to go. Her decision was made. While at the mission, she would relish every moment with the children, for that was a gift too precious to waste. And tomorrow she'd work hard to understand Nick's obsession with the past.

But just for tonight, while the big round moon cast its orange glow over the many domes and arches of this spectacular city, she'd stop worrying about tomorrow and concentrate on savoring whatever precious moments she was given to share with Nick. She'd memorize his laugh, imprint the sparkle in his dancing eyes as he teased the children with the puppets. She'd tuck each memory deep inside her heart.

And she'd leave the rest up to God.

Chapter 7

A week later, Nick leaned one shoulder against the stone wall and watched Emily mesmerize the children who'd gathered for yet another of her puppet shows. She was an expert at drawing out the suspense in her stories so that no one, not even Mario, dared twitch a muscle until she announced, "The end."

Somehow, in ways Nick had only begun to fathom, she managed to touch each of the children, not just with her funny stories, but also with her abundant hugs, the featherlight brush of her dainty hand, and the comfort of her sweet words. It was with her that they shared their deepest secrets, and to whom they came with their needs.

Just this evening he'd watched her slip a sandwich to a boy in the audience whom he knew had not eaten dinner. For another she'd torn up a skirt so that together they could sew the girl's mother a shawl as a birthday gift. They loved her, all of them, and he freely admitted that he was jealous of the attention that she showered upon them.

But he was also worried. What would happen when she left, what would the children do? He'd tried to envision it, but the picture wouldn't appear. Emily was as much a part of the mission as Sister Claudia. In fact, he'd grown used to her presence in his life—teasing her over the breakfast table, watching her care for Cece, listening as she told Maria where she'd been, what she'd seen.

But the highlight of Nick's day always came when her green eyes grew huge and shone with delight when she gazed at the old Roman ruins he loved. He'd drawn upon every history manual he could find, scoured out the most oblique of facts, toured the city to find the best places to show her at night, after they left the mission.

They shared that, at least. Emily might be from a land far away, she might be used to new homes with all the latest gadgets and men familiar with her way of life, but none of it seemed to matter when it came to his city. She savored the past, drew parallels from it to her present life.

What would he do when she left?

The stark bleakness of that question made him push away from the wall and wander outside, to the children's playground. He sat on a rusted swing and stared upward, fixed his eyes on the stars, and remembered Cece's words.

"Emily isn't here by chance, Nico. God sent her to be used when that mission most needed her. I also think He sent her for you. If you'd only open your eyes and your heart, you'd see I'm right."

But much as he loved Nonna, she wasn't right. He'd known that for three years. He'd promised Alexandra that there would never be anyone else, that she alone would hold his heart forever. So many plans they'd made—three children, dark-eyed, button-nose brunets like their mother. Alexandra would continue with her fashion designing, of course. But she'd find a nanny, some-one who would ensure their children had the best of everything.

Like a faithless thief, the thought crept into his brain. Would Emily leave her children to a nanny? He shoved the question away, angry at the disloyalty of it. Emily didn't have a career; she had no plans for the future. She didn't even know what she would do tomorrow. Alexandra and he had made plans for the next fifty years. To turn his back on that would be to betray the love he'd felt for her.

"Alexandra is dead, Nico. She wouldn't expect you to pay homage for the rest of your life."

But Nonna was wrong. He owed Alexandra his loyalty, but Cece wouldn't understand that. She didn't know the questions he'd begun to ask himself in the days before Alexandra's death. She'd wanted them to move to Milan, not right away, but eventually. It made sense, her career would push forward there. But his life was here. Nonna was here. Home was Roma.

But he hadn't told her that. Instead, he'd let Alexandra think he was willing to leave his life behind and begin again, for her. The more she talked about the future, the more he'd begun to wonder if he'd made a mistake. The night she'd died, he'd asked her to put their marriage plans on hold, told her that he was no longer certain of their future together. The love he'd once been so sure of was shaken by a little thing like loca-tion. How could it have withstood the test of time, children, diverging careers?

"Is anything wrong, Nick?" Emily stood beside him, her slight figure barely discernable in the poor light.

"Just thinking." If he turned his head just a bit, the spicy scent of the Persian rose fragrance he'd helped her choose in the market last week assaulted his senses. It was like her—soft, unexpected, yet quietly appealing.

"It must be a rather unpleasant thought."

A hint of laughter resonated through her voice. He twisted to look at her face, saw her smile.

"You were frowning quite fiercely," she murmured. His silence made her frown. "Is something wrong, Nick?"

"Not wrong exactly. I was just thinking about when you leave Rome."

"A week. That's all I have left." The smile was gone from her voice, her eyes no longer danced. In fact, her entire body seemed to droop. "I was just waiting for Cece. I didn't want to leave before I knew she was feeling better."

"I'm glad you stayed." That was the truth. He enjoyed knowing his grandmother had someone watching to be sure she didn't overdo, someone who would ensure she rested at the appropriate times. Someone who could handle the everyday directions for the staff.

And he enjoyed coming home to find Emily waiting for him. They often shared a cool drink on the patio before Maria announced dinner, which had been bumped up a little earlier so Cece could join them, and so that they would have plenty of time to spend at the mission.

"Actually I was thinking of how much the children would miss you. You've grown so close to them. It will be a terrible wrench for them. Have you told them yet?" He glanced up in time to see her blond head shake. Tears welled in her eyes.

"I've been so selfish," she exclaimed. "I haven't been thinking of them at all, but of me, of how much I'm going to miss not being here for Emilio's first birthday or to watch Sophia say her first word. But they will have it much harder, won't they, Nick?"

He felt ashamed by his own words when her head bowed and he heard the words slip from her lips.

"Perhaps it would have been better if I had never come here," she whispered.

"Of course it wouldn't have been better." He bristled with anger at his own carelessness. Why was it that whenever he spoke to Emily, he couldn't find the right words? Time after time he'd blurted out something which she'd taken the wrong way, and he hadn't bothered to correct her impression. Well, not this time!

"They've loved having you here, Emily. You've done so much for them, given them love and understanding that money could never buy. And you've taught them what it means to be a follower of Jesus. That's worth a great deal." He saw her eyebrows rise and stopped. "I just meant that perhaps we should prepare them, ease the shock a bit," he muttered, wishing he'd minded his own business.

"Actually, I'd planned to tell them the ascension story one of these nights. Perhaps I could tie that in to my leaving." Her furrowed brow told him how hard she was thinking. "You know the kind of thing—people leave, but if we all love God and obey Him, we see each other in heaven again." She lifted her head, stared at him. "Would that be all right?"

A wave of tenderness washed over him as he stared into her eyes. She was so concerned for the children, and so careless about her own needs. But leaving Rome would mean she would go back to—what? Cece had insisted Emily had no family in America. What kind of a life would she make there?

"Nick?"

He blinked, saw the question in her eyes.

"Would you pray with me? I need God's help to do this. I love these kids very much. It will be hard to say good-bye when the time comes."

"Of course I'll pray with you." He accepted her outstretched hand, watched her gulp, and wondered if he was doing the right thing by letting her go. Did she know how much he and his grandmother would miss her bubbly presence in their dull lives? How much he'd miss the sparkle she brought to each day?

"Dear Jesus, the children in this mission are special to You. You know the exact number of hairs on their heads and what they long for most in their hearts. I don't want to hurt them, Father. Let me be a lamp and light for You. Amen." She sighed, then glanced up at him. "I'll start preparing tomorrow night."

"I didn't mean to hurt you, Emily," he murmured, fingers still entwined with hers. "I know you love them. I just thought—"

"I know. And you're right. I can't leave it till the last minute. But it hurts to think of leaving." She choked back a sob, tugged her hand from his. "I need some cheering up, Nick. Can we go somewhere bright and happy and fun tonight? I don't want to look at anything from the past, and I don't want to think about the future. I just want to be around people who are laughing and singing. Is that okay?"

He nodded, forcing a smile.

"Of course. We'll have coffee and dessert in one of the sidewalk cafés and watch the world go by."

Later, as they wandered down the Via Veneto, Nick kept her hand tucked into his arm, pausing when she did to look at the wares of the street peddlers. He encouraged her to have a new portrait sketched by a different artist and laughed with her when the balloon she'd been given blew up and away into the night sky.

At her request, Nick drove to the Piazza Navona and stood beside her while she stared into the aquamarine water that spurted out of the fountain of the four rivers. Emily shivered once, and he moved to wrap his arm around her shoulder, cuddling her against his side as they stared at the four figures. He could have told her that the work of Bernini was meant to represent the Danube, the Ganges, the Nile, and the Rio de la Plata. He could have explained that the piazza now occupied the former stadium of Domitian, that it could once hold up to thirty thousand spectators. He could have given her the age of the statue and the piazza and pointed out several artifacts nearby.

He could have, but he didn't.

Suddenly none of that seemed important. The only thing he could think about, the one fact that imprinted his brain, was that in seven days she wouldn't be there to share it with him and he would be lonelier than he'd ever been in his life.

"Emily," he whispered, wanting to tell her something, anything, that would ease the pain he saw on her beautiful face.

She turned to him, her green eyes wide, questioning, molten hair blowing in the breeze. Suddenly Nick knew that whatever he'd hoped to convey couldn't be compressed into mere words. There was only one way he could explain, and he hoped she would understand.

His gaze honed in on her lovely mouth, and he bent his head and touched his lips to hers, praying she'd understand, delighted that his prayer had been answered when her arm reached around his waist and her lips returned his caress.

He eased back, stared into her upturned face as his emotions swirled around him. She was young, beautiful, and she had her whole life before her, a chance to do anything she wished. And he wanted to spend the rest of his life with her.

The shock of that held him immobile.

Then a cool breeze whipped the fountain water in a spray that spattered over them like a hard dash of reality. Emily stared at him, and he watched as the resignation crashed over her like a wave she couldn't avoid. With a sob, she pulled away, turned her back on him.

It was a good thing she did, for Nick knew what had to happen. No matter how deeply Emily was buried in his heart, he couldn't ask her to stay. God's plan for him didn't include that.

"Let's go home, Nick," she whispered when a group of merrymakers invaded their privacy moments later. "Please take me home."

"Yes." But as he drove back to Cece's, escorted Emily from the car and into the villa, he begged God to take away the feelings, to send him back to the self-imposed hermit he'd become before she'd pulled him back into life.

Later, as he sat in his grandmother's garden and watched the sun rise, Nick realized how foolish his prayer had been.

Nothing would ever make him forget Emily.

It was childish to pretend otherwise.

Chapter 8

It was her last full day in Rome.

Ever since she'd risen this morning, each action felt as if it occurred in slow motion. That feeling persisted as Emily filled her water bottle and stowed it in her bag, made sure her map was tucked inside, along with a tissue and an apple. Maybe if she could prolong the day, draw it out to the very last second, she wouldn't have to leave.

"Are you ready, my dear?"

Emily turned to smile at the precious woman she'd grown to love.

"More than ready, Cece. I deliberately left the catacombs till last, but now I wish I'd opted to go earlier. I could have spent today in St. Peter's."

Cece wrapped an arm around her waist and walked with her to the door.

"Because you could have prayed there?" she asked, one eyebrow quirked. She read Emily's eyes and shook her head. "Dear one, you must remember that God hears His beloved children no matter where they are. The catacombs are as good a place to speak to Him as any and perhaps better than most.

They will help remind you that our God is not dead, that the same One who cared for those poor souls is still working today. Think on His goodness, Emmy. You will find the solace you seek."

"I love you." She hugged the tiny frame close, breathed in the sweet lilac scent that would always be Cece.

"I love you, too. Now off you go and enjoy your day." If Cece's smile looked a little forced, she wasn't allowing Emily to see it.

"You're sure you'll be all right?" Emily couldn't help asking. "You wouldn't rather I stay here, keep you company?"

"Watch me while I sleep?" Cece shook her white head firmly. "No. I'm perfectly well, Emmy. You go and enjoy your day. Just be sure to return in time for dinner. Maria has something special planned." Cece kissed her cheek. "There you are, your taxi awaits."

Emily's emotions churned wildly as they drove through the familiar streets. One last day. That's all there was left. Very well then. Hadn't she given her future to God? Now she had to trust that He would not let her stumble or fall.

This morning she would revisit St. Peter's and allow herself one last look. By the time the sun was hot and the day warm, it would feel good to wander through the catacombs. Secretly she'd hoped to see Nick leading a class through the famous basilica, but there was no sight of him in St. Peter's Square, nor did she happen to meet him while pondering the Sistine Chapel ceiling. Perhaps that was just as well, for as she stared up at Michelangelo's magnificent frescoes, she was reminded of God's unwavering love for His children. A sense of peace washed into her soul.

After enjoying a slice of piping hot pizza on the Spanish steps, she sipped her water and watched the couples who filled the piazza. They looked so happy, and for a moment, the impact of leaving grabbed at her. But Emily fought back, whispering a prayer for help. By the time she'd stored her bottle in her bag and strolled to the catacombs of St. Sebastian, she was reconciled to following the path on which God led her.

The solemnity of the catacombs felt sadly eerie. She stood to one side, watching as members of the Franciscan order moved through the underground cemetery in respectful silence.

"A magnificent basilica over this spot was built in the fourth century to honor the apostles Peter and Paul. It later received the precious relic of Peter."

Delighted and surprised by the familiar sound of that whispered voice, Emily whirled to face Nick.

"I didn't know you were coming here," she murmured, mindful of the silence surrounding them.

"I had a few hours off and thought you might like company." He led her down a pathway that wound through the burial grounds. "Excavations began in 1915, but still they continue today. A particularly important series of buildings have been found, which were dedicated to the two apostles at a time when it was illegal to bury the dead inside Rome."

For the first time, Emily heard little of the actual content of Nick's words. Instead she reveled in the pleasure of listening to the timbre of his low voice, of the brush of his arm against her, the gentle way he guided her through the barrel-vaulted complexes. When he finally led her out, Emily knew she couldn't walk away without at least trying—one last time.

"It's early yet. I know Maria is making a special dinner

before we go to the mission, but I wonder if you'd like to see one last thing." Nick's voice was quiet, but brimming with determination, as if he had something he intended to say and would not be put off.

"I'd love to see whatever you'd like to show me," she murmured, trying to quell the tiny flicker of hope that would not be dashed. "Is it far?"

"No." He walked her back to his car, helped her inside, then headed away from the city, climbing steadily to the top of a hill. "It's not much really. Just the *campagna*, the countryside." He waited for her to join him on the crest, then waved a hand to indicate the vista in front of them.

"Not everyone appreciates or understands the Roman countryside," he murmured in hushed tones as the sun blazed its last few red rays over them, then began a slow and steady descent beneath the horizon.

Emily watched, holding her breath until the last faint flicker cast a shadowed light across the ruins in front of them.

"At one time this land was full of patrician tombs, military roads, and of villas where noble families lived. There were great aqueducts just over there that brought abundant supplies of water to the baths and the fountains, and irrigated the gardens and vineyards. The rest of the world benefited greatly from Rome's influence, which was once contained within these seven hills."

"It's a wonderful heritage and a magnificent country," she whispered, unsure of the meaning behind this strange litany. "You have every right to be proud of your city."

"I love Roma." He smiled that lopsided grin that didn't quite reach his eyes. "But that is not why I brought you here."

"Oh."

"No. I had another reason." He turned, pointed to a small cross that stood opposite them, on the other side of the road. "Alexandra died here."

That caught her by surprise.

"I—I'm so sorry, Nick. You must have loved her very much." Why did it hurt so much to think of Nick loving someone else?

"I thought I did. Later, well, I had questions. We had—different views of life. I'm not at all sure a marriage between us would have worked."

"All couples have problems." She didn't quite know what to say, so Emily whispered a prayer for help. "But once you've made the commitment, you work things out. I'm sure the two of you would have learned to compromise."

"Probably."

But he didn't sound certain. Instead he turned his back on that side of the road, stared down at the magnificence that had stood before them and had disappeared with the erosion of time. One hand raked through his hair.

"I came here many times after she died. I didn't know what else to do, and I felt that here, alone, I could talk to God." Suddenly he faced her, his palms cupped her face. "I made God a promise here, Emily."

"Oh." The hairs on her arm prickled, but it wasn't from the breeze. A terrible feeling assailed her, and she clung to the faith she'd found earlier.

"After her death, I realized that God's plan for me did not include marriage. He led me to the mission, and I've found joy there, and happiness."

"Is it enough?" she whispered, wondering if she dared to

tell him her feelings. "Will watching those kids grow up replace seeing your own?"

"It has to." His thumbs brushed against her cheeks, his eyes dark and sad. "Don't you understand? I made a promise to God that I would be content to help at the mission, to do what I could there. His plan for me doesn't include anything more, no matter how much I want it."

"How do you know that?" she demanded, jerking out of his grasp, as the tears welled in her eyes. "How can you be so sure?"

"I just am. Please understand. You are a wonderful woman, Emily. The children adore you because your heart is big and you give constantly. Cece adores you, too."

"And you?" She waited, breath suspended, for an answer she knew he couldn't give her.

"I—I care about you, Emily. Truly." He let out a pent-up breath, his shoulders slumped. "But I have no business doing so. I promised God, and I will not go back on that. Besides, we're worlds apart. I'm years older than you, from a different culture, a different land. I'm a simple teacher, I have nothing to offer you."

He did. If only he loved her, it would be more than she'd dared hope or dream for. But she wasn't going to argue or debate it. If God had chosen Nick for her, He would find a way to work things out. At least she'd learned that much from her days in Rome. Her life was in God's hands. He alone could open doors, or hearts.

As she stared into the night sky and the ruins that lay broken and crushed through the ages, Emily could only rejoice that she'd come to Rome. Tad hadn't been the right man for her, and even though she'd been bitter about his leaving, she realized now that his actions had saved her from making a huge mistake.

"I've upset you. I'm sorry, Emily. You have a right to be angry with me after what we shared."

Though it cost her greatly, Emily reached out, touched his arm with her fingers, feeling the warmth of his skin transmit to hers.

"I'm not angry, Nick. Not at all. You've taught me so much about your country, about the past, and from that, I've learned to look to the future." Emily smiled at the skeptical frown on his face. "It's true. Being here, getting to know you and your grandmother, it's been a chance for me to think beyond my little world and consider life in a broader scope, in terms of eternity."

"You really mean this?" His hand moved to cover hers, eyes quizzical.

She nodded.

"Yes. You know what's in your heart, Nick, and that's between you and God." She stood on her tiptoes and brushed her lips against his cheek. "I'm glad to have known you, Nicolo Fellini. You're a strong, caring man who has trusted God with his future. That's all any of us can do. I respect your desire to be true to your promise."

Then she turned and walked back to the car, climbed inside, and waited to be driven back to the villa.

I've done my best, Lord. Wherever you lead, I'll follow. The prayer slipped from her lips, as she watched Nick survey the hills once more before turning to walk toward her.

I love him, God. More than I ever dreamed. But I want to do your will.

Chapter 9

He'd done everything he could think of to steel himself for the evening ahead, but as they walked into the mission later that evening, Nick knew Emily would not be the only one fighting her emotions tonight.

"*Ciao, piccolina,*" she laughed as a tiny girl toddled over to hug her legs. "It was such a hot day, and yet here you are, brimming with energy." She kissed the downy soft cheek, remaining hunkered down to receive the endless round of hugs that the other children offered.

"I love you, too," she whispered in each tiny ear. As usual, their probing fingers found a way to touch her shining mane of golden hair, eyes huge.

Emily laughed at them, her gaze sparkling with love as they poked and prodded her pockets for the treats she always brought. Nick moved back and simply watched as she showered her attention on each child, listening and nodding as they explained their day in minute detail.

"So much love to give," his grandmother had said after dinner, while Emily prepared for their mission visit.

He could not help but agree.

"You're staring at me," she whispered, as she passed him to

mop up the purple juice a chubby hand had spilled. "Do I have something on my face?"

Nick shook his head, but no words would emerge from his choked throat.

"Well, what then? You look very—odd." She glanced down, saw the spot where a bit of melon clung to her sundress and blushed, her cheeks rosy with embarrassment. "I'm such a mess," she giggled, plucking the fruit off. "You must be embarrassed."

He wasn't, not at all. He was proud of her, as if it were somehow his right to crow to anyone that cared to listen that Emily Cain was a woman to be prized.

Indignation surged inside. Why? Why did this have to happen now? He'd grown accustomed to his lonely life, he'd put aside his dreams and hopes and resigned himself to bypass all the things his colleagues and friends were now enjoying.

"Nick?" She stood waiting, her smile fading as she stared into his eyes.

"You look fine," he murmured, reaching to brush a bit of cookie from a strand of her hair. "You look wonderful."

"Don't be sad, Nick," she whispered, her green eyes brimming with tears. "God is good. He knows the desires of my heart. He will bring things to pass in His own time. But I need you to be strong tonight, to help me say good-bye. Please help me."

How could he refuse her?

"Come, children, gather round. Emily has something to say."

"Thank you." Her hand brushed his for only a second before she turned to those clamoring for her attention. "You all know this is my last time with you." She stopped, controlled the tremble in her voice. "Tomorrow I will get on a plane and fly back to my home in America."

Thirty-five sets of button bright eyes stared at her.

"I'm going to miss you so much," she continued. "And I'm going to pray that one day God brings me back here, to see you again. Will you pray for me, too?"

Nick found a path through the dozens of brown arms and legs, then strode across the room until at last he was outside the building, in the little courtyard where the children played. He tilted his head back and filled his lungs with great gulps of air.

"It isn't so easy to deny your feelings, is it, Nico?"

He jerked around, stunned to see his grandmother sitting on a small chair, wrapped in a thick shawl.

"What are you doing here?" he demanded, automatically checking her color. "You are supposed to be at home, resting."

"Am I?" She shrugged. "I did not feel like resting. Tonight I felt like watching my grandson push away the gift God has given him."

"Don't start, Grandmother. You know my feelings." Anger nipped at him, mingling with guilt that he'd spoken so sharply to his beloved Nonna. "Happily ever after is not for everyone. I am prepared to do what I promised. Isn't that enough?"

"It is if God has asked this of you," she murmured, her eyes dark in the shadowy yard. "But has He asked this, my son? Or is this something you've done—locked away your heart so you won't have to suffer as you did when Alexandra died?"

"How can you ask that?" He paced back and forth across the yard, trying to ignore what she'd said, but the words would not be silenced. "You know that His plan is for me to remain alone."

"I think that was your plan, Nico, and that you've convinced yourself that God had asked it of you."

He couldn't believe Nonna was saying this.

"What is the first thing you learned about God? Was it not

that He is love? Emily came here because you wrote her, yes. But it was an idea that began long before your birth and it was supposed to happen when her mother was alive. Don't you see? God chose to send Emily to us at a time when she needed us."

"Sì. This is true." Nick nodded. Yes, he understood that. She'd been hurting and somehow among the ruins she'd found peace and joy.

"Could not that same God, the one you both serve—could He not have drawn the two of you together for His own plan?" She saw his frown and snapped her fingers. "Think of it this way, Nico. Your trust has been in yourself, in your ability to keep a promise you made. That is wrong. We do not trust in ourselves, but in the God who chose us. 'Blessed is the man who trusts in the Lord and has made the Lord his hope and confidence.' Is that what you've done, Nico? Or is your hope and confidence in yourself?"

"Cece! I didn't know you'd be here." Emily stood in the doorway, glancing back and forth between them. "Have I interrupted something?"

"Of course not. Come. I have brought a huge cake which Maria insists you are to share with the children." She rose and, using her cane, moved slowly across the courtyard. "Come, Nico."

"In a moment," he murmured, watching as Emily threaded her arm through the frail woman's and helped ease her way. "I'll be there in a moment."

Moments later the children's voices echoed outside, but Nick heard little of that. His eyes were fixed on something much farther away.

"But what is the truth, Father?" he whispered. "Please show me the truth. Is Cece right—is it fear that I cling to?"

"I'm sorry you had to get up so early just to drop me at the airport." Emily offered the silly polite words, wishing desperately that she had something wonderful to say, something that would shatter the silence between them and bring back that easy camaraderie of past days.

"It is nothing. I was not asleep."

"No, I guessed not." In truth of fact, Nick looked like he hadn't gone to bed. Black stubble covered his jutting Roman chin. His eyes were bloodshot, with tiny lines fanning out around them. The only things that looked fresh were his clothes, the perfectly tailored black pants and pristine white shirt that emphasized his Latin heritage.

How would she live without seeing him every day?

Emily thrust the thought from her. Faith didn't mean trusting for a moment, or an hour. Faith meant letting go and waiting for God. However long that took.

"It's very busy this morning, isn't it? I'm afraid you won't find a spot to park."

He grunted noncommittal agreement, slowing the car to a crawl as they approached the departure level. Finally, another vehicle pulled away, and Nick directed his car into its spot.

"You can only stay here for five minutes," she murmured, staring at the sign. This was not how she'd planned to say good-bye, but perhaps a quick break was best.

He shrugged, climbed out of the car, and unlocked the trunk, one eye on the policeman who was now headed their way.

"Listen, Nick. There's no reason you should get a ticket. This suitcase has wheels, and I can find my way to the proper gate." She took her suitcase from him and snapped out the handle. "Let's just say good-bye here."

Using sheer willpower, Emily dragged the smile to her lips, all the while her senses soaked up every memory she would need to sustain her in the weeks ahead.

"Thank you for showing me all the sights and for explaining everything. I couldn't have wished for a better tour guide, even though we got off on the wrong foot at first."

He frowned, opening his mouth to reply, but Emily couldn't wait, couldn't listen to the words. Not now.

"Ciao." The policeman stood on the curb, obviously prepared to ask Nick to move.

Seizing her moment, Emily whispered good-bye.

"Thank you," she murmured. But that didn't say all that was in her heart, so she stood on tiptoes, wrapped her arms around his neck, pressed her lips against his cheek, then blurted out the one thing she'd promised herself she would not say.

"I love you, Nick Fellini. I thank God for sending me here to meet you. I wish you only the best. Good-bye, my love." Then she turned and walked into the airport as quickly as she could, dragging her suitcase behind.

By clenching her jaw and walking straight ahead, she managed to find the appropriate gate. But once there, she could control her emotions no longer. Flopping down in a seat, she hunched over and let the tears flow, wishing they could ease the ache in her soul.

She'd arrived here, bitter and angry about a future she wouldn't share. Now she would leave, realizing that what she'd thought was love for Tad came nowhere near the overwhelming tenderness she felt for Nick.

"Please help me, God," she whispered, oblivious to the sounds around her. "Your will be done."

Chapter 10

Nick stared at the policeman, and wondered what he was saying. Nothing made sense this morning.

Emily loved him?

Into his mind swam the picture of her, green eyes shiny with a lambent glow that radiated from deep inside. And that beautiful hair—coiled about her head like a veil of gold. She loved him. Was such a thing possible? Shouldn't he have known, have seen—something?

But it was there, he realized, thinking back on the times they'd spent together. The day he'd taken her to his special place and tried to explain, hadn't he known it then? Wasn't that why he'd tried so hard to make her understand that a relationship between them was futile—because he knew she was different, that she was someone he couldn't walk away from?

So what was he doing?

Cece thought he'd put the barriers there himself. All night he'd struggled with that—begged and pleaded with God to show him the right way. Now with the clarity of the early morning sun flooding the airport tarmac, he understood that God had never asked such a thing of him. It had been his own guilt, his own fear, his own mistrust of love that had tricked him into believing that he could not love Emily, that to do so was to consign Alexandra to some terrible faint memory.

But he had loved Alexandra. Perhaps they would have married; he didn't know. Only God did. And in His infinite wisdom, God had sent him a young woman who cared about the things that he did, who threw herself into life because she believed God was in charge.

And in a short time she would fly away, believing he hadn't loved her enough.

"*Mi scusi*," he muttered to the surprised policeman. He should explain, tell him why he was leaving his car behind. But there was no time.

Nick raced into the airport, scanned the monitors, and headed for the gate he knew Emily had taken. He fiddled impatiently while security scanned him, then hurried down the gleaming walk, his eyes searching.

"Emily?"

She glanced up, turquoise eyes damp with tears that lay on her cheeks. Blond bits of hair stuck to her face, but he wiped them away.

"I love you, Emily. Will you marry me, stay in Rome, help with the mission? Until God tells us to do something different?" He caught her hands, drew her upright. "I steeped myself so deeply in history, I almost missed the present. I almost missed loving you."

"Oh, Nick." She stood on her tiptoes, threw her arms around his neck, and returned his kiss with fervor. "I love you, too. I'd love to marry you."

Several moments later he became aware that they were attracting attention.

"Let's go home to Nonna," he whispered.

The boarding announcement cut off her response.

Emily stared into his eyes.

"Do you trust me, Nick? Do you trust God?"

"Yes, of course." He frowned. "Why do you ask?"

"Because before I can marry you, I need to go home. There's something I have to get."

"But—we could go together, after we're married."

She shook her head, her eyes dark. "Can't you trust me, Nick? Can't you trust Him?"

To let her go, so soon after he'd found her—it was asking a lot. But finally he nodded.

"Go home. Settle your affairs. Because when you next return to Rome, I will never let you go." He held her, cherishing the love they shared.

"I won't want to leave," she reassured him, her smile huge. "It won't take me long. Two weeks, no more. I promise."

The final boarding call separated them. He walked her as far as he could and kissed her one last time.

"I love you, Emily."

"I love you, Nick."

Then she disappeared.

Emily slid a hand over the delicate satin folds of her wedding dress, her eyes riveted on the mirror that showed her grandmother's dress in all its beauty.

"It's a most lovely gown, *Carissima*. I'm glad you brought it. Your grandmother is the one who started this." Cece leaned over to kiss her cheek. "Even now I know she is watching from heaven. I can feel her smile inside here." She patted her heart.

"She always told me that one day I would wear her dress."

A soft rap on the bedroom door broke the silence.

"I've waited a long time to get married." Nick's low growl penetrated the thick wooden door, a hint of worry at its edges. "How much longer, Emily?"

With the help of her cane, Cece walked to the door, opened it just enough to slip through, and wrapped her arm in his.

"No longer. We are ready. Let us go to the garden to wait for Emily."

Emily took one last look, then whispered a prayer. Today she knew exactly where she was going. God had led her on a path filled with discovery, but many more awaited her as Nick's wife.

She opened the door, walked across the hall, and began her descent down the stairs. A sheaf of blood-red roses from Nick waited at the bottom. She gathered them into her arms, sniffed their fragrance, then made her way to the garden where he waited.

Nick took his time staring at her, his eyes widening at the beauty of her gown.

"Was it worth the wait?" she whispered, before the minister could begin.

He lifted her hand to his lips and kissed it, grazing the diamond ring he'd given her on her return.

"You, my darling Emily, are always worth waiting for."

Dear Reader,

A Roman holiday is unlike any other. From the first Bernini statue towering in the piazza, to the soft gush of the Trevi fountain, to the inspiration of the Vatican, to the reverence of the Catacombs, your senses swell and soar as you relive a past long buried beneath the cobblestones you tread.

I wrote this story in the depths of a prairie winter, when all around me the cocoon of swirling snow and icy winds buried everything. Emily Cain believes her life is just such a barren wasteland after her grandmother's death and her fiancé's departure. Bitter, full of resentment, she escapes to Roma—a glorious city in the throes of spring. Years of hearing about the eternal city from her grandmother have made her yearn to be captivated by the past, and yet bitterness prevents her from finding healing and comfort until she lets the lessons of the past teach her a new way to love.

Sometimes it takes the likes of a Coliseum to remind us just how small and insignificant our problems are, and sometimes it takes a glimpse of Michelangelo's Pieta to remind us of how much God loves us.

But one need not visit Rome to see with new eyes. Little boys repeating bedtime prayers, a handmade surprise for an unsuspecting teacher, snow angels pressed in neat rows—my sons did all of these and reminded me anew that God's love heals all, if you let it.

If your heart feels like winter, may I encourage you to take a Roman holiday. Fly away with me to that secret place where our loving Father's arms wrap us in warmth, where the frangipani is sweet, and rest is secure. We can go there anytime, you know. Just by closing our eyes and whispering "Father."

Blessings,
Lois Richer

A Letter to Our Readers

Dear Readers:

In order that we might better contribute to your reading enjoyment, we would appreciate your taking a few minutes to respond to the following questions. When completed, please return to the following: Fiction Editor, Barbour Publishing, Inc., P.O. Box 719, Uhrichsville, OH 44683.

1. Did you enjoy reading *From Italy with Love?*
    ❏ Very much—I would like to see more books like this.
    ❏ Moderately—I would have enjoyed it more if _____
    _____
    _____

2. What influenced your decision to purchase this book?
    (Check those that apply.)
    ❏ Cover   ❏ Back cover copy   ❏ Title   ❏ Price
    ❏ Friends   ❏ Publicity   ❏ Other

3. Which story was your favorite?
    ❏ *An Open Door*   ❏ *To Florence with Love*
    ❏ *The Lure of Capri*   ❏ *Roman Holiday*

4. Please check your age range:
    ❏ Under 18   ❏ 18–24   ❏ 25–34
    ❏ 35–45   ❏ 46–55   ❏ Over 55

5. How many hours per week do you read? _____

Name _____

Occupation _____

Address _____

City _____ State _____ Zip _____

E-mail _____

$\mathcal{H}$EARTSONG ❤ PRESENTS

Love Stories Are Rated G!

That's for godly, gratifying, and of course, great! If you love a thrilling love story but don't appreciate the sordidness of some popular paperback romances, **Heartsong Presents** is for you. In fact, **Heartsong Presents** is the premiere inspirational romance book club featuring love stories where Christian faith is the primary ingredient in a marriage relationship.

Sign up today to receive your first set of four, never-before-published Christian romances. Send no money now; you will receive a bill with the first shipment. You may cancel at any time without obligation, and if you aren't completely satisfied with any selection, you may return the books for an immediate refund!

Imagine. . .four new romances every four weeks—two historical, two contemporary—with men and women like you who long to meet the one God has chosen as the love of their lives. . .all for the low price of $10.99 postpaid.

To join, simply complete the coupon below and mail to the address provided. **Heartsong Presents** romances are rated G for another reason: They'll arrive Godspeed!

YES! Sign me up for Hearts❤ng!

NEW MEMBERSHIPS WILL BE SHIPPED IMMEDIATELY!
Send no money now. We'll bill you only $10.99 postpaid with your first shipment of four books. Or for faster action, call toll free 1-800-847-8270.

NAME _____

ADDRESS _____

CITY _____ STATE _____ ZIP _____

MAIL TO: HEARTSONG PRESENTS, P.O. Box 721, Uhrichsville, Ohio 44683
or visit www.heartsongpresents.com